THE START OF THE STORY

JANE LOVERING

B
Boldwood

First published in Great Britain in 2024 by Boldwood Books Ltd.

Copyright © Jane Lovering, 2024

Cover Design by Alexandra Allden

Cover Photography: Shutterstock

The moral right of Jane Lovering to be identified as the author of this work has been asserted in accordance with the Copyright, Designs and Patents Act 1988.

All rights reserved. No part of this book may be reproduced in any form or by any electronic or mechanical means, including information storage and retrieval systems, without written permission from the author, except for the use of brief quotations in a book review.

This book is a work of fiction and, except in the case of historical fact, any resemblance to actual persons, living or dead, is purely coincidental.

Every effort has been made to obtain the necessary permissions with reference to copyright material, both illustrative and quoted. We apologise for any omissions in this respect and will be pleased to make the appropriate acknowledgements in any future edition.

A CIP catalogue record for this book is available from the British Library.

Paperback ISBN 978-1-83533-231-3

Large Print ISBN 978-1-83533-230-6

Hardback ISBN 978-1-83533-229-0

Ebook ISBN 978-1-83533-232-0

Kindle ISBN 978-1-83533-233-7

Audio CD ISBN 978-1-83533-224-5

MP3 CD ISBN 978-1-83533-225-2

Digital audio download ISBN 978-1-83533-228-3

Boldwood Books Ltd
23 Bowerdean Street
London SW6 3TN
www.boldwoodbooks.com

For Ben.

1

AUGUST 1958

The elderly lady sighed as she pulled herself out of the taxi. 'Just you wait here for me, Dennis,' she said to the driver, tugging a bedraggled bunch of flowers out after her. 'Don't you go leaving me.'

Dennis, looking only slightly less bedraggled than the flowers, and infinitely less fragrant, sniffed. 'Well, hurry up, then, Doris. Nobody likes hanging about out on these moors. You never know what's coming for you.'

The road stretched long and grey, draped over the moors like a tired python. Doris looked up and down it, at the lack of anything bar some sad heather still waving its purple in the breeze and a couple of yellow gorse bushes doing their best to enliven the landscape. 'There's nothing coming for you, Dennis Slaithwaite,' she said, very definitely. 'Nothing except your ma with a rolled-up copy of *News of the World*. Now, you be quiet and wait here. I'll be nobbut a minute.'

Brandishing her bouquet as though it were a cudgel with which to keep anything untoward at bay, Doris picked her careful way out across the moorland, following a path that only existed now somewhere in the depths of memory. Clouds followed her, tracking her progress as a little heap of shadow, until she stopped and looked down.

'There you are,' she said gently. 'Well, my loves, I've come to say goodbye. Off to live with my sister, for my sins. Or hers. I'm not quite sure which one of us is going to suffer most, but there you go. Anyway. I'm heading off to Nantwich.'

Stiffly, as though the weight of her seventy-odd years had congregated in her joints, she bent and laid the flowers on the stone that lay in the heather at her feet.

'I'm the last that remembers you,' she said quietly. 'The others have all gone now. Apart from that Elsie, but she's halfway round the twist, she'd not know you from Pat Boone any more. So it's only me.'

The stone remained unimpressed and continued in its flat, mossy horizontality. The bells of heather flowers dangled around it, past their best now and fading rapidly into withered brown fists. Doris regarded them with sympathy. What was it that Mr Churchill had said, back in those dark days of the war? 'When you're going through hell, keep on going?' Something like that, anyway.

'Keep on going, my lovelies,' she said quietly, more to herself than to the stone. 'I hope you find happiness, wherever you are. If nobody remembers you now, at least you'll know that we knew you once.'

She reviewed that last statement. It didn't sound very pithy, for last words in such a momentous situation, but she was tired and Dennis had started beeping the taxi horn at her, and she'd still got to finish packing up her things and put butter on the cat's paws. She really couldn't think of anything else to say. So, with a small shrug and a settling of her shoulders, Doris turned and began trudging her painful way back towards the road.

Over on the stone, a breeze moved the flowers and revealed a card. It was printed in pastel colours, with pictures of Tinkerbell from the Peter Pan film. On it, in a somewhat shaky hand but with impeccable calligraphy, were the words '*For the little people*'.

* * *

Now

'There's a man to see you, Rowan.'

Chess barged her way into my office again, despite all my best efforts to train her to at least knock gently first. Well, I say *office*, it was a back room in the local library. Chess was my assistant. Well, I say *assistant*, she was the secretarial equivalent of a back room in the local library. Small, dark and hopelessly inadequate for the task in hand.

'Um? Did you get details?'

'Tall. Man. Irish, or something, he's got an accent anyway.' Chess stared over my shoulder at the laptop screen. 'What are you doing?'

'Typing up the notes from the last few days' interviews. These have to be transcribed straight away, before I forget. And I actually meant details like – why does he want to see me?'

'Dunno.' Chess further illustrated her unsuitability by perching herself on the corner of my desk. 'Doesn't it drive you mad? All these people telling you fairy stories?'

'No. It's my job. Can you go and find out what the man wants, Chess, please?'

But it was too late. The door was already opening and a scruffy dark head emerged into the gap. 'Hello? Anyone in?'

Chess raised her eyebrows at me. As she'd got her hair tied back into a ponytail so tight that their starting position was somewhere towards the top of her forehead, the raising took some effort.

'That's the man,' she hissed at me.

'I gathered,' I replied, dryly.

'And you'd be...' the man flapped the door so that he could stare at my nameplate '...Dr Rowan Thorpe?'

I just blinked. Who, my entire posture said, would be sitting in an office with someone else's nameplate on the door? It clearly said it with some force, because the man cleared his throat.

'Er,' he said. 'I was expecting a bloke, y'know.'

'Well, you got me.' I sounded waspish. But then, I generally sounded like that these days; only one step away from a yellow and black jumper and sitting in an irritated fashion on a fruit bowl. 'And who are you?'

He ignored my question, sliding himself through the gap between the door and the frame in one smooth 'nobody ever tells me to go away' move. He was wearing black from head to foot, and a grin that was nine tenths easy charm and one tenth determination. 'So, you're the folklorist?'

I sighed. 'One of them, certainly.' I elbowed Chess in the leg. She was transfixed, staring at our visitor.

'She doesn't like people in here,' she blurted, swivelling away from me. 'Gets really cross at interruptions.'

'And yet, here I am,' the man said, still cheerful.

'It's not the being here that's concerning me,' I carried on, poking Chess quite vigorously now, out of sight of our visitor, 'so much as the *why*.'

I wanted Chess to show him out. I rolled my eyes at her, then at the door and then nodded at our visitor, but she was blithely oblivious to subliminal messaging. 'Do you want a coffee?' she asked.

The Start of the Story

'That...' The man began removing his long black coat. Underneath, he wore a black sweater and black jeans – he looked as though he'd come dressed as a shadow. '...would be very nice, thank you.'

'Chess,' I hissed, trying for reproach.

'Oh, it's okay, I was going to make you one too.' Chess levered herself off the corner of my desk and, pausing only to trip over the rip in the carpet, exited. As she shut the door behind her, one of the screws holding my nameplate on pinged loose and I heard the thud as it slid sideways.

The man draped his coat over the back of the chair opposite my desk and sat down, uninvited. Then he put his elbows on the desk, rested his chin on his hands and eyeballed me.

'You're not what I expected.'

'No. You thought I was a man, for a start. Now, can we go back to who you are and why you're here, please? I've got work to do.' I angled my head towards my laptop screen. It, sensing that something was up, had also gone black.

'I'm Professor Connor O'Keefe,' he said, as though that were all I ought to need.

'How lovely for you.' I was so waspish now that my voice almost knocked itself against the window. 'Congratulations.'

I got another flash of the dark smile. 'And I'm a historian.'

I felt my shoulders rise as the tension crept up my spine, stiffening my back and making my neck muscles rigid. Historians and folklorists. It was like Montagues and Capulets, Mordor and the Shire. We practically had scarves and team songs. We were, in short, natural enemies.

'I'm sorry to hear that,' I said, pretending a smile. 'Still, we can't all be on the right side, can we?'

The easy charm slipped a fraction and a flash of dejection

crossed his face. 'Ah, come on, now. We don't have to turn this into a fight, do we?'

He had big brown eyes and the kind of cheekbones and stubble arrangement that would get him almost anywhere, especially in the world of history where they liked their professors to look as though they could be fronting a TV show about castles, complete with trying on armour and standing on battlements looking sexy. The charming smile and the Irish accent wouldn't do any harm either. And what did I have? A too-short haircut, a complexion built from cheap food and an office behind a photocopier. And Chess.

Standing on battlements looking sexy was *not* in my repertoire. Sitting behind a desk being annoyed was, however, right up my alley. 'As I still have to be told what *this* is, I'm afraid I can't agree with you.'

Professor Connor O'Keefe leaned back on the chair and chewed at his lip. 'And that's awkward, now. I was hoping that you'd have been brought up to speed,' he said. 'I'm here working for the university. We're surveying on a site up on the moors.'

I still failed to see what any of that was to do with me and said so. I kept my voice and eyes steady, he needn't think a whimsical tone and puppy-dog eyes would cut any ice with me, and he was clearly beginning to see that this might be the case, because he'd folded his arms and gained a more combative expression.

'I'm interested in this location.' For a second he leaned behind him and pulled an old paper Ordnance Survey map from a pocket. It was so creased that it took both of us to spread it out on the desk. 'There's a marker – we think it might be Roman. Possibly even pre-Roman. So I'm here to have a bit of a poke around.'

I looked at the site he tapped. It took me a few seconds to

work out where it was, upside down and with the major towns folded underneath, but once I got my eye in I felt my shoulders rise even higher. Any more tension and you could have played me like a harp.

'Oh, no,' I said. 'You can't disturb that. That's the Fairy Stane. And it's not a marker, it's a rock.'

And not just a rock, I thought, but wouldn't add. I didn't know this man and it was none of his business anyway. My emotional entanglement with a stone slab was almost inexplicable even to me and I certainly wasn't going to go into detail with a cocky professor who dressed like a vampire and smiled like a film star.

Connor O'Keefe sighed. 'Oh, I am so going to regret any of this,' he said, almost to himself. 'Look. We think there might be some important lettering on the underneath. I've been doing some research and the thought is that there could be an undiscovered Roman town nearby, close by the Roman road that crosses the moor. That stone could give us an idea of location. Or it may even mark the site of an Iron Age boundary as it lines up with some other potential markers.'

Dark eyes swung up to meet mine. 'So we're thinking that we raise the stone and see what's on it,' he went on. 'I proposed a short dig and someone at the university said that it might be an idea to run it all past you first. As you're apparently interested in the site too,' he added, but in a way that indicated that my work could, in no possible way, be as important, life altering or destiny-fulfilling as his.

'No,' I said.

'I'm sorry, what?'

'I said, no. No, you can't lift that stone. As I said, that's the Fairy Stane. I've been recording stories based in that part of the moors, and it's vital to *my* work that the stone remains in situ.'

Connor O'Keefe bit his lip again and rolled up the sleeves of his jumper, as though he were preparing to go into the boxing ring. Although, given the symmetrical perfection of his face, I doubted he'd ever been closer to boxing than the day after Christmas. '"Fairy Stane"? What's that about?'

I leaned forward across the desk, putting my elbows on the crease that concealed Pickering and Thornton le Dale.

'There's a legend around the name,' I began conversationally, slightly encouraged by the tinge of nervousness in his voice. '"Stane" is dialect for "stone". It's the Fairy Stone, and the legend is that underneath it is the door to fairyland. If the stone is moved, the Little People will escape and wreak havoc in the world.'

There was a momentary silence and then he burst out laughing. 'Oh, come on, now! You're not after believing any of that, are you?'

I didn't smile. Instead I just sat, arms still outstretched almost protectively over the location of the stone on his map, and waited. Then I said, in my calmest, steadiest voice, 'It's not a question of belief. It's a question of lore. Our local folklore says that that stone must not be moved.' Then I pulled my arms back and dragged the map back into a rough approximation of the shape it had been when he'd brought it out. It was as close as I dared come to saying 'so there'. Historians and folklorists might be at loggerheads, but that was no reason to degenerate into playground talk.

Connor sat silent for a moment. I was holding the scrunched-up map out towards him, but he didn't take it. He chewed his lip again and seemed to be inwardly considering several options, one of which appeared to be poking me in the eye. I kept the silence. I absolutely was not going to apologise or explain.

This was *my* territory, and that was *my* stone.

Eventually Chess broke our impasse by bursting in again, this time bearing three mugs of coffee. 'Here we go,' she trilled, oblivious to the atmosphere.

Connor stood up, swept his coat from the back of the chair and shoved the map back into his pocket, all in one move. 'Sorry,' he said to Chess, passing her on the only piece of floor large enough to accommodate two standing people. 'I've got to run. Next time, eh?'

Then he winked at her, glowered briefly at me over his shoulder, and left.

I resisted, with the greatest difficulty, the urge to throw my mug at the closed door.

2

I still, after all this time, called out 'I'm back!' as I arrived home. And, as ever, the reply was nothing but a swirl of disturbed dust in the narrow hallway, a resettling of the silence more comfortably to include me. Outside, the water of the old mill race petered past, reduced to shallows now by undergrowth and lack of dredging, the silty build-up housing weed and the overgrown banks providing cover for a variety of birds, the names of which I had never really bothered to learn.

It was home. An old mill cottage, all that was left now of a small settlement where a ford crossed the little river, and where generations had ground their grain. The mill itself was long gone, lost to fire and years, leaving nothing but a few burned bricks to be turned up in my garden every now and then, and an outline against my riverside wall, to mark where it had once stood.

I'd... *we'd* bought it ten years ago. Derelict, damp and unloved. We'd carefully restored it, with hours of research and study, to as close to its seventeenth-century origins as was compatible with twenty-first-century living. Now – now it was just me. My home. I felt a slight touch of guilt for the things I was leaving undone around it. There was a patch above the back door where we'd never quite got to grips with the water coming in, and peeling paint in the back bedroom. All things I should be getting fixed. The money I had wasn't infinite and I needed to stretch it for living expenses so I'd pushed some of the lesser tasks down the list until now they were beginning to become greater tasks, which niggled at the back of my mind when I let them. One day. I'd find the money and the energy – one day.

I kicked off my shoes, collected the slump of junk mail from underneath the letter box, and shuffled my feet into sheepskin slippers to walk through to the living room, sorting the mail as I went.

'Rubbish, rubbish, an invitation to view a residential care home – bloody cheek, I'm only thirty-five – Specsavers, local free leaflet, advert for takeaway. Why does nobody write letters any more?'

I addressed the empty air. Outside somewhere, ducks fought a quacky battle. I felt the silence and the lack of presence again and turned the TV on to provide a background for me to resonate my anger off.

Bloody historians! I punched a cushion into a more acceptable shape and sat down. Why couldn't they accept that sometimes you had to take local folk stories for what they were, an oral tradition that dated back – well, so far I'd been able to trace some tales right back to the late eighteenth century. Stories simply didn't need anyone poking and prodding and trying to prove this and that.

My phone rang. The display told me it was Chess, so I ignored it. She had a tendency to watch TV and need to unload at whomever was available and I really did *not* want a thriller plotline explained to me when I lived alone, out here miles from anywhere, in the dark.

The isolation of the cottage suited me now. People were kept at a distance and I could face them when I had had chance to gird my metaphorical loins. I couldn't cope with the noise and chat and general detritus of humanity any more. It scratched at my nerves and made me feel like over-chewed gum – stretched and thin and lacking purpose other than just Being There. Here, the silence soothed me. It was my acquired backdrop and I had learned to love it and rely on it, as the thing I deserved.

Over on the wall above the inglenook fireplace, which took up far more space than was sensible in the little living room, was my map. It was browned with age and creased with use, and it had been framed and hung where I could see it, to remind me that this was my patch. Restless, I got up, went over and traced the lines: *1857*, the date reminded me. *Malton and Pickering area.* Not quite my patch, the map went from the outskirts of York and up to the edge of Middlesborough while my area extended from Durham down almost as far as the Midlands, but this bit, covered by the tea-ring-speckled, damp-crinkled map, was where I was based and where I worked. Next to the map was a very old photograph of the mill and cottage, taken when the mill had been working and the cottage had been lived in by the miller and his family. Here they were all lined up outside the cottage, bearded old man, pinafored wife and six children ranging in size from almost-adult to small girl barefoot and clutching a rag doll.

Six children. I looked up again at the beams over my head. The cottage had two bedrooms, three when the family lived here, as one had been turned into a bathroom when we'd renovated. It must have been noisy back then. Now it was almost silent, apart from the trickling of water and the ducks. From a lively family home, children, dogs and the kerchunk of the grinding wheels in the mill, to my quiet little retreat, full of carefully sourced vintage furniture. Once the place had been full of stories. Bedtime stories for the children to soothe them to sleep. Tales of warning and adventure from the miller, who had fought in the Crimean war in his youth. Stories of the local ghosts, goblins and fairies from his wife, told to her by her mother, passing down the generations like a thread that linked them to the area. The folk tales that brought me here and kept me, knitted into the web of words as tightly as if I'd been born here.

Now, just me. But I was making sure those stories stayed alive. Interviewing those still remaining about the tales and traditions of their childhoods, and those of their parents and grandparents. Getting it all recorded, before it was too late. That reminded me, I still had some typing up to do. I'd been interrupted by the visit of Professor Connor O'Keefe and hadn't finished getting my notes straight. I switched on the computer. *Professor* O'Keefe, indeed. He'd only introduced himself with his title to put me on edge, of course, to flaunt in my face that he ranked slightly higher than I did, as if it would make any difference.

I got my recorder out of my bag and set it on the desk, plugged in my headphones but didn't start typing. I was too irritated. That smooth Irish charm accompanied by the kind of face that's used to getting what it wants and a smile that is positive that every female is going to buckle at the knees before it. I hadn't missed the fact that his jumper had very likely been cashmere, and his coat had been wool and expensive. I hadn't examined his trousers, but I would take any bets that they had understated stitching and a designer label and his bloody shoes were probably handmade by elves or something.

I screwed in my headphones so tightly that I nearly burst an eardrum and switched on my recorder with enough force to slide it halfway across the desk.

Bloody historians.

3

The next morning, instinct told me to drive up to the Fairy Stane. I had the feeling that Professor O'Keefe might decide not to wait for approval and might lift the stone to evidence his own research. There was no way I could trust a smile as open and honest as his and I was right. When I drove up onto the high moor, there were Land Rovers and cars parked in the lay-by and the almost invisible path that led out onto the moor, and the stone had been trodden free from undergrowth.

I left my car and followed the trail of bruised bracken and irritated wildlife until I arrived at a collection of students, milling around uncertainly as though a fire alarm had gone off and they'd evacuated the building but had no idea what to do next.

'Where's Professor O'Keefe?' I asked the nearest, a capable-looking girl wearing a Barbour with the sleeves rolled up.

'He's late,' she said, looking me up and down. 'I expect he's on his way. Who are you?'

I walked over to the Fairy Stane. It lay, innocently attracting moss and lichen and half-overgrown with reedy grass, flat on its face on the moor, which was exactly where Professor O'Keefe would find himself if he dared touch it.

'I'm the person who's here to stop you,' I said, and sat down, very firmly, on the stone.

'Stop us doing what?' The girl looked confused.

'Lifting this stone.' I drew my knees up under my chin and tried to look as though this was the sort of thing I did all the time.

A young man wandered over, his hair tumbled around his face by the breeze and a sparse beard decorating his lower jaw. 'I thought we were here to try to suss out the likelihood of a Roman settlement,' he said, trying to hold his hair back with one hand. 'Prof didn't say anything about stones.'

'That's because I'm still making my mind up.' The Irish accent told me who it was, even though I couldn't see on account of my view being blocked by students and my own knees. 'Weighing up our options, you might say. Hello, Dr Thorpe, you all right down there, now?'

'Fine,' I replied tightly.

'Well, then. We'll go over here and talk about Roman topography, shall we? So we don't interrupt your... sitting.'

He was *laughing* at me. The bastard, the smooth, Irish bastard, was laughing at me! Not with his face, of course, he was too clever for that, but he displayed his amusement in the way he stood, and even his words had held that little swing of irony that let me know he found me funny.

Well, let him. He could laugh all he wanted. What he *couldn't* do was lift my stone. Especially not with me sitting on it.

The moss that formed little cushions on the stone's surface held a surprising amount of water, which was now making its way through my jeans. I ignored it and tried to pretend that I came out this way for a quiet sit on it all the time. I leaned back on my elbows and stared up at the sky, which didn't give me much to focus on apart from a few dots of birds gathering for late emigration and some ominous-looking clouds fluffing up the horizon. The emaciated grasses that prodded their needle tips around me prevented me from seeing where the professor and his cronies had gone, but I could hear the echo of voices on the wind: laughter and a brogue that broke over words in an unusual way. Casually, and because I didn't have anything else to think about, I wondered whether he spoke Irish.

Then I wondered whether it was going to rain, because I didn't have a coat on, just my 'sitting in the office trying to look smart' jacket.

Then I wondered what was making that particular scuffling noise in the grass behind me. I didn't mind mice, there were enough mice at the cottage, but I wasn't overkeen on rats.

Then I wondered why it had gone so quiet, and stood up.

The bastard had gone, as had all the students and the cars that had been parked in the lay-by. Only mine stood there now, solitary and distant under a rapidly greying sky. I wondered how I hadn't heard them all leave, although the wind blowing from the moor meant that, if they'd come off the moor from a different direction, I probably wouldn't have heard the engines start.

I brushed myself down awkwardly. My bottom was soaked from the mossy sponges I'd been sitting on and one of my feet had gone to sleep. Beneath me, the stone lay bland and stretched like a sunbather on a beach. Featureless, just another lump of millstone grit, the same as most of the boulders and rocks dotted around this piece of moorland, different only because of the regularity of its sides. Four feet by two, the dimensions were imprinted in my mind, I'd read them so many times in the stories that gave the place its name and reputation.

Four by two. Too regular to be natural. A stone covering the entrance to fairyland. It was said – those words that led me into much of my research – that if you lay down at midnight and put your ear to the stone, you could hear the fairies partying away down in the depths. I was halfway through a rather neglected piece of work for a folklore magazine about the loose connections between fairyland and hell and the associated tales.

All was quiet and still around the stone now. No signs of fairies, partying or otherwise. Not so much as high-pitched singing or the buzz of tiny wings, unless you counted the lone bee, trundling its way through the last of the heather flowers with the determination of a shopper at the final sale of the season.

The first spots of the rain that had been bubbling under the horizon began to fall.

'Ah, you'll be heading back now, then. Can I beg a lift?'

The voice came from behind me, where the moorland devolved into bog, and tussocks jutted out from waterlogged soil, unnaturally green. I didn't turn around.

'Can't you go back the way you came?'

'Not really, no. And you and I ought to have a word, unless you intend to live on that stone for the next six months.' Connor O'Keefe moved around to stand in front me, his big black coat billowing in the wind so he looked like a buccaneer on the deck of his ship, stubbled and with the breeze pulling his hair back. He'd done it deliberately, I knew, and I guessed that the windswept piratical look usually had the girls falling at his feet.

'I'm not going back to York,' I lied. 'I'm driving over to Glaisdale. I want to take some pictures of a farm that featured in some stories I've been recording.' I gathered my jacket more closely around me. The rain was beginning in earnest now and the mossy damp had got right through my jeans to my buttocks.

'All the better. More time for us to talk,' he said cheerfully. 'I think you may have got the wrong end of the stick somewhere along the line, Dr Thorpe, and I don't want you to be giving yourself the pneumonia sitting out here on that stone worrying I'm going to do the dirty and lift it without telling you.'

It had been beginning to dawn on me that I couldn't, realistically, sit on the stone forever, and that I was going to have to find a more practical solution to the Fairy Stane problem, so I let him fall into step beside me as I turned to head back along the path to my car. I figured there was no point in giving permission, he was going to come anyway, and this way I could always throw him from the moving car.

'I tried to get your mobile number from your assistant,' Connor went on, monologuing relentlessly in the face of my silence. 'To her credit, she refused to give it to me.'

So, that had been why Chess had been ringing me last night – to tell me he'd asked. I should have answered the phone, then I could have used all my saved-up invective.

'Good,' I half grunted. I wanted to think about what to do next and this man and his talking were getting between me and the peace and quiet I needed.

'So, I figured I'd run into you soon enough, and that you'd be wanting to keep an eye on me now. I did think it might take a wee bit longer, but – here we are.'

'Apparently so.'

'Ah, you're a hard woman to get around, Dr Thorpe.'

His words were almost gleeful, as though he were utterly relishing my monosyllabic replies and my distinct lack of enthusiasm for his company. He sounded happy and cheery and completely at ease and his entire personality got so far up my nose that it was wheeling around my sinuses at this point.

'Look.' I stopped suddenly and was mildly appeased when

he skidded alongside me in an attempt to stop too. 'You aren't going to "get around" me. I have no intention of being "got around". You want to lift the Fairy Stane, I cannot and will not allow that to happen. There is no middle ground here, Professor O'Keefe. The stone is on my territory. I'm working on the stories based around it, and, therefore, lifting it is out of the question.'

I'd turned around to face him down, horribly aware that the rain was beginning to drip from the ends of my hair and it had got through the seams in my jacket. He, on the other hand, had his coat shrugged up at the collar, hands in pockets, and the rain was decorating his hair with uneven beads of moisture rather than sliding down to run down the back of his neck.

How the hell did he *do* that?

'Well, now,' he said, tipping his head to one side, 'and why don't you tell me what you really think?'

He was so utterly infuriating that it took all my willpower not to run off and try to beat him to the car, so that I could have the satisfaction of leaving him on the moor in the rain. But he'd probably stand by the road looking billowy and craggy and get picked up by the next car, which, I thought with my teeth gritted, would be driven by three supermodels who were heading to Monaco for the weekend and who'd invite him along.

Every single aspect of Connor O'Keefe ran down my nerve endings like an electric wire.

'If I told you what I *really* think,' I snapped back, 'you'd have me arrested.'

'Ah, I reckon we're only about ten minutes from that happening anyway.' He started walking again. We were very nearly at the car and the thought of being able to sit down out of the rain made me speed up a little. 'You really don't like me much, do you, Dr Thorpe?'

'You do yourself an injustice, *Professor* O'Keefe. I don't actually like you at *all*.'

I unlocked the car, slightly smug at my comeback, and he swung into the passenger seat in a move that looked as though he would have preferred to slide in through the window like Starsky and Hutch.

'Where's Glaisdale?' He didn't follow up on my expressed dislike of him, but his tone was a little less cheery and his chin had a set to it that implied he might be clenching his teeth slightly.

'It's near Danby. In the heart of the moors.' I tucked my jacket as far under my bottom as I could to protect the seat from the warm damp that my moss-soaked behind had become. This pulled the neck taut as a straitjacket and made me sit more rigidly than I might otherwise have done.

'And you've a farm to take pictures of, y'said?'

'Yes. I've been recording folk memories of the area round abouts, and there's a farm still standing where there were stories of a hob working.' Then, because I couldn't resist the opportunity to know more than him, 'A hob is like a brownie or a pixie, a helpful house spirit.'

'Ah. A bowl of milk and they'd clean the kitchen for you.'

'That sort of thing, yes. And I want to put photographs in to illustrate locations. It might be valuable in the future, when some of these sites are gone.'

'No such luck for me. The Romans were not ones for the camera, sadly.'

'I imagine not.'

We lapsed into silence. I was wondering why the hell I hadn't admitted I was heading back to York. Well, because I'd thought he'd decline a lift that was apparently going to take him miles into the depths of the moors, that was why. Now I had to drive pointlessly up to the old farm, taking photographs of a place I'd photographed only the other day so I didn't look like a liar.

The rain pounded against the car while the cloud gathered itself around us as we drove higher and higher into the moors. The occasional sheep passed into view, black faces against the fog, floating above the grass at the sides of the road, but there was nothing else. No other traffic, no walkers, no scenery. I toyed with the idea of turning round but he'd only ask questions, wouldn't he?

It began to feel like one of those films where you realise the characters are actually dead and in Purgatory.

'Are you sure you're going to be able to take any pictures in this?' Connor turned to look out of the passenger window. Because of the fog outside, I could see his face in reflection and he looked unsettled. Being driven he knew not where by a woman whose dislike filled the car like petrol fumes must be finally getting to him. 'It's a touch filthy out there now.'

In reply, the rain thrummed on the car roof and we drove through some standing water so deep that the car bucked like a resistant horse. 'No, not really,' I said grudgingly. 'It's worse than I thought this far up.'

But I drove on. Turning around, admitting defeat and heading back to York would be – well, admitting defeat. And I could *not* be defeated, not with Mr Swanky Pants in my car, waving his professorship and the Romans at me. Folklorists keep going. It was practically a motto. In fact, I'd have got it on a T-shirt, if I ever wore T-shirts, which I didn't because one thing about being a folklorist is that everyone expects you to wear tie-dye and kaftans and lurid T-shirts and listen to Steeleye Span. So I defiantly wore Levis and tidy shirts with tailored jackets and pretended to like drum and bass and The Weeknd. The fact I preferred silence, I kept to myself.

The fog thickened to the extent that I had to drop my speed to fifteen miles an hour. I wanted to turn around so much that I had to fight my hands' desire to take over and spin us in the road, but in the face of Connor O'Keefe's presence, I could not. My jacket was almost strangling me and the moistness of my jeans was giving me a very unpleasant warm chafing sensation, but I'd told him I was driving up on the moors, so drive up on the moors I would. Besides, if this extended trip was inconveniencing him in any way other than keeping him away from my Fairy Stane, I was going to maximise his discomfort. My own I could ignore.

Eventually, when it would have been quicker to abandon the car and get out and walk, the decision was taken from me. We were flagged down by a man in a fluorescent jacket.

'Lorry's blocking road,' he said quickly through the tiny gap that I opened in my window. 'You'll need to turn round.'

I could feel the waves of self-satisfaction coming from the professor in the passenger seat, almost as though he'd psychically caused the accident so we'd have to go back, but obediently I U-turned and we headed back the way we'd come, inching along the road with two wheels practically on the verge.

'So, shall I be telling you what my plans actually are now, then?' he said, cheerful again now that we weren't apparently falling off the edge of the world. 'Or wait until we get back to your office?'

I didn't answer. I was having to concentrate hard on not driving off the road and onto the boggy moor. But, of course, he went on anyway.

'I'm on secondment to York University from Dublin, because my speciality is lost Roman settlements and the archaeologists have LIDAR evidence of something that looks like a small town out to the east there.' He glanced quickly at my face, but I kept my expression impassive. 'That would be a big deal – there's not a lot of evidence of Roman settlements out here. A few villas, and, of course, they had York and Malton, to secure the river crossings.'

My interest in the Romans and their enjoyment of bridges knew no beginning.

'So I've got a team out from the university to look into it. The archaeologists are doing their test-pit thing, and I'm leading the landscape people, plus lecturing on Roman daily life out here on the fringes of empire.' Connor went on, seemingly not caring that I was not contributing to the conversation. 'And I found out about your Fairy Stone—'

'Stane,' I interjected. 'It's called the Fairy Stane. I know Yorkshire dialect probably doesn't mean a lot to you, but it's important that places keep the names that the locals give them – a lot of history can be tied up in naming.'

There was a moment's silence. We were dropping down now, away from the higher moor and back towards the stone's location, with the fog thinning all the way.

'You're right, of course,' Connor said, turning to look at me properly now. 'You're very passionate about the subject, aren't you?'

'Someone has to be,' I half muttered. 'History isn't all treasure hoards and kings in car parks. Oral history that's passed down through the generations, even if it's in the form of folk stories, can tell us a lot about how real people lived. They are important too, more important than your glittery Romans or buried treasure.'

'Hang on a minute.' Connor held his hands up. 'I'm not saying that they're not, now, am I?'

'You want to lift the stone!' Finally my composure broke. 'You want to ruin a piece of folkloric history just to prove your own! What's that, if not thinking that your fancy-shmancy centurions take precedence over what the ordinary farming families believed?'

We cleared the fog level and the whole of the Ryedale valley was spread out before us, from the smooth chalk rise of the wolds along the flat plain of the ancient glacial lake. A land of myth, of story. *My* land.

'It's not that I'm wanting to lift your stone.' Connor sounded weary now. 'It's more that I might have to. It could be a boundary marker, as I said, or it could be a waymarker or even mark a burial place. Wouldn't you want to know, if you were me?'

'Not if it meant desecrating something that's special to others,' I muttered. 'Lift the stone and release the fairies, that's how it goes. Prove that there's no entrance to fairyland and you destroy the oral history.'

I flipped the indicator and we pulled out onto the main road. I turned for York.

'It sounds more like a folk retelling of the myth of Pandora's box,' Connor said thoughtfully. 'A mangled recital of a half-understood Greek tale. You do realise that I could lift the stone, check the underside and put it back and you'd never be any the wiser?'

'That,' I said tightly, 'sounds like a threat, Professor O'Keefe.'

We drove the rest of the way back to York in silence.

4

'So where *did* you leave him?' Chess asked, so utterly absorbed in my story that she'd been standing with her finger on the print button for nearly five minutes and the little green light had given up and gone out.

'At the traffic lights on Huntington Road,' I said, with my head in my hands. 'I couldn't stand him sitting there all "I've got the upper hand" any longer. So I told him to get out and walk from there.'

Chess sighed. 'He seems really nice, though.'

'He was lucky that I didn't order him out ten miles earlier, or he'd be trying to find a bus stop in Sheriff Hutton. Honestly, Chess, it was *horrible*. He's so smug and so self-satisfied and sure that he's right and all I'm doing is writing down stories and he doesn't even *realise* how insufferable he is.'

'You don't think that might be a "you" thing, rather than a "him" thing?' Chess admired her reflection in the printer screen for a moment. 'You can be a bit...' She pulled a duck face, which was further exaggerated by the streaky glass. 'A bit touchy.'

A thorn of shame drove through my heart. She was right, I

was touchy; short and snappy and impatient these days. Not enough sleep and bad dreams would do that to a person, plus the worry of bill paying and the other intricacies of solo living. It all wore away at the back of my head until it felt as though bare nerves reacted to every draught, like ice cream on a tooth. It was nobody's fault but mine. Nobody's responsibility, but mine.

'Sorry, Chess.' I tried to sound conciliatory rather than annoyed. 'I do try.'

'You go in your office and I'll bring you a cup of tea,' she suggested, forgetting, Chess-like, that she might have said something to upset me.

'I can't. I can't sit down. My bum is still all wet and I'm not sure that chair can take any more unpleasantness without disintegrating.'

'Go and hover, then. I'll find you something dry to put on. *And* make you a cup of tea.'

I gave in and went down the tiny narrow windowless corridor that led to my office behind the main rooms in the little library. My encounter with Professor Smuggo had had the same effect on my nerves as a night of tossing and turning. It made me feel as though my skin were too small and the inside of my head were too hot. A kind of sensation of the whole world being wrong and nobody could tell except me.

At least the office smelled familiar – of cheap fibreboard, sun-scorched papers, dust and carpet squares cannibalised from, from the smell of them, a cats' home. I nearly made the mistake of sitting down, but managed to pull myself back at the last moment and went to lean against the desk. I was lucky to have a desk. I was lucky to have an office and Chess, and a grant for 'Recording Local Oral Traditions and Tales and Maintaining Social Historical Artefacts and Material Culture relating to Tradition'. Most folklorists had to freelance, recording and writing as and when they could whilst having a day job. I'd drawn the long straw, got a council grant, a workspace and the budget for an assistant. Even if the assistant was someone with no real interest in the subject, a desire to try all the hair-colour products in Boots and a somewhat *loose* approach to actual working hours.

As for the office... I looked around at the walls and the windows, which showed only a view of more walls. We were slightly below ground level; folklore hadn't been relegated quite as far as the basement, but there was an air of damp fernyness about this room that let me know that basement dwelling was still a possibility, should I not manage to keep my work sufficiently within the public view. Or, I thought in my more charitable moments, the room was sinking slowly under the weight of information inside it. All those years of oral history, all those stories of grandmothers who'd 'turned' the butter using charms, or healed wounds with certain herbs and told bedtime stories about exactly *why* the children shouldn't go out onto the high moor after dark, weighted even the air and added gravity.

I gritted my teeth. It was important. Recording these memories before they were subsumed beneath computerisation, globalisation and the generalisation of a population who moved every five years was important. I was already hearing the memories of memories, one more generation and most of it would be lost or diluted by popular fiction and television.

I looked around again, at the stacked box files of written evidence donated by families who hadn't known what to do with granny's notes, recipes and charms; at the cupboard that contained artefacts like someone's great-uncle's water-divining rods, corn dollies, a jar of home-made ointment for keeping the snow from balling in horses' hooves. And I couldn't help the feeling that I was drowning in it all.

'Here!' Chess burst in, dragging an air of enthusiasm and a carrier bag with her. 'I borrowed these off Magda. They're all I could find.'

I opened the carrier bag to reveal what looked like a set of curtains. 'What is it?'

'She's got her belly-dancing class tonight, but she says you can borrow the trousers for the rest of the day if you want.' Chess gave me an encouraging smile. 'Better than getting your chair seat wet and having to sit on damp for the next week or so, isn't it? I'll go and make that tea now.'

Okay, I thought, with the sense of resignation that often overcame me when I was here. I had a meeting later with a lady who was coming down from Durham with some tape recordings of her father's reminiscences of growing up in the wilds of High Cup Nick. I needed to get my jeans dry for that.

There were little brass discs that chimed to contend with, I discovered as I clambered into the borrowed trousers to the accompaniment of hundreds of little metal castanets. Luckily I had emergency knickers, kept in the secret lower drawer of my desk where most researchers would have a bottle of whisky, against those months when nature didn't play ball, so at least I wasn't having to go commando in the voluminous trousers. Having dry, warm buttocks again was comforting. I hadn't realised how much of my ire at the professor had been occasioned by the unpleasant chafing of damp jeans.

Then I put my headphones on and set to work typing up some more memories from the tape I'd made a few days before. Properly evidenced, collated and dated material was the bedrock of my life. It would all make a book one day – at least that was what I'd told the grants committee, and maybe it would, but I needed to find an angle first. Nobody was going to read this loose collection of stories, memories of the elderly who sometimes wandered back into times when their tales had been current or third-hand retellings of family reminiscences, not as it currently stood anyway. I had to find something concrete to peg it all to, a loom to weave the stories so that they felt as though they all came from the same cloth, rather than disparate recollections from varying locations.

Then the thought came to me – I had the Fairy Stane. Though I'd told Professor O'Keefe that I was researching the area, obviously I'd lied to give him second thoughts about raising the stone. But what if I actually *did* write that book? If I used the stone, the idea that fairyland lay beneath the North York Moors, the theory that disturbing the fairies would bring doom and destruction... yes, it might work. And it might put another obstacle in the way of his interfering with my landscape.

I found I'd stopped typing and put my chin in my hand as I thought. My face was reflected in the bland blank screen and I could see my hair hadn't benefitted from the rain any more than my bottom had from sitting on the damp stone. Both ends of me were rebelling. At least my lower regions were recovering slowly, now encased in the capacious and startlingly coloured belly-dancing trousers, but my hair wasn't so lucky and was twisting upwards into the kind of dreadlocks normally seen in illustrations of Grendel from *Beowulf*. No wonder the professor had been giving me those covert, amused looks right up until I'd slowed down at the traffic lights and told him he could find his own way back from there. I looked less fey and more forty thousand volts.

But the Fairy Stane... yes. I could do it. I'd got enough general material on belief in fairies, hobs, boggarts and sprites from the locality. If I could link it all back to the late nineteenth century generalised acceptance of the liminality of the moors and the accessibility of the fair folk and their propensity for hanging around human farms... I teased a hand up and through my hair, thoughtfully. Yes, it could work. Plus, that would give me a legitimate reason to hang around the stone and make sure that nothing untoward happened to it.

Of course, he *could* lift the stone, examine the underside and drop it back down again without telling me. But the disruption it would cause to all the overgrowing lichens and bog grass would be an absolute giveaway and I could, and would, raise not only fairyland but merry hell if he tried it. I didn't think that whoever had seconded him down to York to look into the Romans and their possible settlement would be too keen on that kind of publicity. They'd at least knock his charm back to Ireland and he could go and brood and wear his expensive wardrobe over there.

The thought made me smile, and my reflection softened at the edges.

'Here's your tea.' Chess wafted back in again. 'And he's here again.'

'Who is?' I shifted around in my chair to take the tea and my trousers clattered and chimed.

'Our hunky professor. He looks a bit annoyed, mind.'

'Tell him to go away. There must be something he has to do apart from hang around being a pain to me. Doesn't he have lectures to do or a modelling contract to fulfil or something?'

'No, he bloody doesn't. Right now he has the little matter of being lost to take up with you,' came the ringing tones from the corridor outside. His voice echoed off the walls like someone shouting into a trumpet. 'You left me. I've only been over here three days, I have no idea where I am most of the time, and you *left* me.'

Guilt instantly washed over me, flushing my skin and

making me cough on my tea. Three *days*? He'd only been here three days and I'd ordered him out of my car well beyond the city centre and where, if memory served, there weren't even any helpful signs.

'I had to stop a bunch of kids and ask them the way into town!' Connor burst through the door looking hot and dishevelled. '*And* the cheeky gobshites pretended they couldn't understand my accent.'

'I think you'd better make another cup of tea,' I said weakly to Chess as the professor slumped wearily into the spare chair, as though he'd hiked fourteen miles up a vertical slope, rather than walking the mile and a half to my out-of-the centre library and office.

'I'm sorry,' I said, genuinely, once Chess had returned to the little kitchenette, probably to evict the library volunteers, who tended to cluster around the kettle and any biscuits or cake that had been donated. 'I didn't know you were new to York.'

'Well, I am. I only know my way from the house I've rented to the university, and even that's a bit of a stretch still. There's too many turns and roads and they all look the same out there!' Connor was unmollified. He gathered his coat around him like a villain's cape, drawing himself in until he was one pencil-slim tube of blackness. 'I could be anywhere in the world, and yet here I am looking at some quite frankly shaky evidence for another Roman town somewhere where it never bloody stops raining, like you don't have Roman experts of your own.'

The words came out of him in a torrent of pent-up exasperation. I still felt too guilty about making him find his way back to town to really appreciate the fact that I'd finally managed to wipe the charming smile off his face. There was also that tiny tickle of shame that Chess had engendered in me with her accusation of touchiness. Whilst I didn't really care what people thought of me, I couldn't afford a reputation for being hard to deal with. It might put people off from coming forward to tell me their stories if they heard I was testy and grumpy.

'You're Irish, though,' I pointed out, trying to sound a little more friendly. 'You must be used to rain.'

'Not,' he enunciated carefully, 'Yorkshire rain. *We* have proper rain, the sort that makes everything soft. *Yours* just goes through fifteen layers of clothing, and then you're wet and cold and it still doesn't stop.'

I couldn't, and wouldn't, apologise for the weather. It was autumn in North Yorkshire. What had he expected, thirty-degree sunshine and barbecues?

'It's cold and it's wet and I'm living in a house with neighbours who've got the Hound of the Baskervilles one side and what sounds like a family of fifteen the other.' He hunched forward now, hiding his face in his hands. 'I've not had a night's sleep since I arrived, and I'd book into a hotel only I've signed up to be here for six months and a professor's salary isn't up to it. I've only got two more days before I have to sign for the house for the full six months and I don't think I can stand the torture, but it's that or a tent.' He raised his face, and I could see the shadows under his eyes now I wasn't being misled by the cheeky grin and the incessant upbeat chat. 'I don't suppose you know someone who's renting a room out, do you?'

I mentally combed through my list of acquaintances. It was short. 'Not really. I might know someone over in Helmsley who's looking for a housemate...'

'Helmsley.' Connor slumped even further into the chair. 'That's one of those places about a hundred miles from York, yes?'

'Twenty-five. On a good day. You could rent a car. It's a very pretty drive.'

'Is that where you live?'

The question surprised me. My domestic situation had absolutely nothing to do with the present circumstances, but the backwash of guilt made me answer. 'Er, no, I live out in the middle of nowhere, about ten miles from Helmsley. On the moors,' I added, just to reinforce the idea that I might spend my days sitting on the Fairy Stane, in case that had been featuring anywhere in his thought processes.

'Only I don't drive, y'see.' This admission startled me almost as much as his question about my living arrangements. 'I've no sense of direction at all, and I'm a danger to myself and every mortal soul when I'm behind a wheel.' The merest hint of a return of the charm began to tinge his words. 'And I shouldn't have come over here without even knowing where I was going to live or how I was going to travel around, but...' He shrugged. 'Ah, y'know, life happens and it's good to be out of Dublin for a while.'

Chess came in with the extra mug of tea and perched herself on the edge of my desk, looking from one of us to the other. 'What's wrong with the house you're in now?' she asked, interestedly. Then, seeing my slightly taken-aback look, 'I was listening. It's really quite hard not to, when he's yelling and the kitchen is only half an inch of plywood away.' She made a 'sorry-not-sorry' face.

Connor took the offered tea and stared into it as though the answer to Chess's question might be inscribed on the surface.

'Ah, it's not so bad,' he said. 'It's only six months. How long does it take to die of sleep deprivation anyway?'

'Stop it,' I said firmly. 'What exactly *is* wrong with your current place?'

I got a return of the smile now. It seemed that Professor O'Keefe couldn't keep dissatisfaction up for very long and his usual upbeat demeanour was bouncing back. 'On the left they've got a dog that sits outside and howls all hours, and on the other what sounds like the population of a small town, all under the age of seven. So all day it's competitive shrieking on the one side, and then when they go quiet, out goes the dog and starts up with the howling. It's like one of those modern novels,' he added.

'Wow.' Chess fiddled with her updo. She'd retouched her eye make-up whilst she'd been making the tea, I noticed, and now looked like an Amy Winehouse album cover. Connor O'Keefe was clearly on her radar. 'That sounds dreadful.'

'Do you know anyone who's got somewhere the professor could rent for six months?' I asked her. The problem of his housing situation had blended with my sense of remorse and become something I needed to remedy. 'You've got loads of friends, Chess, you must know someone.'

Chess stuck her tongue out, thinking. 'No, not really,' she said slowly. 'Not that would be suitable, anyway. Students are back and everywhere even halfway rentable has gone to them.' The tongue wiggled. 'You can make a lot of money, renting to students.'

'Ah now,' Connor sighed. 'There's always the earplugs. And headphones. And probably the pillow. I'll be fine.'

'What about your place?' Chess turned to me, the tongue making a sudden withdrawal as she was struck with inspiration. 'You've got a spare room, haven't you?'

I had a sudden flash of my quiet, peaceful home. That air of undisturbed silence that was sometimes my greatest friend and sometimes my worst enemy. 'No,' I said, quickly, and wriggled so that my borrowed trousers tinkled in emphasis.

Chess frowned against the considerable strain caused by the updo. 'You have,' she said accusingly. 'You're always saying you've got a room you never even go in. And you're coming into town most days, so transport wouldn't be a problem.'

'No,' I said again, even faster this time.

But Connor was sitting up straighter now and the protective coat had fallen away to flop over the sides of the chair, like a valance. 'You say you live near the moors? So you'd be handy for the work out there?'

'"No" is a complete sentence,' I said, a rising sense of panic making me speak breathlessly.

There was a short pause. 'No, it isn't,' Chess said eventually. 'There's no subject or object, so it can't be.'

'Well, I don't want to impose or anything.' Connor was still sitting up, alert, looking like a greyhound waiting for the hare to come by. 'But it wouldn't be for too long, just until I could find something more convenient?'

Mental images tumbled in. A man's coat over the back of my sofa. Toiletries in the bathroom, singing on the stairs, the radio tuned to something I never listened to. Alexa randomly playing music I didn't know. Laughter. Proper meals.

'No,' I said again, but aware that my tone lacked the rigour it previously had.

'Oh, go on,' said Chess. 'Something's bound to come up in York soon.'

'Something affordable,' Connor mitigated. 'But I can pay you something for the room. To cover electricity and – stuff.'

The thought of the occupation of my house was pushed out by the thought of my bank balance. Not dire, not yet, but the grant was tiny and petrol costs were rising again, along with electricity and food costs. The thought of the damp patch over the back door jabbed me with a sharp corner of guilt. I *did* need the money, damn him. If I played host to Connor O'Keefe for a short while it might earn me enough to fix those niggling issues without having to empty the savings account.

It needn't be for long. It had better *not* be for long. I needed my silent solitude.

'The house is tiny,' I said, and now I sounded as though the whole thing was a fait accompli and I was making excuses. 'The spare room isn't much more than a bed. The hot water can be unreliable, and it's very quiet, there's nothing to do in the evenings, and there's no public transport at all. I'm quite often away too.'

'But the neighbours don't howl or play "Who can scream the loudest?" all night?' Connor looked hopeful. As I'd been so resolutely sour-faced at him on the earlier drive back from the moors, I could infer that boarding with me would be the lesser of two evils by not very much, and the other evil must be very unpleasant indeed. 'It really would be kind of you, Rowan. Oh, and I like the trousers, by the way. Very – er, colourful.'

I restrained myself from poking him in the eye. He'd actually used my name! Not the vaguely derogatory 'Dr Thorpe' that he'd been calling me up to now, as though a doctorate were something to pity. Bringing the belly-dancing gear into the conversation was a touch below the belt, although any touches below the belt would currently make me chime like a clock shop at midnight.

It was the guilt, that was what it was. Guilt, or hypnosis, one or the other. Because I found myself agreeing to host Professor Connor O'Keefe in my spare room, temporarily, mind you, only until he could find something more suitable in town, where the neighbours were reasonable human beings and the rent wasn't eye-watering. The trousers didn't help, because I didn't dare stand up and hold the door open to invite him to leave, as I really wanted to do. The waist was looser than it should have been so I was forced to remain sitting or risk him getting a very close look at my underwear. I was disadvantaged in every way.

'You'll need to use taxis,' I warned sternly. 'I won't always be coming into York, or I might need to work late some nights, and I sometimes have to attend conferences and things. I'm not going to be at your beck and call for running you back and forth.'

I carried on sitting, even though it made me feel like an interviewer with a difficult candidate, and very much at a disadvantage.

'Understood.'

But as he stood up to take his leave and go back to get his things together, I felt a sense of impending doom as deep as though the stone had already been lifted and the grief of the fairies had been let loose on the world.

This was such a bad idea.

5

'And this is the kitchen,' I said, awkwardly, leading Connor down the hallway and into the room at the back that overlooked the river. We'd knocked down an outside toilet and extended out, so the walls were bare brick but the windows were huge, with what an estate agent would call 'extensive river views'.

'It's lovely,' he said, lugging his large case along with him. He had a suit bag draped over his shoulder and another bag dangling from a wrist. I wasn't quite sure where it was all going to go; if he put all his clothes in the bedroom there wasn't going to be a lot of room for him. 'No, really, the cottage is lovely, thank you for this.'

'I'll show you your room.' I backed along the hallway to the bottom of the stairs.

'So, you renovated the place yourself, then?' The question was a polite one, the standard query from visitors, usually followed by, 'How long did it take?'

I hesitated, halfway up the staircase, bracing myself with a hand on each wall. The cottage had been built along the same plans as the mill, narrow steep stairs and rooms of exceptionally odd shapes, and it could take some getting used to. With luck, I thought, he'd find the wobbly layout and ceilings low enough that he'd have to duck in doorways so annoying that he'd be back in York by supper time.

I murmured something vague in response to his question and opened the door to the little spare room. To myself, in my head, I still called it the nursery, but really it was a proper adult spare bedroom: double bed, small chest of drawers and a bedside cabinet. Not enough room to live in for long, but fine for occasional occupation, the odd guest.

My very odd guest put his bag down on the bed and moved to the window with a soft whistle. 'Wow. Overlooks the river.' Then he turned to me. 'Seriously, Rowan, I know we may have got off on the wrong foot back there, but I can't thank you enough. I'll be able to get a proper night's sleep finally.'

An urge to discomfit him overcame me. 'As long as you're a heavy sleeper,' I said. 'I do Morris dance practice in the kitchen at four every morning, and then my death metal bandmates come round for rehearsals every night. No neighbours to disturb, you see.'

He stared at me for a moment, and then seemed to work out that I was joking. 'Morris dancing, eh? That explains your trousers earlier. Didn't know that needed so much practice. Isn't it mostly flinging your hankie?'

'It's the bells,' I replied, straight-faced. 'They take a lot of work.'

'And death metal?'

'Oh, yes. We're working on a twenty-minute drum and tuba duet,' and then even I couldn't keep it up, and backtracked. 'No, you're right. It's very quiet out here, only the ducks really make much of a noise.'

'It's perfect.'

'There's no transport, as I said, so if you need to be in York on days I'm not going, you'll have to book a taxi pick-up.'

'Ah, it'll be fine now.' He sat on the edge of the bed and bounced experimentally. 'And I don't snore, so I won't disturb you. I'm well mannered in the house, clean up after myself and all. Mam brought up five boys and she knew what she was doing.'

I imagined that life. A busy house full of children, the noise and the chatter, toys strewn around floors and a smell of cooking always in the air. I often found myself doing this when I talked to people, as though I were seeing through a window onto another life. It stood me in good stead when I was working, this ability to imagine how people lived, stepping back through time into homes with no electricity when an evening's entertainment was stories around the fire. It was almost as though the past existed in two parallels. One was the actual way of life, cooking and cleaning and milking the cows – the practicalities – and the other gave insights into the beliefs and nightmares. So it was really my training that made me pick up on his throwaway comment. 'Five boys? That's quite a handful. Where did you all grow up?'

'Mostly outdoors.' Then he smiled. 'We're Dublin born and raised, a good Catholic family, at least, the others are. Me, I'm secular to my fingertips, much to their disappointment, although being a professor helps make up for it. Mam nearly died of pride when Eamonn went into the Church.'

'Er...' My mind wheeled around the image of someone's walking through a church doorway being a cause for family celebration.

'He's a priest,' Connor explained with a grin at my baffled expression. 'It's a bit like being related to royalty. I tell them all that I'm a worshipper of Mithras now. I'm not, of course, but it's worth it to see their faces, even if it does mean I only get half as much dinner when I pop home for the weekend.' The boards of the bedroom floor squeaked as he got up again and went over to the window. 'Can I open it?' he asked.

'Of course. It's not just for show.' I stood back to allow him room and was mildly pleased by his temporary confusion at the apparent lack of window opening mechanism. 'It's a Yorkshire sash. It slides sideways, like this.' I demonstrated. 'We kept all the original features when we restored the place.'

Connor nodded and slid the window a few times, experimentally.

'I need to...' I made vague hand signals towards the door as though I had to wave to a crowd or scatter grain. 'So I'll leave you to settle in.' Then I berated myself all the way back down the tiny staircase. *Why* had I agreed to this? The cottage already felt too full of people. There were noises I hadn't made, creaks and bumps overhead, presumably Connor unpacking, although hopefully he wouldn't be here for long enough to *need* to unpack. I'd sent Chess some fairly pointed texts on the subject of finding him somewhere more convenient to stay for the remainder of his six months. Guilt might have provoked me into making my spare room available, but his stay absolutely could *not* be anything more than fleetingly temporary. There was nowhere for him to sit, for a start – the loveseat sofa that faced the fireplace was only meant for one. Two if they were physically close, and I did not intend to be physically any closer to Professor O'Keefe than the driver and passenger seats in my car.

And where was he going to work? My computer took up the dining table and there wasn't room in the kitchen for him. Outside? I briefly entertained the idea of Connor O'Keefe sitting dismally out on the step, or on the narrow fringe of garden that fronted the river, overgrown and matted with weeds as it was.

The vision of him sitting there damply, making muted duck-call noises, with his feet dangling in the river, was unexpectedly amusing and I found myself letting out a little giggle, which made me feel better.

When had I last giggled? Chess made me raise the odd smile now and again with her pronouncements, but actually *giggle*? Or laugh? When had that been? Too long ago now for me to remember. I worked too hard to have time for levity: long solo hours recording, typing up notes, compiling and collating. Being a folklorist was a solitary occupation. We roamed the peripheries of life armed with voice recorders and notebooks, grumpy and aloof. There's not generally a lot of laughs in listening to eighty-year-olds reminiscing over memories handed down from their parents and trying to sort out the tales that might be important, stories that might interleave with others of a similar nature to give a base to local legend. There's a lot of drinking tea, looking at photo albums and going back over how much better things had been before computerisation. Or decimalisation. Or the car.

In short, it was a job that involved dedication, attention to detail and a kind of detached sociability. None of these things seemed appropriate to being forced to share a house with a Roman historian. A historian who wanted to destroy a local folkloric totem, at that.

I felt my face shrug off the smile and assumed my normal composed expression and went to look busy.

6

Connor had been right about not being a noisy guest. He was almost completely silent, from early evening when he retired upstairs after eating a pack of sandwiches he'd brought with him, until the next morning when he called down from the stairway to the kitchen as I was blearily making myself a cup of tea.

'May I use the bathroom? I could do with a shower before I start the day. Is that all right now?'

I blinked over my mug. 'Of course it is.'

'I didn't want to interfere with your bathroom schedules, that's all. Getting ready for work and everything.'

His consideration took some of the irritated wind out of my sails. 'No, that's fine. I'll shower tonight when I get home. Are you wanting a lift through to the university today?'

I put the mug down and began popping bread into the toaster. Two slices – and then another two slices. He must be *starving*.

'Oh, yes, if you're going through, that would be great.' His voice receded along the landing as he headed bathroom-wards.

'I'm not lecturing but I want to meet up with the guys who are surveying the land.'

A couple of minutes later he was in the kitchen, hair wet and weighted long with the water, towel over his shoulders and dressed in his usual black.

'Toast?' I pushed the plate towards him. He'd been quicker than I'd expected, so I was still sitting on the window seat with my toast dropping crumbs into my lap, staring out across the river to the other side of the disused ford. I *had* been intending to be washing up when he came down, or tidying the kitchen, showing how generally full and busy my life was and how much of an imposition he was upon it. But it was seven o'clock and my annoyance hadn't had chance to crank up to visible level yet.

'Thanks.' He grabbed the plate, looked around and saw the butter and jam on the worktop. 'Is it all right if...?'

His politeness notched the annoyance up one setting. 'Of course. You don't have to ask. You're paying to be here, that gets you use of shower and snacks.' Moodily I bit into the remaining toast, then threw the crusts out of the window to the assorted duck crowd that had gathered, paddling furiously against the current, for just this occasion.

A quacking, splashing battle ensued. When I glanced away from it, Connor was looking at me, frozen in the act of buttering his toast.

'I know this is awkward for you,' he said so quietly that his words were almost lost under the noise of a large white duck dive-bombing one of the mallards. 'I'm sorry you got talked into it. But I'm really very grateful, truly. I slept last night like the dead for the first time since I arrived over here, and I'm beginning to feel human again.' One eyebrow lifted and his mouth twitched into the customary smile. 'So, please make use of me while you've got me. Any jobs need doing about the place, I'm your man.'

I closed the window. 'I do my own jobs,' I said stiffly and then, aware of how ungracious I'd sounded, 'but thank you for the offer.' The damp patch above the back door gave the lie to my words, but I ignored it.

'Ah, only a thought.' A buttery moment ensued, and then he went on. 'I'm fully house-trained, so you can leave me to my laundry and washing up and all that. I'll make my bed and keep the crumbs to a minimum. Mam ran a very tight household, what with five boys and Da, she wasn't up for martyring herself to the house.'

I had a vision of Connor's mother, like a cross between Mrs Doyle from *Father Ted* and every stereotypical Irish Mammy I'd ever read about. Plump and censorious, strict about Mass on Sunday, cooking up a storm and fussing over her sons to the extent of them struggling to find girlfriends. Apart from the priestly Eamonn, of course. I could see her ruling the household with a rod of iron amid the chaos of all those boys, having them clamour to make her a cup of tea when she settled herself into an armchair.

'What with her job, and all,' Connor went on, biting happily into the toast.

'What does she do?' I asked, trying to keep the conversation going.

'She's head of the biochemical sciences department,' he said, turning back to tidy up the jam, so at least he couldn't see my expression. I was glad, because my mental attempt to overwrite Irish Mammy with Scientist was scrambling my face.

We finished our breakfast in silence. Connor stood and looked out of the window while he ate and I drank the rest of my tea while reading an article in a magazine about the Fairy

Census, which collated current belief in the world of the Other. I made a note of the name of the author, in case I needed to contact someone about the future of the Fairy Stane. If Connor and his ranks of students made any attempt to disturb it, I'd rally everyone in the folklore world in an attempt to protect it. He needn't think he could ride roughshod over lifetimes of belief just to prove a historical point, not without a fight, anyway.

Then I drove us to York.

It was a busy day. I had a meeting with the people who awarded the grants who wanted to see the current stage of my research, so I went armed with some of the more hair-raising tales I'd recorded. Stories of haunted bridges, cursed lanes, the black dog that accompanied travellers on the high moor all went down well. Apparently the Most Haunted influence was still strong among the general public and real-life tales were incredibly popular tourist attractions. Those words, 'tourist attractions', made the hair on the back of my neck prickle – what I was doing was collecting oral history, social commentary and myth, all gleaned from lone farms high on the moors as tales told on long dark nights before electricity had come to the villages.

If the fairies had ever danced on that isolated stone, or if their land was captured beneath it, then I was their guardian. And even though I had no personal belief in the Little People, I was still going to make sure their stories and their haunts were marked.

7

The grants people seemed happy enough with the way things were going. The mention of a potential book – which could be displayed in shops, with an atmospheric cover and the possibility of earning real money – cheered them immensely. They fed me custard creams and coffee and released me back into the real world where, buoyed up by relief, I did some shopping and headed back to spend an afternoon forcing Chess to do some actual work while I made phone calls to set up more interviews and tracked down some old paperwork from the library's archive resources.

I emerged from the office as the sun was going down, to find Connor and Chess sitting together in the library, forming a book club of two around the history section. Far too late I remembered that Chess's degree was history and that she was only my assistant because there weren't any folklore graduates in York. Or at least none who wanted to work for a pittance and a grouchy boss.

'I find the writing approachable, but a little bit lacking in intellectual rigour,' Chess was saying. As I hadn't seen her read anything apart from *Cosmo* in the time that I'd known her, I was slightly surprised by her assessment. Unless she was covering the subject of women's magazines, of course, which would have fitted her evaluation just as well as some of the modern takes on historical subjects.

'A bit populist, you're right.' Connor put his cup down and then noticed me. 'Ah, and you're here.'

'Why? You're not talking about my work, are you?' I prickled.

'We are not. You're a sensitive soul, Rowan.' He grinned at me, but I wasn't going to be appeased that easily and kept the scowl I'd assumed as soon as I'd seen him out there, drinking coffee. Nobody had offered *me* coffee.

'Pragmatic. I prefer pragmatic,' I said, glancing at their cups in a meaningful way. 'It's been a long afternoon and I'd like to get home, so if you two have finished slandering some poor struggling author...?'

'I'm meant to be going out tonight.' Chess pulled her phone over and glanced at the screen. 'Yep. Time to go.'

She collected her coat, bag, keys, hat, scarf, glasses and other accoutrements as though she were a self-assembly version of an assistant, and waved us a cheery farewell, leaving Connor and I in the silent and dark library, surrounded by watchful books.

'We really weren't talking about you,' he said jauntily.

'I should hope not.' I prepared to lock up. 'You need my spare room and Chess needs the job. If you start ganging up behind my back, then she's looking at going back to shelf-stacking in Tesco and you'll be sleeping on her sofa.'

'That really does make you sound a bit sensitive, y'know,' Connor said in a tone so reasonable that I wanted to punch him. 'And you can't afford that, not if you're putting yourself out there. Publishing theoretical research is a bloody brutal business.'

'I'm well aware.' I still sounded stiff and unlike myself.

Connor O'Keefe had that effect on me – from his casual but expensive clothes to his jaunty air of ever so slightly having the upper hand, he made me defensive and wary. To be honest, most historians brought me out in clenched jaws and narrowed eyes, so he was ahead of the crowd there. 'I'm multi-published in my field.'

'So, then, why folklore?' He followed me out and then stood while I set the alarm. I had no idea why the alarm was necessary – the library's underused nature indicating that the population of this part of York had no insane desire to seize all the books they could carry home, and hit-and-run folklore students were thin on the ground.

'Someone has to remember,' I said shortly.

'Chess said your doctorate is folklore, but your main degree was history, so you switched some time ago?'

I stopped, staring unseeing at the keypad. Here, on this busy street with the dark hustling me to hurry, the memories seemed to press more tightly, provoked by the layers of history that York possessed. Roman, Viking, Norman, Tudor... I could recite the eras as easily as I could rattle off my full name.

'Someone has to remember. Otherwise the memories die. I started to see that history was folklore written by the winners of battles and backed up with paperwork.' I pressed the final button and started the march around the soggy corner to where my car was squeezed into the tiny library car park, hopefully giving the full and final impression that this conversation was over. Connor jogged alongside me, seeming not to be cross at the unsurfaced nature of the car park, which sent spatters of mud up my legs with every squelchy footstep.

'Oh, I'm not saying it's not an interesting subject. I'm wondering why you chose to switch allegiance.' He grinned at me, his expression caught for a moment in the lights of a passing car. 'You could have been one of us.'

'I *was* one of you,' I couldn't help but retort. I needed to learn to bite my tongue and cultivate a serene air that touchy subjects bounced off, but I wasn't there yet. 'That's how I know it's all *evidence*, no room for conjecture, it's walls and measurements and original sources. It's just all so damn *concrete*.' Then, ashamed of my outburst, I threw my bag onto the back seat of the car and got in behind the wheel. Connor was still standing at the passenger door. 'Don't hang about. I've got work to do at home.'

'You haven't unlocked my door,' he said, with a curious inflection in his voice, almost as though he was trying to stop other words from coming out.

I pressed the button that opened the other doors and he got in. 'There you go now,' he said and his voice was cheery again, with something that sounded almost like relief. Had he thought I'd been going to drive away and leave him?

But then, I thought, steering carefully out into the traffic, I'd done it before, hadn't I? Maybe he'd been traumatised by being left. After all, *I'd* known that he was only a mile from the centre of York, but *he* hadn't, when I'd ordered him out at the traffic lights.

'I'm sorry,' I said, in a small voice that didn't really want to be heard, just so I could say I'd said it.

'For maligning my profession? You're all right, I do it a fair bit myself.' Connor raised a hand and scuffed through his hair. 'I've no illusions about the way we work, Rowan. But there has to be evidence, otherwise it's a load of people, each with their own opinions, and that's not history, that's a shouting match.'

We reached the edge of the city and the countryside began to unfold on either side of the road in huge patches of black broken by the lights of occasional farmhouses. Trees leaned over the car, skeletal in their winter uniform of branch, twig and owl, whilst beneath our wheels the lost leaves of autumn formed a frictionless carpet.

Neither of us spoke. I wanted to – there were justifications and accusations that I had lined up and ready. I'd used them before, they were a well-trodden path for the arguments that frequently broke out, usually when funding was involved, but for now I kept them stoppered up behind concentration. The winding roads with their impromptu tight bends and suicidal wildlife meant that I didn't want to be distracted by explaining to Connor why I'd switched from history to folklore. No, scratch that. It wasn't the distraction. I just didn't want to talk about it, particularly not to him.

Finally we breasted the last hill and began the descent towards Mill Cottage. I'd left a light on in the porch, as I always did at this time of year, and it glowed, a welcoming beacon in the pool of darkness that was the ford, the river and the house.

'You don't mind being so isolated?' It was the first thing Connor had said in miles. Perhaps he felt he'd said too much earlier. I could only hope that tact and shame were beginning to creep into his make-up.

'No.' I steered into my parking spot. Then, feeling that maybe a degree of rapprochement might be called for before we spent an evening together in chilly silence, 'And there are always the ducks.'

We got out of the car, into the cool and the quiet. There was no sound apart from the plop and gurgle of the river, and a distant wind running its way through the reeds, as though searching for something.

'They're not exactly popping round for a drink and a bowl of peanuts though, are they?' Connor, too, was keeping it light. I felt my shoulders drop a little and realised I'd been tensing myself against a continuation of his questioning about my life choices.

'They sit outside the window in the morning waiting for toast,' I pointed out. 'And things can get quite heated if there isn't enough to go round.'

'Like our old neighbours in Dublin. You should have heard the rows when the sherry ran out.'

That made me smile and the smile made me loosen up sufficiently when I unlocked the front door to offer to put the kettle on and make some tea. 'What about food? Have you eaten?'

'I'm a history professor. I'm lucky to catch the last pack of sandwiches in the shop down on campus. I've had a few biscuits, in the meeting.'

'How are you still standing?'

'I had toast.' He pointed at my toaster. 'This morning. You made me toast, remember?'

The kitchen light came on, bright and invasive. 'I was going to make a stir-fry,' I said. 'Would you like some?' Then I wanted to bite my tongue again. It wasn't my fault that he didn't feed himself properly – I'd had a fair few of those meetings myself, the ones that went on for hours and ended with you feeling so wrung out that you could barely sip a Cup-A-Soup afterwards. I'd had evenings where I went to bed with a bowl of cereal and realised I'd had nothing else since breakfast.

Connor was watching me under the unforgiving glare of the fluorescent bulb. I knew it washed out my skin and made me look pasty and couldn't work out why it didn't do the same to him. Probably because there wasn't enough skin showing between the barely shaved cheeks and the flopping hair and the coat collar, I decided.

'Look,' he said. 'Show me where the stuff is, and *I'll* cook. You sit yourself down, you look a wee bit...' He tailed off.

'Frazzled,' I supplied. 'I look frazzled. It's how I end every day.' I waved a hand to indicate the fridge, where all the stir-fry ingredients lived, and he bent to open the door and investigate.

'Ah, I didn't like to say,' his voice came muffled from inside the fridge. 'Chicken, veg and some sauce, that right?'

'There's some noodles in the cupboard.' I leaned back in the kitchen chair and closed my eyes, only to jerk back upright with my eyes pinging open like untethered blinds. 'Can you cook? I don't want you setting my kitchen on fire and ruining practically the only food I've got in.'

A snort. 'Course I can cook. Mam was away at conferences more often than not, and Da thinks cooking is making a cup of tea, so the lads and I learned defensive cookery at an early age.' A moment's fumbling later and ingredients began to hit the counter. 'Except young Eamonn, of course.'

'The priest,' I said, wanting to show that I had, at least, listened to him.

'That's your man. I think he has parishioners bringing him hot meals most days. Like offerings.' The wok hung from a rail above the worktop, and Connor unhooked it deftly and swung it onto the stove. 'Why don't you leave me to this and you go and have a shower or get changed or whatever it is you do when you get in. I'll earn my keep here.'

How long had it been since someone had cooked for me? I asked myself the question as I wandered out of the kitchen and up the stairs without even raising the energy for arguing. A long time. A *long* time. I couldn't remember the last time I'd been able to shower with the smell of cooking wafting up the stairs and the sound of dishes clanking, a voice singing and muttering

The Start of the Story   55

in the kitchen below and lights randomly going on and off as someone moved from room to room.

For a moment I tasted memory. A cup of tea brought in bed. A fried breakfast before a winter walk. Home baking. *How long?*

I knew how long, of course. I knew, almost to the day. And sometimes that time felt like a lifetime, and sometimes only yesterday.

When I got back to the kitchen the air was full of the blue haze of hot oil and the smell of soy sauce. Connor had opened the window and the chill of the intruding breeze contrasted with the heat of the cooker so sharply that I half feared it would snow on the table.

'Good timing. You look brighter.' Connor plonked two plates on the table, without ceremony. Veg and noodles flopped over the edges and a piece of pak choi left the launch pad to fly onto the floor.

'Presentation from the University Canteen school of cookery?' I asked, but I half smiled as I said it.

'Ah, when you've four starving brothers sitting waiting with their napkins tucked in and their forks raised in a threatening fashion, you care more about getting it onto the table than Instagram.' He sat opposite me, fork already in hand.

The food was good. I'd been half afraid that Connor's idea of 'cooking' might have involved burning everything to a uniform 'hard brown and crispy', but he'd got it just right.

'Garlic salt,' he said, pausing from his eating like a starving peasant. 'It's the secret to everything. Apart from Victoria sponge.'

'I didn't even know I *had* garlic salt.' I was eating in a more decorous fashion. 'But you're right. It's good.'

'I'm softening you up. In case I have to stay longer than intended.' He gulped down the last forkful. 'I had a quick look around properties to rent between meetings, and there's not much about.'

I felt the shutters come down again. I didn't altogether relish the feeling as I might have done before, probably because I'd been half enjoying this relaxed conversation over hot food, with the cottage illuminated and the glow from the lights shining out over the water. 'You can't,' I said shortly and picked up my plate. I hadn't quite finished eating, but I wanted to indicate that the matter was indisputable. 'We agreed.' I scraped the remains of my food into the bin with enough noise to drown out any comebacks.

Connor nodded over his last forkful. 'Of course. I was teasing.'

I relaxed a fraction again. 'I knew that.'

'You're very easy to wind up, y'know.'

'So there's no challenge in doing it,' I retorted, putting my plate in the sink and running water onto it, which resulted in splashing myself up the front.

'Touché.' Connor got up and stood beside me. 'Let me wash up. Why d'you not have the dishwasher?'

'Because there's only me.' I felt oddly exposed standing there next to him. I'd put on a fleecy tracksuit after my shower, while he'd taken off his coat and hung it behind the door but was otherwise still wearing his usual black jumper and jeans combo. It made me feel as though I were unfinished, unprepared, whilst he was ready to face anything. I sat down again. He'd seemed too tall, too intrusive to be close to.

'And what do you do in the evenings around here?' He washed up efficiently and stacked the pots and pans to dry as though it was his usual task. All those brothers, I thought. If they were all this domesticated, that house in Dublin must be immaculate. 'You've a TV, I notice.'

'The signal down here is dreadful though,' I said. 'We're in a dip. I stream stuff on my laptop, but usually I'm working.'

'Isn't that what daytime is for?' Connor dried his hands on the kitchen towel and sat down opposite me again.

'Daytime is for recording, for visiting people. Collecting their stories, going through various libraries, old papers. Evening is when I type stuff up, collate, cross-reference. That kind of thing,' I finished lamely, aware that this did not make it sound as though I were hosting riotous gambling evenings with exotic cocktails.

'No socialising?' He rolled his sleeves down.

'I socialise.' Now, that sounded defensive. 'I sometimes go out with Chess, or – friends.' *And how long since that happened?* 'But I'm busy. I've told the grant board that I'm going to publish some of our stories, the more local ones, and they're very interested in that, so I need to have something to show them at the next meeting. I need the money,' I finished, hoping that some overt vulnerability might make him back off.

'The overhanging bogeyman of the grant board.' Connor leaned back in the wooden chair, stretching his legs out in front of him. 'Now that's one thing we *can* agree on. I'm trying to raise the funding for a full investigation of that potential Roman settlement up on the moor there.' He shifted about, crossed long legs ankle over ankle. 'It is no secret to say that they are not keen.'

'Oh dear,' I said, with a lack of sympathy exuding from both syllables.

'Which is why it would be good to lift your stone there. I'm still thinking it could have Roman origins. Or even pre-Roman, they sometimes re-used Iron Age or Neolithic artefacts as grave markers, and the cemeteries were usually on the road outside the settlement, so that might be even better.'

'You're not lifting the stone.' My words were heavy, individually enunciated to leave no room for doubt, and he went quiet, tugging at the day or so's growth of stubble that adorned his chin.

We had sat in this self-imposed sullenness for a minute or so, when there came a most tremendous crash from the living room, as though someone had thrown a brick through the window, and we both leaped up, wide-eyed.

'What the hell was that?' I'd frozen, clutching the edge of the table as though, should this be some kind of zombie attack, I could upturn it and hide.

'Dunno.' He looked at me and then at the dark doorway to the room beyond. 'Shall I go and look?'

'It might be dangerous.' I grabbed at his arm to prevent him walking into whatever-it-was. 'Someone trying to break in.'

'Are you breeding attack-ducks out here?' Connor gently removed my hand from his sleeve. 'If they're breaking in then they're already here, and unless we barricade ourselves in the kitchen, we're in trouble. Besides, it's quiet now.'

He was right. Bar the odd tinkle of glass falling, there were no further sounds of onslaught, and together we shuffled our way over the threshold into the living room. I switched on the light.

'Oh no.' My map had fallen from its hook on the wall, slid down to smash on the metal of the log burner and lie face down on the carpet amid a glittering fallout of glass fragments. The frame had come apart, the mitre corners showing the nails that had held them together, newly exposed like internal organs.

'What was it?' Connor edged into the room now, as though the broken map might be concealing burglars.

'It's my 1857 map of the area. I use it for research. It shows the farms that were around then, the field boundaries and the old watercourses. The stone is marked on it too.' I picked up the map by one side of the frame and more glass twinkled its way in shards onto the carpet. 'It's... I've had it a long time.'

'Hmm.' He looked at the hook, now distinctly sideways and with the lower portion bent. 'This was never going to support that weight for long.'

'It's been up there since... It's been hanging perfectly well for the last five years,' I snapped. 'I have no idea why it would choose now to give up the ghost, unless it's under the sheer misery of having a historian in the house.'

'I don't think you can pin this on me,' he said, equably. 'Mind you, I don't think you can pin anything much on a hook like that.' He bent down beside me and gently took the frame out of my hand. It was only then that I realised I was cut and bleeding where tiny fragments of glass from the edge of the frame had sliced into my fingers. 'Put it down, it's sharp.'

I tightened my grip until blood oozed. The shock of the breakage had gone now, replaced by the helplessness of losing something with so much memory bound to it. The map poked a corner from the frame, horribly bare now its glass was gone, looking cheap and like just another piece of paper, rather than the historic overview of my area it had been when it had been flat and weighted and captive.

Connor looked into my face. 'It's not any old map now, is it?' he asked, but it wasn't really a question, more an observation. 'What is it, sentimental value?'

'Something like that.' I ground the words out. 'I'll sweep up the mess.'

He lifted the map, thrusting its way clear of the broken bits of frame like a geographical tongue, and spread it carefully on my dining table. 'Ah, it's fine. No damage at all.' I watched him from the kitchen as he carefully picked away the split frame and the razor edging of glass splinters until they sat in a flat pile so he could pore over the old map. 'I see it now. There's your stone.' A finger jabbed down almost on the dead centre of the map. 'And over here, that's where we think the Roman settlement traces are.' He squinted close to the paper. 'Looks like there was something above ground when the map was drawn up – those could be the lines of walls.'

I came in with the dustpan and brush and a tea towel around my cut hand. 'They could be field boundaries,' I said.

'Mmm. Could be, I suppose. And what's this over here?'

'Oh, that's Evercey Manor.' I began to collect the pieces together with the brush. Although my heart was still hammering, the worst of the shock and despair had worn off now and I didn't feel as though I might burst into tears at any second. 'A mid-fifteenth century place that got added to and built on right up until the Second World War, when there was nobody to inherit it and the place was demolished.'

He pulled a thoughtful face. 'That's good. Shows the land has been lived on, which bodes well for the Romans, who might have been the ones that cleared the land in the first place. We could have a villa and associated buildings – not quite as exciting as a full settlement, but it could be worth bringing the archaeologists in on.'

'Leave the stone alone,' I said almost automatically, trying to make sure I got every last twinkle of glass from the carpet. 'I'll get the hoover over this.'

Connor straightened up. 'Why do you care so much?' he asked. 'On the one hand you're this aloof personality who doesn't want interference and on the other – no, wait a minute, actually I think I've answered my own question there.'

I stood for a moment looking down on the map, my hands full of dusty sharpness and cracked wood. The urge to cry was still pushing vigorously at the backs of my eyes. 'It's not the stone *per se*,' I said, carefully managing the words so that no emotion came with them. 'It's what it stands for.'

He sat down suddenly on my chair, at my dining table work desk. I bridled at the liberty. 'Go on, then,' he said. 'Convince me.'

Stiffly I took up station on the other side of the desk, carefully placing the dustpan full of glass in the middle, on the top of the map. Did I deliberately want to block him from looking at my map? Or did I want to make sure I didn't knock the sweepings back onto the floor? I wasn't sure.

'I could say the same to you,' I said. 'Convince *me* that looking for Romans takes precedence over my work.'

Connor rolled my chair back so that he could lean back at an angle so acute that he was almost a straight line. I could have laid him on the map and measured distances. 'You're good at this,' he said admiringly. 'You've argued with a lot of historians, then?'

His lack of confrontation, his happy acknowledgement of my proficiency in this particular struggle and his expression of surprised enjoyment took the wind completely from my sails.

'I've had to fight my corner a lot, yes,' I said, and the desire to beat him into submission with the dustpan faded. 'Quite a lot of people don't take folklore studies seriously. It's all fairy stories and rubbish as far as they are concerned.'

Connor was looking down at the part of the map still visible now. He traced his finger over the dark shading that was the moors. 'Try me,' he said, in a slightly softer voice. 'I'm Irish. The fairy stories now, they're practically part of my genetic make-up.'

The light glowed off his hair and he looked relaxed and comfortable, as though he belonged there in my wheelie chair, at my worktable, and I managed to grip onto the rapidly vanishing edges of my annoyance and distrust. 'My work is not your business,' I clipped out rapidly. 'I'm going to bed now. I need an early start in the morning, so if you're going into York, you'll need to get a taxi.'

That had done it. The open interest vanished from his expression and he frowned it into a closed look, eyes narrowed and his mouth a lip-chewing twist. 'Hmm, okay,' he said thoughtfully, then, 'I'll not be needing one. Tomorrow I'm walking up onto the moor and having a bit of a poke around. I'm meeting a guy to put up a drone and take an overview of the proposed site.'

'Oh.' My heart dropped a little. Was that *disappointment*? Or annoyance at his assumption that he didn't need to tell me his plans? Had I, perhaps, been looking forward a bit too much to continuing my acerbic confrontations in the car on our morning drive? 'I'll be back around six.'

'Could you leave me a key?' He was tracing those lines again, a slow finger hovering too close to the site of the stone for my liking.

'What for?'

He smiled at me now, but there were still traces of that tightness in his eyes and the smile wasn't quite as easy and open as usual. 'I'm sorry. I know you don't know me from Adam and I might have my mates hanging around the corner with a lorry to strip out your valuables, but, truly? I want to be able to sit down and drink coffee and not have to spend all day in the company of the drone men who can, let me tell you, be a touch too single-minded for the likes of me.' Another, slightly wider, grin. 'Besides, it's dark by the time you get back and I don't want to have to hide in the bushes so the ducks don't get me.'

I couldn't help it. I smiled at the image of Connor crouching in the undergrowth with his coat over his head. It was only sensible for him to have a key, after all. I was sometimes away at folklore-related events or couldn't get home. Never for exciting, fun reasons; more for lecturing or grinning-halfheartedly-whilst-standing-at-the-back-of-a-crowd-holding-a-glass-of-cheap-warm-wine reasons, but even so. Giving Connor a key was reasonable. 'Sorry. Of course. I'll dig out the spare key.'

His face seemed to relax a little. 'Thank you. And goodnight now.'

I had forgotten that I was taking my high dudgeon and retiring. I'd got caught in the net of his interest, and having someone here occupying space in my home. 'Yes. Right. I'll hoover the bits up tomorrow.'

'I can do it, while I'm drinking my coffee and hiding from the dual threats of drone-men and ducks.'

I flicked him a short smile of farewell and took myself off up the stairs, not sure whether to feel affronted at his casual assumption of duties in the house or happy that I wasn't going to have to wield the hoover.

Connor was making himself far too much at home for my liking, that was it. I resolved to get Chess to spend tomorrow finding him somewhere else to stay, even if it was in Sheffield.

8

1870

The women, shawls over their heads and crying, gathered inside the cottage as the men clustered outside. This was something the men must do, alone. The women would make their own journey out there to the stone, tomorrow maybe, or the day after, carrying their little offerings. But tonight was only for the men.

Jack, whose cottage this was, gathered the box inside his jacket. It had been an heirloom, given to him by his father when he'd married, containing a silver spoon – the family treasure. Now it was going to the stone, containing the weight of their hearts within it.

'Now then, lads.' John, who looked after the horses up at the house, was in charge tonight. 'Stay together. If anyone asks... we're off to greet the fairies, all right?' He rested a heavy hand on Jack's shoulder in a moment of solidarity. 'All right?'

Jack nodded and adjusted the box. The torches were lit and the procession started, out along the sandy trackway that joined the estate to the neighbouring towns, and then swiftly branching off to cross the moor to where the stone waited for them.

* * *

Now

Now that autumn was vanishing, overcome by the onrush of a rapid winter, I was doing less driving about in search of first-person tales, and more cold hard research in warm, soft libraries. Many of those with tales to recount lived in deserted hamlets high in the hills, holding on to a way of life that had vanished twenty or thirty years ago with the coming of computerised farming. Elderly men still carried hay to barns full of cattle, women who'd been born before the war still baked and cleaned farmhouses and drew water from the well. It was a generation that was disappearing rapidly. Each cold winter took another few, and I had to seize my chance to record their memories of traditions and superstitions. But driving fifty miles along sleety lanes to sit in unheated rooms with my recorder during the snatched moments of daylight had taught me to do the recording during summer and spend the winter compiling and cross-referencing with other folklorists in other parts of the country. Plus, I had a cupboard full of donated diaries and observations to sort through. These cold months were a time for hunkering down, drawing the curtains and reading. I drew the line at making jam though.

But being in the office meant being in the forefront of the onslaught that was Chess. 'He's good looking, though. How are you getting on?' Her questions were relentless.

'He's a good guest so far, but he can't stay with me, Chess. He's the enemy, after all.'

'History isn't the enemy, Rowan.' Chess pursed her prim lips. 'We're complementary regimes.'

Nothing complimentary about Professor Connor O'Keefe, I thought mutinously. I'd tried to figure out various ways in which he could have sabotaged my map but couldn't work out how it could have been done and grudgingly had to accept it as an accident. I even found myself wondering why the hell I had left him that spare key this morning whilst I was sorting through some donated papers and sneezing at the dust. He couldn't stay much longer. He just *couldn't*.

This was not right. This had to stop. I couldn't work if I was going to be second-guessing the motives of a man whom I half suspected was already up on the moor with a crowbar and a notebook. He wanted to lift the Fairy Stane. And I wasn't going to let him.

I realised I'd skimmed several pages of handwritten notes, taken by a lady who'd been an amateur collector of local tales, which had been given to us by her granddaughter who'd found them in the attic. There could be loads of as yet undiscovered tales amid the cramped and crinkled pages, but I wouldn't know because I'd been too busy dwelling on having Connor O'Keefe as a lodger, and this just wouldn't do. I needed to pull myself together and... and he needn't think that trying to get me to open up about my reasons for studying folklore would soften me towards his attitude!

Folklore was folklore, it informed and expanded recent social history. I didn't need to justify myself or try to explain. If he preferred to stick to solid and concrete evidential history, then good for him.

Good for him. I turned a page so quickly that it nearly tore and I carefully placed the book down onto the desk. I needed to be calm. Methodical. Chess had gone over to the main library to order some research materials so I couldn't even go and relieve myself of some of the irritation by listening to her recitations of last night's TV or what someone I didn't know had said about somebody else that I'd never met and how it had caused a feud that was set to take to social media.

I put my coat on and went out into the windy, rainswept street to try to clear my head. The buildings of York leaned in, crowding above my head in their medieval glory, whilst patches of the old wall shone in the brief sun. At least my office was in a picturesque location, I thought, stomping down the road towards the coffee shop and letting the breeze cool my ears and untangle my hair. Roman, Viking, Norman, Tudor. If it hadn't been for those pesky Scandinavians it would sound like a litany of past boyfriends' names, I thought, resisting the temptation to poke the wall vigorously for its historical persistence. Whereas my branch of history was ephemeral, fleeting. Stories of lives that touched the supernatural, or, rather, gave supernatural shape to the as yet unknown. Stories of social warning – grey lady ghosts were *always* girls who'd got pregnant out of wedlock and drowned themselves. Unmarried pregnancy and suicide, those twin dark threats that hung over girls, the dual transgressions.

I bought myself a sturdy coffee to give myself an excuse for the walk, and headed back for the office, moving slowly as I sipped, aware of myself moving alone through this crowd while I daydreamed about ways of forcing Connor to leave my cottage. I wanted my space back. I wanted to be left alone in the evenings with my thwarted dreams and my books. I couldn't mutter to myself as I moved from room to room while Connor was there, he would think I was mad – or even more mad than he obviously currently considered me to be.

I wanted my life back the way it had been.

I even stooped to reading estate agency window adverts of houses for rent, only to find that anywhere on a bus route was prohibitively expensive, and he'd been right, mostly already rented. Then I berated myself again. His accommodation problems weren't my problems. I'd got enough on with this book that I'd told the grant providers I was writing in order to justify them continuing to pay for my research. Now I had to get on and write the wretched thing, but how was I going to do that with my brain circling around the issues of having an argumentative historian in my space?

No. He had to go.

I drained the coffee, threw the cup in the recycling, and went to tell the returned Chess that I was heading back to the cottage to work from home for the rest of the day. With a bit of luck Mr Smuggo would still be out, striding around the moors like Heathcliff in better clothes, possibly falling into a bog and drowning. I smiled to myself at the thought.

'Heading home to spend more time with the good professor?' Chess was tapping desultorily at her keyboard whilst really reading a fashion blog.

'Working on a way to get him gone,' I said. 'And I haven't ruled out pushing him in the river or giving him a tent either, so keep your sofa free.'

She chuckled in a way that was designed to make me angry so I snatched up my car keys and stormed out through the back door so as not to upset any of the library patrons who might be innocently browsing the shelves. I stomped across the car park, careless of the splattered mud, and threw myself into my car, seething with resentment again at the fact that I was heading back to an uncertainty of historian and having to think about meals and bathroom time and clean towels instead of my calm isolation.

Chess was obviously trying to set us up, which meant she was also now the enemy. This was ridiculous! All I wanted was peace and quiet, a useable office – which it was more or less, and nicely central – and a snug place to retreat to and finish off my work. That was all! Not too much to ask! And now I'd got – I swung the wheel sharply and the car oversteered, nearly clipping the grass verge – my assistant playing matchmaker, my downtime disturbed and my cottage...

I remembered the cottage as it had been. Raised voices, as we'd called up and down stairs for advice or tools, evenings spent looking up the best type of walling to install, the most period-appropriate paint finishes. When it had been a project, a proper historical restoration and something that had...

No. Stop it. Now was what was important. And the now contained Connor O'Keefe.

I couldn't properly appreciate the loveliness of the storm-scoured countryside, the newly planted brown earth sprouting with a thin cover of green, like a hair transplant on a gigantic scalp, or the way the distant sun touched the tops of recently bared trees and highlighted them against the vigorous blue of the sky. But I did, as ever, catch my breath at the top of the rise that led down to the ford, when the thin silver strand of the river at the bottom captured the light and the little cottage glowed in all its whitewashed finish, snug in the landscape as it had been for centuries.

There was no sign of Connor and the door was locked. Hugely relieved, I flopped onto the little loveseat, not even taking off my coat or hanging up my bag. He wasn't here. Good. I could actually do what I'd said I'd do and start some work before I was interrup...

'You're back early.'

'I thought you'd be out.' My eyes had found the gap on the

wall where the map had hung, and they caught on the bare painted space, refusing to look at him.

'Just popped back to pick up a delivery.' He hesitated, as though he wanted to engage me in conversation, but the way I kept my eyes on the empty wall must have put him off, because he went back out again. I heard clattering in the kitchen for a moment and then he was outside to greet the arrival of a white van, bearing something big and wrapped in cardboard.

'Just go away,' I whispered. It sounded like a plea or a prayer and I hadn't realised how much I'd been banking on having the place to myself.

He came back in. 'Tea?'

'No, thank you. I've got work to do.'

'Oh. Okay.' A pause while he rummaged and I heard the kettle boil. Then, 'I put the hoover over the broken glass, by the way. It should be fine down there now.' A clank of mugs and a pouring of water. 'And I'm off out away back up on the moor. We've found something that could be the walls on your map, or what's left of them.'

Almost apologetic at its appearance, a mug of tea slid into the edge of my vision, backed by the dark cloud that was Connor, and then he was gone to a slam of the back door and a raised voice of greeting. The tea steamed, puffs of vapour floating across to add to the ghosts of the cottage. The miller, his wife, those children – how many others might still be around?

Not the right ones. Not the wanted ones.

I sighed and it let out some of the annoyance, then I picked up the mug and began drinking the tea almost without thinking about it but imagining instead the investigations going on up on the moors that teetered above my house. In fact, if I got up and went to the window, I could almost see them, where the sand track that had once been a road crossed the ford and rose up to become another hill on the far side. Out on that ridge was the track that led to the Fairy Stane and from there, presumably, on to this putative Roman settlement.

I turned away from the window and forced another mouthful of tea between clenched teeth. At least Connor had made lifting the stone sound like a last resort. If they got concrete results from the drone search to add to his no doubt exhaustive, in-depth and scholarly previous research, then he wouldn't *need* to lift it, would he?

And, really, why *did* I care so much?

The thought hit me, barbed and vicious. *Why did I care?* The stone could be lifted, checked for any revealing lettering and put back. Who would know? Only whoever lifted it, Connor O'Keefe, and me, and I'd only know if I checked for disturbed foliage. Unless... unless it turned out that the stone really was a Roman relic, and then what? Would they take it to a museum, to preserve its ancient writing? And leave me with nothing but a bare space on the moor and a huge hole in the legends? I couldn't really write a book of local folklore based around a stone that wasn't there any more, could I?

Besides, whatever the professor might think, memory, folk history, was important. It had to be kept. It had to be guarded and curated because otherwise what use had it been to all those people who'd kept it for all those years? To us in the twenty-first century, muttering charms as you churned the milk was pointless. Unnecessary. We knew the cream would turn to butter regardless, as long as the fat content was sufficient, the temperature was right, the cows had eaten good grass and you kept on churning. But back before science stuck its fingers in farming, so much was experience and guesswork. And charms? If someone like me didn't keep a record of such things, if notes weren't kept about the words used and the beliefs behind them, then they'd vanish as if they'd never been. Folklore was *important*. It was memory and the past and ways of life long gone, *and it couldn't be allowed to die.*

The silence in the house sang in my ears. There was nothing but the gentle gloop and gurgle of the river as it caught on the edges of the ford and then swirled free back to the depths of the mill race, and the hum of the air trapped in these small rooms.

I sighed again, carefully lifted the old paper of the map off my desk and turned on the computer.

9

Connor didn't come back that evening. I went to bed and lay awake, alert for the sound of his key in the lock, but it never came. In the morning I got up to a quiet and empty house, made myself tea and was throwing the crusts from my toast out to the ducks when I thought to check my e-mails.

> It's late, I've been out for a drink with the drone boys, and I don't want to wake you by coming in, so I'll sleep on one of their sofas tonight. Don't want you to think I've fallen in a bog and drowned!
> Connor

I wondered if he knew that was what I'd been silently planning for him, and felt my cheeks get a bit hot. Was I really *that* obvious? Then I shrugged and decided to have a quick morning shower, just because I could. The house was mine again, in all its polish-and-old-wood-scented glory.

The gap on the wall where my map had hung snagged my

eyes again as I walked past, and the map itself flopped half its length from the bureau where it was currently resting to leave my work desk clear. Would I rehang it? I ought to, it was useful in the way it showed me sites known only to folk tales and maps like this, but I didn't know if I could. This wasn't just a map, it was a memory-story, leading from that secretive bookshop near the minster where we'd met over the ancient volumes, to the day we'd hung it on the wall. The day we'd moved into the cottage and looked around at all that had to be done and hugged and laughed at the hard work waiting for us.

'God, Elliot, I miss you.'

The words felt heavy and obvious. Of *course* I missed him, that went without saying, so why did I feel the need to breathe the words aloud? To keep his memory alive, somehow?

I shook my head and sat, damp and rosy from the shower, on the edge of the bed. This gave me a prime view, too high for the river to feature, so it comprised the brownish ribbon of track, pimpled with chippings and acned with the red of broken brick that the farmers scattered every year to try to stop the whole thing degenerating into mud. Then, further up, the greying sticks of heather and whortleberry and the occasional blast of colour from gorse, as though some wild impressionist had been by and decided that what the moors needed at this time of year was more yellow.

I was making lists in my head, which was hopeful. A mental track of all the sites that I'd either written about, recorded or found among my paperwork, everything centred on the Fairy Stane, and I had about enough to fill a book. A small book, to be sure, but then nobody would read a four-thousand-page tome of scholarly research into the whys and wherefores of some of the stories. Whether the drowned maids were a cautionary tale to keep young girls from going astray with the farmers' boys, or the hobs and goblins were distant memories of the Celtic hermits living wild in caves – the reading public didn't care. They wanted spooks; they wanted places they could go on the moor and put their ear to the ground in the – hope? Expectation? Fear? – of hearing the fairy world partying beneath.

They wanted, in short, *local colour*. I could do that, and hopefully in such a way that the grant committee would keep funding my research, because the book would pay for itself. It might not reach the dizzy heights of *The Times* bestseller lists, but it would sell regularly in the independent bookshops and tourist information places. People could take home a souvenir of 'that time we went to North Yorkshire', put it on their bookshelves and occasionally dip in to laugh at how funny we'd been in the past.

Outside, the sky, which had previously been bell-clear and cloudless, was becoming oppressed by the weight of incoming cloud. Time for me to drive through to York, see if any of those books that Chess had ordered had come in yet, and perhaps venture across to the university, where the music department was running a short course on Folklore through Lyrics. I'd promised to drop in for a chat with the students.

I gave one last long look out across the high moor and started to get dressed.

By late afternoon I was feeling proud of myself. I'd ticked off the things I had needed to do, listed some potential chapter headings for the book, given Chess a bulk of handwritten pages to start transcribing – which had interrupted her novel-reading at a vital page – and tidied the office so I now knew roughly where everything was.

There was no sign of Connor. I'd half expected a head around the door, or a text asking me what time I was leaving, but there had been no indication of his existence all day. He was probably hung-over, I thought with a degree of grim pleasure. Out drinking with his cronies and then sleeping it off on an uncomfortable sofa, then spending the day holding his head and moving slowly. It would be one less day that I had to worry about the Fairy Stane anyway.

So it came as something of a surprise to arrive back at Mill Cottage and find him firmly in residence, in the kitchen. There was a pleasing smell of garlic in the air, the back door was wide open and the pool of light that spilled out to illuminate the approach was studded with hopeful ducks.

'Ah, there you are, now.' He whirled around from the hob with a wooden spoon in his hand and a tea towel around his waist. 'I hope you don't mind but I made dinner.'

I wanted to ask how he dared take such a liberty, but I was hungry, and the food smelled good and the kitchen was warm and well lit in comparison to the bleak dark beyond.

'What is it?' I asked cautiously, hanging up my coat.

'A recipe of my granny's. There's pork and garlic and – well, you'll find out. You're all right with those things?'

It really did smell nice and I found I was smiling. 'I'll eat anything someone else cooks,' I said.

Connor looked at me, his head tipped slightly to one side and the steam from something boiling making his hair frizz. 'That's good,' he said. 'Because I've no idea what it tastes like.'

'It smells edible.' So, he wasn't hung-over to hell, he wasn't moping drearily around whilst swallowing paracetamol and slumping in corners. 'How was your evening yesterday? You could have come back; you wouldn't disturb me.'

'We got to talking history – they are all Cavaliers in the local Sealed Knot brigade, they do reconstructions of Civil War battles and things. So, we spent most of the evening playing "my army's bigger than your army" and drinking beer. It was great.

By then I was over in York, and it was late and a taxi would be expensive so I slept on a sofa.' He turned back to the stove and stirred something that bubbled. 'Not entirely altruistic on my part.'

He served up the food and we sat in the kitchen and ate, without much chat. I didn't really want to talk anyway; I'd used up all my words during the day and he seemed to be similarly sunk in thought.

'How did the drone go?' I asked eventually, after we'd cleared our plates in silence.

He shrugged. 'There's some interesting indications. The crop marks I saw online last year weren't visible, of course, but there are walls that could be the remains of buildings over a broad area that could have been a trading post.'

'Not a town, then.'

He shrugged again. 'We've got roads going up over the moors, we've got forts, but we've not got anywhere that people could have been living. The army would be in the forts, but what about the families? The followers and the workers?' Now he shook his head. 'A previously unknown Roman settlement, now that would really make Mam proud.'

'You're doing all this to please your family?' I looked at him over the table. This was the first sign I'd seen of any kind of personal vulnerability.

'Four brothers, one in the Church.' Connor gave me a smile. 'It takes a fair bit to rise to the top of that pile.'

Then, as though he felt he'd said too much, he got up and began clattering plates into the sink and scraping saucepans, leaving me feeling as though I had been prying into secret places. 'Thank you for dinner,' I said, sounding stiff and obligated. 'It was very nice.'

'No problem. You can wash up though.'

'Of course.' Then I felt awkward that I hadn't offered straight away. 'Absolutely.' I got up and went to the sink.

'Oh, and I got this.' Connor went into the living room and came back with the cardboard parcel that I'd seen him take yesterday from the van driver. 'I thought it might be useful.'

'What is it?'

He slit the card that wrapped the large rectangle, and pulled out more packing material. 'It's a new frame. For your map.'

I froze. My arms were up to the elbows in sudsy water, cutlery was chiming and clinking off the crockery as it floated to the bottom and, for a second, it was the only sound in the room. 'What.' It wasn't a question.

'You're right, it's a useful resource, that map. I'd never have heard of Evercey Manor if it weren't for that, and the Civil War history guys had some interesting stories to tell about that place. D'you know that it stayed Catholic? Apparently the family that owned it had some dirt on Henry, or possibly Elizabeth, and they carried on being Catholic pretty much underground, throughout the Reformation.'

The frame slid out of the bundled packing material. It was modern pine with protruding metal staples, a thin poor replacement for the heavy original framing that had encased my map before. No weight to it at all.

'And I think it might well be necessary to lift your stone,' Connor continued, as though everything he was doing were perfectly normal. 'We won't do any harm, we'll lift and photograph, maybe a TLS scan of the surface so we can recreate—'

'You are not lifting that stone.' I pulled my arms back out of the water, feeling angry that I'd allowed myself to be lulled by his cooking, his seeming to care. 'You can't.'

'We could replace it with an identical stone,' he carried on, sounding as though this were perfectly reasonable. 'No one need even know it wasn't the original. But we'd only need to do that if the stone has some detailing on that needs preserving. Come on, even you must know how important it is to make sure that we guard against the stone's weathering into illegibility, if it gives us any clues as to what was going on out there.'

'No,' I said again, my voice as tight as a straitjacket. Tiny domestic bubbles of froth spilled further up my arms until my sleeves were wet. 'You can't.'

Here it was. Everything that separated folklore from history. Everything that showed that I stood for the people; the lost and the voiceless out on those moors, wandering in their stories, whilst he stood for the surgical, factual demand for answers.

We stared at one another for a moment, then I turned and dashed the frame from his hand. I couldn't have told if it was an accident, a mere contact of body against the pale, thin wood, or whether I'd intended to catch the corner and sweep it to the floor. Either way, it fell, spinning, from his grasp and broke on the tiles.

'My husband made the old frame.' My voice was so swollen by all the extra, unsaid words that it came out an octave lower.

Water dripped. We both stood and looked at the wreckage on the kitchen floor, a tangle of pine strips, staples and cracked glass.

'You have a husband,' Connor said. Then he turned and, without another look, opened the back door and walked out into the night

I cleared up the second wrecked frame of the week and waited for him to come back in and explain himself. Why *shouldn't* I have a husband? He'd never, at any point, asked about my domestic arrangements or, more importantly, how someone who lived on a grant for folklore research could afford a cottage and a car. And why should he care? He was living here against my better judgement until he could find somewhere closer to the university, not mooning at my heels like a lovesick swain. My domestic arrangements, my life, *were none of his business*.

So why *should* he care? Walking off into a dark, although unfortunately for his internal narrative not stormy, night – what a total overreaction! I put the twisted cardboard and fragmented mess into the bin and looked out across the ford, up the valley side where the track ran, and saw the slim shape of someone silhouetted by the bright light of the full moon into a stick form. He was heading to the stone, I realised. He was going to go up onto the moor and lift my stone, just because I'd mentioned that I had a husband. Why? Had he been hoping that he could somehow use Irish charm and sex appeal to persuade me to let him ruin an item central to local folklore? Had he been trying to get round me with his cooking and chat?

Shit. I could not let that happen. He hadn't got a coat on – the big black coat was still hanging from its hook on the back of the kitchen door. He'd waded the ford and he was walking up onto the high moor in a black sweater and jeans, and from the way the moon's light was crystallising out on every sharp angle out there, there was going to be a frost. November didn't mess about out here, it could be sub-zero in an hour and if he stopped for any length of time the cold would get him, if the bogs didn't or he didn't break a leg.

'Bloody idiot.' I pulled on my own coat, pushed my feet into boots and headed out to the car. All the time my mind was full of the confusion of the last ten minutes, and I dropped the car keys in the mud, which necessitated a few fumbling minutes while I patted down the ground all around the car door until I found them. *Why* had he walked out? The normal response to hearing that someone was married would be – Oh? I didn't know you were married. What's his name? Where is he at the moment? I *wondered* how you'd managed to bag yourself a lovely cottage in the wilds... Then my mouth dried as I realised that any of those questions would have meant a conversation. About Elliot. A conversation that I still wasn't sure that I was ready for, full of words I wasn't sure I could say.

The car splashed reluctantly through the ford, the water spraying up the sides after the rain of the previous couple of days, and then gained purchase on the track beyond. Connor was gone and when I reached the top there was no sign of him further along, so I knew he'd gone out over the moor. There was only one destination point out here, unless he was going to stride moodily through knee-deep heather all night. The stone. He really *had* gone out to the stone, the utter shit. I spared a momentary thought for him scrabbling about at its corners, trying to find something to act as a lever. Eight square feet of heavy local gritstone would not be an easy lift solo, but he might decide to try it, and the thought had me leaving the car and sprinting out along the almost invisible path by the inadequate light of the moon, now filtering through cloud like a Halloween illustration.

I knew the route. I'd been out here so often that I didn't slip on the very wet patch of peaty mud where the moor sloped gently downwards, or sprain my ankle on the loose gravelly part, where scree could take your feet from under you and sprawl you into the wet undergrowth. I ran until I could see Connor's form, hunched into a hook shape as he looked down on the stone. The moon was relentless. There was nothing gentle about its light as it rendered the moor stark and endless and the stone a black slab.

'What the *hell* are you doing?' I was a little breathless after my dash.

He kept his back to me, head bowed like a mourner at a

graveside, and didn't speak. The moon caught in his hair, in his clothes. He looked like an illustration in this monochrome landscape, a dark, upright foreground figure against the tangled shaded background.

'Connor?' His silence disturbed me. I walked across and ended up facing him across the Fairy Stane, both of us looking down on its pitted surface.

Finally he spoke. 'I didn't know you were married,' he said, and now it was his turn with the low octaves. An owl hooted atmospherically from the trees near the river, and it echoed through the night like emphasis.

'Why should it matter?' I asked, pushing my hands into my pockets to try to warm them, and shrugging my shoulders up. It was definitely going to be frosty tonight. There was already an element of crunch about the long reedy grass at our feet. 'My marital status is nothing to do with you.'

Connor sighed and sat down on the edge of the stone. This made him hunch even more, so that he looked like a grasshopper taking a break. 'I had to leave Dublin,' he said.

'Yes, I know. Otherwise you wouldn't be here, would you?' I walked around the stone now so that I could face him, and I could see that he was shivering slightly. Good. That would teach him that you couldn't do 'moody stomping about the night' in North Yorkshire in November – it wasn't practical.

'No, I mean...' He looked up at me. His face was stark in the moonlight. 'I *had* to leave Dublin. I got... involved with a girl and I thought it was getting serious. Turned out she had a husband who thought *very* differently about our relationship.'

He looked so miserable and pathetic that I didn't laugh, even though I half-wanted to. I blinked at him until he realised that this probably wasn't sufficient to explain his walking out.

'We met in a bar, she was very chatty, great company, so we

started meeting up the odd evening and it – well, it turned into overnights and dinners and I thought we... I thought it was turning into something that could *be* something, if you know what I mean.' Now his expression was almost pleading. 'I took her home, everyone loved her, the brothers, Mam, Dad, she was a real hit with the family, and I thought, *This is it.* I really thought I'd got myself a good one. And then...' He took a deep breath. 'Then one day, I was at work, up at the university, and this bloke walks into my office and asks if I'm Connor, so I say yes, and he takes a swing at my head, puts a load of photographs down on the table and tells me to lay off his wife.'

'Oh dear,' I said, inadequately.

Connor slumped forwards and put his face in his hands. 'She'd been telling him she was away with girlfriends,' he said, his words filtered through his fingers. 'She'd got two wee ones at home, and she was telling him she was helping a friend with an emotional crisis.' A half-laugh. 'Well, the emotional crisis came later, and there wasn't any helping.'

I didn't know what to say, so I sat down next to him. The stone was very, very cold.

'So, I not only lose the woman I was falling in love with, but I have to face that everything she told me was a lie. She wasn't a photographer, she was a mum who'd worked as ground staff for Aer Lingus. She wasn't orphaned, she didn't want me to meet her parents because they'd have spilt the beans, and, more importantly, *she wasn't fecking single.*' I heard him swallow hard. 'So, you can see, I'm a little bit sensitive when I suddenly hear that there's a husband who might be home any minute, swinging his fists and demanding to know what the hell I'm playing at.' He looked across at me and there was a long, and slightly desperate, pause. 'But I'm looking at you now and realising that I might have gone off the deep end and overreacted just a touch. I'm sorry. It was a shock, y'know?'

I could feel my face had frozen and it had nothing to do with the temperature. 'He won't be home,' I said. Repression was practically my middle name by now; the feelings stayed locked down where I could see the very tips of them, waving up at me from beneath the heavy weight of suppressed memory. I wasn't about to let them out now.

Connor kept looking at me. It was hard to read his expression in this blank light, when his face was eye sockets, the shadows under cheekbones and a tangle of hair.

'Okay,' he said slowly. 'Divorced?'

I kept my chin up and switched my focus to the moon, a watching circle poised above a mountainscape of cloud. 'Widowed,' I said, and stopped.

'Okay,' he said again. And then, 'Okay,' as though he were talking himself down from a precipice. 'I'm sorry.'

I wasn't sure what he was apologising for. Bringing all this up? Walking out on me for a simple misunderstanding? Making me sit here on this bloody hard and freezing cold stone in the middle of the night?

My fingers traced the edge of the stone, where it ended in softly rounded contours and mossy beds. They curled into the lip of stone, almost as though I were about to lift it myself, and neither of us spoke. The owl called again, a lost and lonely note that wailed into the silence like a siren.

'We need to go back,' I said at last. 'It's going to freeze out here tonight.'

'Did you drive up?' He sounded almost conversational now.

'No, I got a bloody piggyback – of course I drove.'

'Why?' He turned so I could see his face fully and it was washed pale by the moonlight.

'I couldn't be sure of catching you if I walked.'

'You seriously thought I'd come up here to turn your stone?' Connor slapped at the stone between us. '*Really?* I mean, I'm pretty keen on my job but I'm not *that* dedicated that I'd be up here in the dark and the cold.'

'But you *are* up here in the dark and the cold,' I pointed out, and he sighed.

'Fair play.' He nodded and then looked down at the stone's mossy granulated surface. 'And fairyland is really supposed to be under here?'

I didn't know what to say to that. It was what the stories said, those legends of the moor, but right now, here, in the dark with an owl being atmospheric and the moon breasting the cloud banks like a schooner in a dark sea, I didn't really want to think too deeply about it. 'Yes. You're supposed to be able to hear the fairies, if you put your ear to the stone.'

'Have you tried?'

I didn't know what to say. Did I admit that, yes, after Elliot died, I'd come out here in the deep of another sleepless night and lain on the stone? That I'd begged and pleaded with the fairies to come and take me so that I didn't have to exist any longer in this world that had lost all meaning for me? 'No,' I said, reasoning that admissions like this would open a can of worms that would wriggle all over my carefully cultivated calm exterior. 'What are you doing?'

Connor sprawled the length of the stone, with his head at the top and his legs bent at the knee so that he'd fit entirely onto it. 'I'm going to listen. Come on.' A hand reached out and pulled me so that I half toppled next to him. There wasn't a lot of room. 'Let's see if we can hear them partying down there.'

'It's just a story,' I tried to reason with his new and energetic mood. He seemed to have flipped from the sadness of his disappointing love life to a more whimsical turn of thought.

'Yeah, but stories come from *somewhere*, Rowan. All stories come from somewhere. Maybe not fairyland, maybe there really was a Roman buried out here, under this stone. Maybe they had a reputation for being a bit wild and the story has come down, word of mouth, generation after generation.' He stretched his legs off the end of the stone and out into the heather. 'Every story has a beginning,' he said again, quietly now into the night.

I lay with the cold biting into every joint. All I could hear was the sound of Connor's breathing, the distant sound of the river running over the ford, and the owl that was becoming really rather insistent.

No fairies. No parties. No midnight abduction of humans, taken underground and kept. You weren't supposed to eat fairy food, because that meant they had power over you, but how long could you stay hungry?

'They aren't there,' I said when the cold got too much. 'It really is just a story, Connor. There are no little people out here.' The tears of an unaccountable sadness rose up my throat and threatened my eyes. 'There's nobody here.'

'Ah, now. We're here.' He rolled onto one elbow and looked over at me. 'And you're awful sad now, Rowan. I'm sorry.'

The tears were falling, pushed out by the weight of my heart. 'No, it's all right,' I said, all the words in a rush to be said. 'I – I don't often think about it now.'

'Can you tell me?'

Oh, it was the voice, that soft Irish lilt that gave his words gravity. The gentle accent put an emphasis on his sympathy and it cut right through those memory barriers like a welding lance.

'He got up to go to work one day and said he didn't feel well. Collapsed at lunchtime, they called an ambulance and then me.

By the time I got to the hospital, he was dead.' The tears felt divorced from the emotion now, as though I were crying over something else. 'Some kind of cardiac incident. I don't know.' I wiped a hand over my eyes and then my nose on my sleeve. 'I'd done a pregnancy test that morning, and it had been positive. I was waiting to tell him when we got home that night. We'd been trying for months,' I finished, as though Connor needed to know that.

'Oh, Rowan.'

'It didn't last. A chemical pregnancy, the doctor said. Or maybe I misread the test – I was so keen for it to be positive I may have made a mistake. But I never got to tell him.' I sat up now, curling myself over my knees as I tried not to fall back into that awful litany, those words echoing inside my head and squeezing themselves out with the tears – I never got to tell him.

'I'm so sorry.' Connor spoke quietly. 'Truly, I am. When did… I mean, how long ago was this?'

'Three years. We'd been married for two years when he died, together for five years before that. We wanted to get the cottage restored and liveable before we got married, I've no idea why now, but it seemed a good idea at the time.' I gave a snotty half-laugh and wiped my face again.

'And the stone?' Connor looked down at it for a moment and then leaped up as though an electric shock had gone through him. 'Oh, Lord, he's not under here now, is he?'

That made me laugh, properly, for the first time in a very long time. 'No! Of course he isn't! He was cremated and his ashes were buried in the church over there.' I pointed in the general direction of the tiny parish church, which snuggled into the valley about three miles further down the river.

'Thank the Lord for that.' Connor watched me clamber inelegantly to my feet. 'You do seem very attached to the stone though, so I wondered.'

'When we bought the cottage I came up here.' I led the way onto the track so we could leave the moor. I'd had enough of the cold biting me through my clothes. 'Just to explore. I found the stone, of course, I didn't know what it was then, and I sat up here, on my own, looking down the dale. It was summer and the sky was so blue it looked like china, and you could hear the river trickling away in the valley bottom. We'd got our little house, even if it was falling down, and we were in love and it was all so... perfect.'

I kept my head down, eyes on the tricky path. Even in the moonlight, filtered now through running cloud that dashed across its face and away, I could see glimpses of Connor's expression and I didn't want to. There was compassion there, and a kind of sad horror.

'I decided to find out what the stone was doing here, it looked so odd, so out of place. I'd been a social historian since I left university and – I kind of slid sideways into folklore from there. The stone and the cottage, they've always been made of stories.' I was hanging on to those stories now as hard as I could.

'So, this is your happy place? And you don't want those memories disturbed, yes, I can see that.'

'It's more than that.' I trudged on. 'Elliot was...' I could do it now, I could speak about him in the past tense. 'He read a lot. He was the one who told me the stories about the fairies, when he read up about the area as we were taking on the cottage. He did all the research, you see. For the restoration. So the stories, the fairies, it's like...' I shrugged.

'Part of him,' Connor supplied.

'Then there was this day...' My memory rushed in to fill my words with the emotions of that day, the sun hot and full overhead. The sky so blue that it felt as though darkness would never come. Elliot leading me up to the stone, our hands clasped, for a 'surprise'. 'He brought me up here and when we arrived he'd already been to the stone and he'd laid out a picnic on it.'

The birds had sung to us from the gorse bushes and the air hadn't moved as Elliot had told me that the picnic was fairy food provided by the Little People from their land under the stone. It had been a surprisingly fanciful statement from my normally pragmatic boyfriend and had made me laugh as we ate thick-cut ham sandwiches and drank warm cordial from a bottle.

Then he'd produced the ring and a speech he'd obviously spent hours rehearsing. He'd carefully sat me down on the edge of the stone and gone down on one knee – disconcerting a passing sheep and putting his foot in the remaining sandwiches – and proposed. 'We had to be together always,' he said. 'We'd eaten in fairyland.'

'Oh, Rowan,' Connor half sighed, as though he didn't want to be heard.

I shrugged yet again. 'So, that's it. That's me. A widowed, accidental folklorist, living in her tiny old cottage in the middle of nowhere.'

'But there are ducks. I feel you are overlooking the ducks, somewhat.'

Surprised, I stopped walking. 'What?'

'Ducks. You know, quack quack, splash splash. You feed them your morning toast crusts and they hang around outside waiting for it. Incidentally, you're not meant to give bread to ducks.'

'I have to, otherwise I'm worried they might attack *en masse* and have my eye out.' But I could feel my mood rising with his levity. I was almost smiling now. 'And the fish get most of the bread, it's the dinner leavings the ducks really want. They just like fighting over toast.'

'But it does go to show that you're not quite the nihilist that you'd want me to believe. Anyone who can save their crusts for the ducks is not completely gone to the other side.'

Then Connor walked off ahead, leading the way down the invisible path back towards my car, leaving me to follow and wonder what on earth he was talking about.

10

The next day I had to drive to Aberystwyth, where a colleague had requested that I take her place at a literary festival. She'd had to drop out because her young son had had an accident, and the associated mother-guilt meant that she'd felt obligated to find a replacement. I was clearly the only person she could think of who had no ties and could swan off to north Wales on a whim to spend six days being the resident expert on folklore literature. I hadn't been fast enough to come up with a decent excuse and so I found myself filling in for her with inadequate preparation and a slight feeling of guilt of my own.

The talks were mostly based around folk horror, so huge preparation on my part hadn't been greatly required, but at least I was there and able to give some opinions on whether the early fairy stories were really a primitive form of folk horror. It was interesting, I got my expenses paid to stay in a lovely hotel, was able to mingle with famous authors – some of them interested enough in my research to engage me in conversation – to browse around the festival, and buy too many books.

I felt a little bit guilty at leaving Connor alone, but only briefly. He was my lodger, that was all. It was none of his business what his landlady got up to, and my disappearing from his life to be An Academic wouldn't affect him. It was also quite nice to be away, after our night of confessions up on the moor. I wasn't quite sure how to face him again now that he knew about me and my sadness. Packing and driving off very early without telling him felt a little like a thumbed nose; a bit of a 'fuck you' to any thoughts he might have about using my revelations for his own ends. Distance was good. Being away from Connor was good. Let him wonder.

I'd carefully mentioned my work on the Fairy Stane to anyone who would listen at the festival, so if he'd chosen my absence to interfere with it, I had an army of bestselling fantasy authors who could help me raise hell too.

I was late in to work when I got back, after a terrible early morning drive back from Wales. 'Good trip?' Chess asked, wafting into the office a good twenty minutes after my arrival.

'Not sure I converted anyone to our cause, but the back seat of my car is full of paperbacks, so depending on how you measure "good", then yes, or no.'

'Your professor's been hanging around.' She hung up her coat, hooked her bag over the back of the chair and then hitched a hip onto my desk. 'He wanted to borrow some of your books.'

I glanced over at the bookcase. 'Which ones?'

'Not your books, *your* books. Books that you wrote.' Chess announced this with a degree of satisfaction.

'Why doesn't he use the library, like a normal person?' I grouched.

'Doesn't have library membership. He's Irish.'

'Well, he could buy them, then. I presume being Irish doesn't preclude him spending money?'

'I dunno.' Chess fiddled her hair into an updo, checked her reflection in the glass of the window, pouted like a guppy, then pulled it back down again. 'He's cute.'

I thought of that night on the moor, the unexpected confidences. We'd gone back to the cottage and headed straight to our respective rooms, and I hadn't seen him in the morning before I'd left. Perhaps he felt as embarrassed about opening up to me as I felt about telling him about Elliot, a kind of cringey weight in the back of my head whenever I remembered. Hopefully we'd never speak of it again.

'Any sign of a place to let coming available for him?' I asked. 'A basement would do.'

'Uh-huh.'

'Catacomb?'

Chess suddenly realised that I was joking and snorted. 'Anyway, I've finished typing up that diary thing that you had.'

'Brilliant, thank you. Anything interesting in there?'

Chess frowned. 'I don't *read* them; I type them up. A few interesting bits, maybe. Trees coming alive, that sort of thing.' She said this as carelessly as though it were an everyday occurrence. 'Up on the moors.'

'I'll check it through when you email it over. And can you find me some books on the buildings up near the stone – Evercey Manor and the village, please?' I needed to find information about where and when the stone was sourced. If it turned out that the whole thing had been dragged in from somewhere else on the moor because it was the right size to fill in a hole, that would be the end of Connor's theory about it having markings on the underside.

'Yeah, yeah.' Chess slithered forward off the desk. 'Have you got any copies of that last book you did? The one about ghost stories being folk memories of morality tales or something? The professor was looking for it – there isn't one here.'

I stared blankly at the bookshelves. That had been the book I'd been working on when Elliot died, and it had gone out unedited. 'I'm not sure. There's one about somewhere. I might have it at home.'

Chess grinned broadly. 'That's good. You can give it to him tonight, then, when you get back.'

'Just finish typing up the memoirs and get to the archives, Chess.' I sighed. 'There's a dear.'

After she'd sauntered out, smug as someone who'd had the last word, I slumped down across my desk, arms outstretched and my face buried in my elbows. I hadn't slept well for my final night in the hotel, there had been partying in the bar which had kept me awake and the drive back had been horrific. I was still getting over appearing in public where I seemed to be regarded as a self-deluded fairy believer, and all I really wanted to do was go home, put on a disreputable tracksuit and slob around with a packet of crisps. Thank goodness it was Friday was all I could think.

Except... except Friday meant the weekend. I usually spent the weekend doing a little cursory housework, walking on the moors and, at this time of year, lighting the fire and curling up on the loveseat to remember how things had been when Elliot had been here. Not, I knew, the healthiest way to behave, but anything else required an energy I didn't have. The literary festival had offered me a change of routine and now I could go back to my 'normal'. I was looking forward to it. But this weekend, unless I was lucky and he'd wandered off with his mates, Connor would be there and that would curtail my slobbing about. I wouldn't feel comfortable lounging around in my holey hoodie if he was going to be bouncing around in his cashmere, all legs and enthusiasm. And, horror, he might even start telling me details from his thwarted love, and what I really did *not* need on a rainy Saturday afternoon when I wanted carbs and comfort, was a lanky Irishman following me about to give me chapter and verse on his gorgeous, cheating ex.

I might do some writing. Yes, I thought, sitting back up. I could write. That would keep Connor away – even *he* wouldn't be so self-absorbed as to interfere with someone who was writing, would he?

I looked around the room. I had small parcels of material dotted all over the tiny space – an old dairymaid's apron, some butter presses, an ancient kettle, donated by those tellers of tales. I could photograph those ready for inclusion in the book, and my cottage would be a perfect backdrop. Then I could go through my typed-up notes and sort out the stories that were particularly local, maybe find a way to reference everything back to the stone and its locality. I could work on the 'fairy' element – if I broadened the category to include the hob and the boggart and elaborated on my theory of these being linked to ancient memories of *genii loci* then I'd practically got enough to fill a book already. I hadn't written anything much of note since Elliot. I hadn't really felt like it. But the thought of protecting the Fairy Stane was giving my imagination and my enthusiasm the kicking it needed.

That was a cheering thought, and it gave me enough energy to start working through some of the older notes.

I opened the first document. There was the date right at the top. Because dates and attribution were so important in this field, I made sure that they were the very first things I noted. The name of the person who was telling me their family story, their age, the place in question and... dates, dates, dates. When did this happen? How old were you? How old was the person telling you? That way we could trace tales back, sometimes a hundred years or more.

This document was dated six months after Elliot died, which would have been the first thing I did when I returned to the office. Because Elliot's death had been sudden and unexpected, there had been all kinds of legal hurdles – he'd had no will, and the mortgage company had really not wanted to pay out on the insurance. There had even been a brief attempt to prove his death an uninsured suicide, although I'd had a storm of doctors who'd come to my rescue over *that* one.

Death was never simple, I knew that. Maybe it shouldn't be. Some of the stories coming down from the high moors told of people dying and included the habits, myths and traditions that were followed and meant that bodies weren't buried for sometimes up to a week. There were bodies placed on the kitchen table for the neighbours to come and view, there was the construction of the coffin – which had to be the right material – the procession to the churchyard, which could often consist of a six- or seven-mile walk over treacherous land, and the burial itself, then the wake.

Perhaps, I thought, still staring at that date, things had been better in the 'old days', when friends and neighbours were as much a part of the bereavement as the family. I'd been left to grieve alone, once Elliot's workmates, our few friends and our scattered and distant families had paid their respects. Not for me the collective gathering, storytelling over the coffin the night before burial and the quiet assistance of the entire community. There had *been* no community. Only me, the silent cottage, the rushing water.

It had taken me some months to be ready to get back to

more than the most superficial tasks. And here was the evidence, in these badly typed notes, where my mind had obviously not really been on them, although training and habit had made sure that the basics were covered.

I started skimming, highlighting anything that seemed relevant to what I intended to write. I'd select my material and then work on chapters and grouping by type or location once I'd got an outline sorted, I decided.

'Hello?'

'Oh, it's you,' I said, less than delighted as Connor's head appeared around my door. 'Don't you have your own office?'

'Yep.' He cheerfully slithered the rest of him inside. 'But I'm declaring it closed for the weekend.'

'I thought I told Chess to not let anyone in?' I was determined to show him that I wasn't one whit softened towards him by our previous confessions. This was me, unemotional, detached, aloof. If he didn't like it, well, someone somewhere would have a damp room in a noisy house that he could move in to.

'Chess has gone home. It's half past six.' Unabashed, Connor leaned against the opposite wall and swirled his coat around him. 'I was going to get a taxi back, but I decided to swing by to see if you were still here. You're cheaper,' he added. 'The lights were on, so I popped in and here you are.'

Half past six? How could it be? But he was right, it was dark outside, which gave this subterranean room a measure of borrowed cosiness. I'd been so absorbed in my work that I hadn't noticed the time pass, although the soggy remains of a cheese and lettuce sandwich sprawled across a plate showed that I'd at least eaten lunch. I couldn't remember doing it. Chess must have brought it in whilst I was writing. She must have come through to tell me she was leaving too, but I hadn't noticed that either. I only hoped the book was going to be as compelling as the writing clearly was.

I shook my head to try to clear the feeling that I'd been woken from a dream. 'Um. Yes, I suppose I ought to... yes.'

'You look tired,' Connor observed, and it was a good job he was across the room because it meant I could glare at him. 'Bad week?'

Guilt poked me in the ribs. I should have told him that I was going to Aberystwyth. 'A literary festival,' I said shortly, wondering if I'd secretly wanted him to suffer alone, without transport, in my cottage miles from anywhere. But he was an adult. I was his landlady, not his taxi service...

'There was me thinking you'd been swept off your feet and taken to a luxury hotel for a week of passion and debauchery,' he said.

I could *not* work out whether he was joking, teasing or had seriously assumed I'd gone off on holiday with my lover, so I 'hmm'phed at him, then added, 'Chance would be a fine thing,' in case he really *had* thought I'd been whisked off for sex and spa baths. 'Anyway, you're just lodging with me. I don't have to account for my movements.'

'Of course you don't,' he replied, robustly. 'I texted Chess, to make sure you weren't dead in a ditch, and she told me you'd gone to Wales.'

So he *had* been teasing about the 'mysterious lover'. I felt relieved but didn't know why.

Connor waited while I locked up and set the alarms, and then trod as quietly as Barghest alongside me to my car in the puddle-festooned car park at the back. My gritty-eyed tiredness meant I didn't remark on his unusual silence until we were almost back at the cottage.

'I'm sorry,' I said, rather grudgingly. 'I should have told you I'd be away.'

'Ah, you're all right. Like I said, I checked with Chess to make sure nothing had happened.'

'How did you manage to get in and out of York?'

Connor gave me a grin. 'I'm a big lad, I can sort myself out with that kind of thing. I have students keen to do me favours, and there's taxis and all.'

Guilt prodded me again. 'I shouldn't have left you to find out from Chess, though. I'll give you my mobile number. It will probably be easier if you can text me. I don't always pick up my emails when I'm at home, and you can't trust Chess to relay information, particularly if she's out for the weekend.'

'That's very sensible.' Connor kept his eyes on the bleak darkness outside the car. 'Thank you.'

'No drunk dialling, mind.' I tried a smile and got one back, a lot wider and more appealing than I was sure mine had been.

'Ah, you great spoilsport. What's the point of having your number, now, if I can't phone you in the middle of the night slurring about how much I love you?'

'Don't you dare.' His tone made it plain that he was joking. 'Anyway, we're in the same house. You could open my door and tell me. Only,' I added with new sternness, just in case, 'you'd better not try it.'

He continued the smile but twitched his head as though he'd made me do something against my will. 'I'm a lot of things, Rowan, but sex pest never made the list.'

I reached out to change gear and my hand brushed against his leg. He moved away at the contact. 'And I'm very glad to hear it.'

'You've been very brave to assume it up to now.'

'You're a professor. One word of accusation from me and you could lose everything, so maybe it's you who's brave.'

He did the smile and twitched-head again. I was clearly surprising him tonight.

We pulled up in the usual spot, but the cottage was in darkness. 'I didn't think to leave a light on,' he said. 'I was in a bit of a hurry this morning when I left – the taxi turned up while I was beating off the ducks. I didn't have toast,' he added, in explanatory fashion.

I opened the front door and wandered through, putting on lights as I went. The cottage began to hum, from the deep rattly purr of the fluorescent kitchen light to the high-pitched squeak of the table lamp in the living room – it was as if the place were talking to me, through illumination. Although Connor was still at my shoulder, I began to feel the relaxation of Friday night settling over me.

'I can't really be bothered with food. I'm shattered,' I said. 'I might go straight to...'

The map was back. Hanging on the wall, in its original frame, in its original place. I stared at it.

'Did I hallucinate the whole thing the other night?' I asked, faintly.

'Oh, the map? It was important to you, so I found a framer in York who did me a favour yesterday.'

I stared some more. The frame was definitely the original, but completely repaired and with new glass. 'But... how?' I stroked the wood with one finger. 'I mean, you only had a few days...'

'Ah, I didn't say it was a *cheap* favour now, did I?' Connor looked – well, it was hard to place his expression. It wasn't *happy*, it was more self-satisfied than that and wavered in the direction of *smug*. 'They came over last night to fix it in situ.' He looked down at the floor. 'Actually, they gave me a lift.'

'You got the frame fixed and a ride home?' I wanted to turn it around to check the repairs on the back, but it seemed ungrateful, so I settled for a bit more staring.

'The amount I was paying, they should have flown me back on a silver unicorn,' he said, but sounded as though he was trying not to laugh. 'But it looks all right up there now, does it not?'

'It does indeed,' I half breathed the words. The map was smooth, the frame was intact, it was as if nothing had ever happened.

'I got the fastening reinforced. Quite frankly it had been hanging by one tack for months. Accident waiting to happen.'

We stood for a moment together. The single lamp gave the room more corners than it should have had.

'Thank you, Connor,' I said softly, still keeping my eyes on the map.

'You're not upset? After what you said before, about – well, about your husband making the frame, I didn't want to do anything that might make any of it worse.'

'I'm not upset.' My voice was still very level. 'It was a very kind thing to do. And I'm sorry that I got so angry with you over the other frame, but...' I tailed off.

'No, no, you were right.' Connor adjusted the hang of the map, where my touching the frame had unbalanced it and made it list towards Pickering. 'That awful pine frame wasn't good. Like hanging the Mona Lisa in something you picked up from IKEA.'

'I wouldn't go quite *that* far,' I said. 'It's just a map.'

'But for you, it's memory, isn't it?' His voice was soft now.

'Everything tied up with everything else, all leading back to the one thing. Your husband, in this case. The stone, in another.'

I began to move towards the stairs. 'Can we not talk about the stone for now? I'm going to have a shower and go to bed with my laptop. The house is all yours. Turn the lights out when you go up.'

I left him standing in the middle of the barely lit room. He stood very still and quiet and I couldn't see what he was looking at as I trod my weary way up the steep staircase towards a hot shower, my bed, and some rubbish on YouTube.

11

For a few weeks Connor and I co-existed without seeing too much of one another. We shared the odd meal, but I was sorting out the contents of my forthcoming book in earnest, so spent much of my time at home in front of my computer or shut in my bedroom. Connor came and went, students seemed to have been persuaded to pick him up and drop him off, so he rarely travelled with me, heading into the university early and coming back late, sometimes after I'd gone to bed. Now he had my mobile number he assiduously messaged me to let me know when he would be late or needed a lift back. He paid up on time, bought the occasional takeaway, was quiet, punctilious and clean.

It was almost uncanny.

He also didn't mention the stone. But I'd told him not to, so I couldn't really get suspicious. Besides he was still deeply involved in attempts to identify the possible Roman construction, which seemed to absorb much of his time and energy, I was grateful to note. Apart from catching him sometimes staring at the map and muttering about the ideal placement for a cemetery, he'd gone completely quiet on the subject of stone-raising altogether.

Then I got home one evening to find him singing.

I could hear him as I parked the car. It sounded like an Irish folk song, plaintive and deep, the syllables rolling out across the frosted dark like invisible clouds, to meet me at the door. I stomped my way inside and he stopped, suddenly, seeming embarrassed.

'Oh! I didn't hear the car. And you're early.'

'Early' was a strange concept now that the evenings grew dark before five and my tendency to work until bedtime meant that I was eating at my computer anyway. There was no 'early', only 'home' and 'bed'.

'Chess was full of cold, so I sent her home and then thought I might as well be gone too.' I unwound myself from coat and scarf. 'It was chilly in the office.'

'Okay.'

'You were singing?' I didn't know why I phrased it as a question. Since there was nobody else here it had to have been him, either that or the ducks had formed a choir.

In the bright white light he flamed a sudden pink. 'Er, yes.'

'It sounded lovely. Was it Irish?'

Connor turned away now and began fiddling with the fridge, bending to look at supplies. 'My granda taught me the songs. Long time ago now, he's been gone, oh, twenty years or more. But when I was a child and we'd go down to the farm in Lahinch, he'd take me out on the land and we'd carve wood and he'd teach me the old songs.'

He straightened up, a pat of butter in one hand and an incongruous cucumber in the other, with his eyes looking somewhere in the long past. 'Dad's Da,' he said. 'Dad grew up on a farm. Not much of a farm, all bog and potatoes as they say.'

Then he seemed to realise what he was doing and the cucumber was tucked back in between the packages and he swung the door closed. 'Anyway. Good day?'

'So-so. They want the first few chapters of the book before the Christmas holidays start, to read over.'

'The grants people? You must have enough to show them, surely, you've done nothing but write for weeks.'

I waved an arm to airily indicate that this would probably be the case and anyway I wasn't in the least worried about having enough material of the quality that would keep the money coming. 'How about you? You sound happy.'

'I think I've finally done enough work for us to be able to send the archaeologists up on the moor there.' He pointed with an elbow in the direction of his disputed 'settlement'. 'They won't go out without a good chance of coming down on some decent archaeology. It's too expensive to start digging with no idea if there's anything there.'

'Oh?'

'Yep. I found documents that talk of tracks and buildings that seem to have been laid out in a grid pattern, typical of a small Roman township.' He put the butter down and rolled up his sleeves. 'Could be the discovery of a lifetime,' he said, hunting down the bread.

'Yes, you've stressed the life-changing possibilities.'

Now he turned around. My expression must have given away what I felt, because he took half a step towards me, then clearly thought better of it. I could get up quite a swing with my handbag, if I needed to.

'We'll not be touching your Fairy Stane, Rowan.'

'Good.' I sounded short, as though the word had been snipped off from a much longer unsaid sentence.

'Unless we absolutely have to,' he went on. 'But I'm pretty confident we'll find what we need without disturbing your site.'

I stalked past him and went upstairs to change. It wasn't fair, this constant making me aware that he could ruin an entire lifetime's worth of storytelling with one casual order. All right, the stone could be an important proof for his work. But wasn't it *equally* important that it remained a mystery? All those stories of the Little People, the fairyland parties, the possible release of the fey into the world, they'd all be blown out of the water if it became known that the stone had been lifted and proved to reveal – what? Nothing but dirt? A small hole filled in by a farmer so his cattle didn't break a leg?

Stories are important too.

I changed slowly and went back down to find that Connor had made a sandwich and was sitting at the table with a book open, flipping pages with buttery fingers. 'I finally got around to reading some of your material,' he said, swallowing vigorously. 'It's pretty good.'

I pursed my lips and put the kettle on. 'Yes, well, they don't give you grants for this kind of thing if you can barely string two words together.'

He closed the book up and I saw the cover. It was one of mine, an early publication that had been part of my PhD. 'You've got butter all over it,' I said, mildly for an author watching their work despoiled with dairy products.

'I'll give it a wipe. So, why the fairy stories? Nieces and nephews queuing up to listen to you read?'

I shook my head. 'Only child,' I said.

'That's lucky.' Almost without thinking, Connor opened the window and flung his sandwich crusts outside. 'Two of the boys are married, and there seems to be a new offspring every fortnight.' Then he smiled at me. 'Ah, they're grand really.'

It wasn't so bad now. After Elliot died, when it had turned out that I wasn't pregnant, I'd found it hard to hear tales of others seemingly spontaneously giving birth. Friends, acquaintances, workmates – for a while it had seemed as though everyone was sporting a bump or wearing a baby strapped to their chest. Part of the whole feeling of loss, I'd reasoned, once I'd managed my way out of the grief-imposed sensation that the whole world was carrying on to spite me. There was absolutely no reason why everyone I met should stop breeding because I'd lost my husband and my chance.

'How lovely,' I said politely.

'Mam's beside herself with joy.' He seemed to realise that I was not cooing and wanting details, pictures, names. 'She'd like all of us to repopulate Ireland, if it was up to her.'

'Apart, presumably, from Eamonn.' I began making two mugs of tea, and Connor laughed.

'Well, yes. But it's interesting, y'know, how Catholic things were up here too. That manor you talked about, the one on your map?'

'Evercey Manor?'

'That's your man. The family there managed to slip under the radar. Presumably they paid lip service to the new official religion but stayed Catholic. Most of their tenants out here were Catholic too.'

'Well, they would be. You didn't go against the lord of the manor,' I said tartly, putting a mug down next to him. 'Way out here I shouldn't think they were bothered too much. It was too isolated. Three miles or more to the church, perhaps they had their own chapel.'

'Keep quiet, pretend to do as you're told, worship in your own way when nobody is looking.' Connor raised his mug to me. 'Thank you.'

'Why are you so interested in the old manor?' I was glad to move away from the subject of the stone. The more he dwelled on his Roman town, the more chance there was that he'd decide to lift my stone on a whim. 'Bit outside your area of expertise, isn't it?'

He leaned back in his chair, sipping from the mug and looking out into the blackness of the night that lay beyond the window. 'I was raised a Catholic,' he said. 'I'm interested, that's all. You don't think that the past religious history might have an impact on some of the folk stories out here? Oppression of the old religion, being forced underground, living your lives in a state of denial? Maybe a nasty case of guilt about having to pretend to turn your back on your religion while you practised in secret?'

'Maybe. There are lots of reasons why people create myths. To make sense of the unknown, as cautionary tales, to put things into perspective, to account for losses. Back before the days when science ran riot, people had to find their own reasons for things they didn't understand, and they did it through stories.'

Connor looked at me over his mug, eyebrows raised. 'And this is where we're both on the same side, Rowan. Memories. Yours are embodied in the stories and mine are trapped in the stones and the documents. We don't have to fight over it.'

'We do if you try to lift my stone.'

'Well, all right. Our disciplines aren't *entirely* compatible, perhaps, but we're still fighting the same battle, to remember the past. And sometimes it feels as though no one cares about what went before.'

'At least you get television programmes.' I tried to drink my tea too hot. 'Digging up gold hoards or building castles, it's all glamorous and attention-grabbing. I'm lucky if I get the odd podcast and a few panels at a literary festival where they only wanted blood and gore and descriptions of wolf kills.'

'Ah, that's rough now.'

We lapsed into silence, or as much silence as can be obtained by two people drinking tea that is rather too warm to go down smoothly, whilst outside waterfowl fight to the death over a Warburton's crust.

'Well, I'd better...' I nodded towards the living room and my computer.

'Yes, and I ought to...' Connor indicated his bag on the floor, bulging with paperwork.

'Right, then.'

'Right.'

But we continued to occupy the kitchen, sipping our tea, him sitting stretched at the table and me standing leaning against the countertop, feeling the roughness of the wood surface.

'You rebuilt this place yourselves, then?' Connor stared out of the window, towards the black night, where occasional wavelets in the passing water caught the lights and gleamed like the eyes of freshwater sharks.

I found myself less reluctant to answer this question than I usually was. 'Yes. It was a ruin when we bought it. We lived in a friend's camper van for a year until we got the roof on, and then without water for six months after that. It's as accurate as we could get it, only we put a bathroom in because there's a lot I'm prepared to do for historical accuracy but pissing in a bucket is out.' I smiled at the memory. 'Elliot could turn his hand to anything, and he had friends who are electricians and plumbers, that kind of thing. He was the sort of person who made friends easily.'

Connor met my eye in our reflections in the window. 'He sounds like a useful guy.'

'He was lovely,' I said, realising that this was probably the first time I'd actually really spoken about Elliot since his death. Being here in this house that he'd done so much work on helped, as though I were being protected from the worst of the memories by being surrounded by evidence of his existence.

'I can see you miss him.' There was a note of sadness in Connor's voice, as though he wasn't really talking about me but was looking inwards.

I looked at him, but he continued to stare out into the dark. 'Do you miss her?' I asked softly. After all, he'd had his hopes and expectations for the future dashed, not quite as definitively as mine had been, but it had still happened.

'Yes. No.' He swung around, catching me looking at him. 'I miss what I thought she was, and what I thought we had.' He sighed. 'But none of it was real, I know that now. All the promises and the stories – they were all inventions of the person she wanted to be.' Another sigh. 'I feel bad for her husband. Telling me what she'd been up to must have been the worst day of his life.' He stood up. 'God knows, it was the worst day of mine.'

'There will be other women,' I said.

I got raised eyebrows for that. 'I'm sure people telling you that you'd find someone else after your husband died didn't help,' he said tartly.

'No. Actually it didn't. I'm sorry, I didn't mean to sound so glib. It really isn't that simple, is it?'

'You have to admit a whole lot of stuff to yourself before you can begin to heal and move forward,' Connor said, picking up his bag. 'I have to learn that I can be gullible and stupid when a woman tells me what I want to hear. I am clearly not great at sorting out the truth. And you...' He stopped.

'Me? I'm not sure I have to admit anything to myself,' I said, bridling. 'Apart from don't let your husband blithely go off to work when he says he's not feeling well.'

'I think you have to admit that memories are all grand and that, but you can't hang on to them forever.' He swung his bag up. 'And I'm off to my room to do some work. Goodnight.'

Leaving me open-mouthed with annoyance, he was gone, quietly, up the stairs. I waited until I heard his door close and then threw one of my shoes at the wall.

12

1898

Betsy was on her way back to the village when she saw May.

Bit of a stuck-up so-and-so May was, everyone thought so. Had 'ideas above her station', Mam always said, just because she was a lady's maid to the young misses up at the house. Always said her haitches, like she was proper posh, and stuck her nose in the air when the parlourmaids tried to talk to her.

So, when Betsy saw her, standing up at the Fairy Stane, she was of half a mind to stick her own nose in the air and keep walking. Let madam stand there on her own, doing whatever, pretend she hadn't noticed. Until she drew closer, curious as to what May could be doing, and saw that she was crying.

'All right, love?' Betsy was a soft-hearted lass, Dad always said. She had no reason to talk to May at all, but she couldn't leave a girl up there, crying like that, not without trying to make sure she wasn't hurt.

Obviously surprised at being addressed, May took a step back. 'I'm well, thank you, Betsy,' she said, stiff as a broom and trying to hide her face.

'You don't look well. You look mazed, lass. What's up?' Then, with a growing suspicion, 'It's not Master Jack, is it? He been trying to get you round the back in the laundry room?' There had been rumours about the son of the house and his tendency to try to bed any of the maids that couldn't run fast enough. 'Just tell him to get to...' Betsy lowered her voice so that nobody passing would hear her use of bad language and tell Dad, '...*hell*.'

May gave a straight-mouthed smile through her tears. 'I shall remember that,' she said, then added more quietly, 'for next time.'

'Ah, lass, you come on away with me.' Betsy took May's arm. The girl resisted at first, then relaxed. 'Come on. Me mam will have tea on, come and have a cup with us and a warm by the fire. It's nithering out here tonight. What were you doing up at the stone?'

May looked down at her feet, and Betsy saw a small rag doll flopped face down in the sharp needles of reeds that grew up around the stone. It looked home sewn, loosely stuffed limbs and a stitched petticoat with an embroidered face. 'Leaving a gift,' May almost whispered.

Betsy was wise for her years. She'd heard a thing or two that went on up here, the men coming out late at night and the women following a few nights later with flowers and little offerings. Sometimes women came alone, stepping heavily along the worn path that led to the stone. Nobody asked. Nobody talked about their reasons. The fairies took their offerings, that was all anybody needed to know. Things were kept safe.

Betsy looked at the doll again, then picked it up. 'You know that little Cecilia has just lost her ma,' she said, straightening the doll's skirts. 'Her sister has taken the four little ones and the boys have gone up to Home Farm to help their pa with the cows and the rabbits.' She didn't look at May. 'But little Cissy has gone to old Mother Sleightholme.' Now she did look up. 'Reckon she'd love a little poppet like this to play with.'

May opened her mouth as though she was about to speak, but then closed it again and rubbed her wrist over her eyes.

'After all, the fairies has got each other up here,' Betsy went on. 'Little Cissy now, she's got no one.'

There was a long moment. Eventually May stretched out her hand and took the doll from Betsy. She tweaked its skirts straight and knocked out some grass that had got tangled in the string hair. 'Yes,' she said, tiredly. 'You're right. Poor little girl.'

Betsy looked at the stone. 'Aye,' she said quietly. 'Poor love. It can't be easy.'

'No.'

The two girls shared a look of understanding. Then May gave a small, thin smile. 'I think a cup of tea sounds like a very good idea,' she said, linking her arm through Betsy's. 'Thank you very much, Betsy.'

Arm in arm they walked off the moor and down towards the village, where smoke spiralled from chimneys into the autumn air. Betsy noticed May look back, just once, but she kept her counsel, as the fairies would, no doubt, keep theirs.

* * *

Now

In the morning I took one look out of the window and decided to work from home. Chess had texted me to say that she was poorly and wouldn't be in. I had everything I needed for the work I was currently doing, and I honestly didn't fancy spending the scant daylight hours alone in that subterranean office, watching the rain run down the brickwork outside and pinging off all the little green ferny growths.

I'd dreamed of Elliot again. The dreams had almost stopped – those awful, cruel dreams where I'd had him back with me and we'd been doing ordinary, domestic things, or the dreams of him leaving, where I'd watched him pack for a long journey and not known how to say goodbye. This dream had been different, in that he was here, but I was angry with him. In life, our arguments had been few and mostly annoyances about wet washing left in the machine or similar stupid domestic upsets. This time, however, my anger had boiled and ricocheted and turned on Elliot, whilst he had been unconcerned and blank-faced about my fury, carrying on his normal routine as though I weren't there.

I woke with the anger still scratching at the back of my neck, the rain cascading down the window, a text from Chess in which I could almost hear the snuffling, and decided that I'd stay right here.

I could hear Connor moving about, a bumping presence in the other room, and felt, oddly, better. After three years, I'd come to terms with waking up from dreams of Elliot to a house that echoed with the lack of him, the absence of his bleary face next to me and no random movement of limbs under the duvet. He was gone. But I didn't have to like it, and hearing Connor shuffle his way to the bathroom and then begin a muttered mumble to himself under the whine of his shaver was somehow comforting.

He couldn't stay, obviously. I didn't want him here, and he was irritating in the extreme, but at least I knew what was happening with the dig on the moor and my stone when he was under my eye. Maybe I could get a cat when he went? Just another living presence in the house, so the emptiness didn't feel so, well, *empty*. It would be something to come home to, something to greet me at the end of a long day and be pleased to see me. Yes. I would get a cat, in the spring, when the days were lengthening.

I pulled on a fleecy dressing gown and slouched downstairs, past the bathroom door where Connor was now sluicing water in a fashion that boded damp patches on the carefully sanded and sealed floorboards, although he did always clear up after himself in an almost unnaturally assiduous way.

I flipped bread into the toaster, put the kettle on and went to stand by the window, where the large white duck that seemed to be the ringleader of the avian gang eyeballed me sternly from the water beneath. It was paddling ferociously to maintain crust-grabbing position, an arrowhead pointing upstream, as the water rushed past, its level raised by the night-long rain pouring down off the high moor, swirling it into the colour of bad coffee.

'You not in today?' Connor said over my shoulder. 'You're usually dressed by now – you not well?'

He sounded surprisingly concerned. 'Given the weather, I thought I'd work from home; there's no need for me to be in the office.'

'Okay, good. Don't want you getting ill, now. D'you fancy taking me to the site of the old manor up on the moor today? As you're not going in?'

I sighed. 'What part of "working from home" is passing you by, Connor?' I turned around to see him catching the toast as it popped out of the toaster. 'It's not a day off. Anyway, why do you want to see the old manor site? There's nothing left, a bit of a hole where the cellars were, maybe, but all the material was taken down and sold to anyone who needed medieval brick. They bought...' I stopped. I'd been about to say that the reclamation yard where Elliot had worked had bought several tonnes of the brick and, despite the fact that this had been back in the sixties, there had still been some there. We'd bought a load to repair the back wall of the cottage. This cottage was part of the manor, and I'd liked that idea.

But after that dream, bringing Elliot into conversation felt unnatural and I was half enjoying this casual breakfast. It was warm and domestic with Connor scraping butter over toast while I made tea and I had a sudden wish that it really *were* a day off and we could sit and chat at the table without the relentless pressure of time; that I didn't have to switch on my computer and spend a day alone digging through old documents. With that dream still haunting my memory, I wanted someone to keep me from going back over it and pulling out emotions that had already faded, brushing them down and examining them with an intensity they didn't deserve.

'Yeah. Sorry, I wasn't thinking.' Connor was already dressed for the moor, his long black coat gone in favour of some unattractive waterproofs that made the noise of an entire campsite being disassembled whenever he moved. 'I'm away up there anyway. I'll have a wee poke around by myself.'

Suddenly I couldn't face a quiet house. 'Look, I'll give you a quick tour around the manor site,' I said. 'If it's important. I could do with a bit of atmosphere myself.'

He laughed and glanced at the window, where light was beginning to break over the far hills in a bluster of storm-driven cloud. 'I don't think we're short of that.'

'I'll just get dressed. Why do you want to see the manor anyway?' I picked up my toast and my tea and prepared to head up the stairs.

'I was thinking – what if the manor was built on the site of Roman remains? It's the way people go – a good spot is a good spot and people have a tendency to build where there's stone and a good flat site that's sheltered from the wind. It would be within the boundaries of my possible location, so it might be worth checking out in case there's any indications. Clues.'

I scampered up the stairs, dressing gown swinging and trying not to spill my tea, mentally rearranging my day in my head. A quick walk on the moors would be good for me anyhow, to get the remnants of that dream blown away, and then I could come back and get to work without this lingering feeling of resentment. And I hadn't lied, I really could do with a little bit of local feeling in my writing – I'd got so wrapped up in the legends that I hadn't really put much colour in; all those bits that people liked to read about when they got home from their holiday, reminders of the moors they'd walked or even admired from a distance. A pouring-wet day with a force eight gale probably wasn't the reminder that they'd want, but I could edit it down to a smell of peat, the gurgle of streams and the occasional grouse clucking its way into the air.

I came back down the stairs to find Connor lounging around near the front door. 'Wow. I thought *I* was dressed for it,' he observed as I rustled my way into the hall.

'You're wearing tourists' clothes,' I said, adjusting my oilskins. 'If you want to do any real work up there on the moor through winter, you need *proper* waterproofs.'

'I'm going to check on a potential site not... not... gut herring on a trawler.' He opened the front door and wind drove a particularly intrusive squall in to examine my furniture.

I raised my eyebrows at him and gave him a 'you'll find out' smile. The rain up here wasn't a soft, view-obscuring drizzle. On the high moors it came at you from every direction simultaneously and, at this time of year, it had ice on its edges too. Connor was wearing good walking gear, waterproof trousers and a half-decent coat, but I knew the way the rain got in through seams and waistbands. Our rain was the mosquito of precipitation, it got everywhere, even when you thought you'd protected yourself against it.

We splashed to the car, Connor rustling lightly whilst I walked like a reanimated corpse, as the oilskins meant bending my arms and legs was difficult, and climbed in. Visibility was almost nil in the driving rain.

'Are you sure you want to go up there today?' I asked, starting the engine and staring out through the windscreen wipers' frantic attempts.

'Ah, it'll be grand. I'm only here for six months, two of which are nearly gone. I can't imagine the weather is going to improve mightily in the next few weeks, so might as well do it now.'

He smiled again, and I felt a little jolt. Of course. He was only here for six months, presumably until the memory of his transgressions in Dublin had faded safely into the past. By the spring, and the slow, gradual improvement in the weather, he'd be gone.

'Oh, yes. And we ought to get up there before the ford gets too full to drive through and we have to go the long way round. Right.' I let the clutch out and the car slithered onto the more solid surface of the ford edge, crept through the building water, and began the climb up onto the moor, throwing gobbets of sandy mud around us as we went.

'They're forecasting it getting colder. Does it snow often out here?' Connor asked idly.

'Most winters we get some. We're pretty high up, so it dumps on us in preference to the towns lower down.'

'Do you get snowed in?'

'Once or twice.'

'Cosy.' Connor went back to staring out at the bleak grey

expanse. The low cloud meant that the rain had less distance to travel so was even heavier up here and the view was cut to what was immediately in front. 'Cosy' was not the word that sprang to mind when I considered being stuck in the house with a questionable electricity supply and no idea when a passing farmer with a plough on the front of a tractor would get around to clearing the road to the cottage.

'Don't you get snow in Dublin?' I asked as I pulled the car onto the edge of the track so that we could walk out to the manor site.

'Ah, it's like any city. It snows, now and then, but you don't really feel it, other than that the bus comes late and the bars get busy early.'

I opened my door, and the wind took it from my hands and snatched it to its furthest extent. I'd grown up in a city. Elliot and I had met in Leeds, got jobs in York, and decided that we wanted to live – I tried very hard not to think 'and raise our children' – out in the countryside. Right now, with rain trying to get into the car with me, I couldn't quite remember why.

'Remind me again why we're here?' I had to half shout the words above the noise of the wind, which hit our ears like the sound of a practising piper. 'Are you going to want to dig around the site of the old manor? Only I don't think you'll be able to get much of a hole before it becomes a pond.'

'I'm a historian,' Connor said vaguely, shrugging his back to the wind. 'Not an archaeologist. I mean, I've done my time on digs when I was a student, but I mostly deal with digging in libraries and archives now. I'm the person that points the archaeologists at places.'

We tramped along a small trackway that once would have been the approach to the manor. It lay at the top of a shallow valley and away towards the bottom of the slope I could see signs of activity. A dig tent had been erected, blown down, and was being stared at by a group of people as it flapped its collapsed edges in the wind like a half-manifested ghost.

'They're getting started, that's good.' Connor shaded his eyes against the driving rain and peered out through the mist at the group. 'They won't get much done at this time of year but it might be enough for them to establish what they need to do when the weather improves.' He wriggled his shoulders. 'About July should do it.'

I was pleased to note that all the activity was a decent distance from my stone, which was about a quarter of a mile away from us, stretching its length invisibly in the tangled and waving undergrowth.

'This is roughly the site of the manor,' I said, my pointing finger describing a rectangular shape. 'Foundations were fifteenth century, but I think the site was originally established in the fourteenth. Wooden then, of course, but rebuilt in locally made brick around about 1520.'

Connor looked at me. 'It's all right, you don't need to give me the lecture, now,' he said, pulling his hood further forward over his head so that he was not much more than a nose tip and some hair. 'I've got the degree.'

A hot rise of embarrassment made the inside of my waterproofs damper than the outside for a moment. 'Yes. Sorry, of course. I was forgetting for a minute.' My oilskins cracked in the wind like sails. 'I was thinking of...'

Elliot. I'd been thinking of Elliot, who'd worked for a heritage building company, sourcing materials to rebuild and repair ancient houses. He'd come down more on the 'builder' side, where I was on the 'historical' side, and he'd look at stone and tell me where it was quarried and where to look for masons' marks. I'd tell him about the people, the changing fashions, the building to 'keep up with the de Joneses'. Actually, it was nice to have someone who already knew. It cut out a lot of the talk, which was difficult anyway because of the wind.

'The terracing could be original Roman.' Connor held his hood in place. The gale was not cutting his toggles any quarter.

I nodded. I was dry enough but the oilskins were like being a boil-in-the-bag cod and I was heating up. I hoped Connor wasn't going to take too long.

'I'm going for a walk around. You'll wait here? Only if you move, I might not be able to find you again and I can't bear the thought of trudging around calling pathetically.' He gave me another smile, which I could only see the edges of, and set off away across the manor site, with his hood pointing downwards to indicate that his eyes were on the ground.

Mist swirled. The far-off group of archaeologists came and went as the air thickened and then dispersed, cloud settling over the hills for a good long downpour but being displaced by the constant pressure of the wind, and Connor became a black shape crouching occasionally over the peat. I could have called over to him, but the wind was too strong for my voice to have carried. It was currently whipping the hood of my oilskins, so the material dipped and bulged and flicked water into my eye.

I turned my back to the wind and leaned into it with my hands in my pockets. The pressure was somehow pleasing, pushing at me until I had to step or lose my balance, almost like another presence. Almost like a hug, I caught myself thinking. Almost as though the wind were a crowd, a shoulder against mine here, a force in my lower back there, making me move along with it.

How long since I'd had a hug? A long time. People had hugged me at the funeral, but those had been brief arms across me, embraces of sympathy. Since then I'd actively repelled any attempt at bodily contact, because it hadn't been Elliot. The last time I'd had one of those full-on squeezes that threatens to knock the breath from you, it would have been that final day. Elliot, leaving for work because 'I can't let them down, we've got wainscotting up to our eyeballs', despite the fact that he was off colour and lacking in his usual energetic frenzy.

I stepped again, one foot landing in a peaty squelch where water was wearing away at the moor's surface. I'd thought it all through before. If Elliot had stayed at home, would I have stayed with him? Would I have been there when his heart had stopped so catastrophically? Could I have got help to him in time, while I punched and pummelled away at his chest trying to keep him alive long enough for an ambulance to arrive?

Or would I have trusted that he'd be fine and left him in bed with a thermos of tea, instructions to call me if he felt worse, and gone to the office anyway? To come home and be faced with...

I shook my head and the rain splattered off my hood in a mist of diamond drops. I went over this regularly, less regularly now, of course, but still, whenever I dreamed of Elliot the dreams would be followed by this relentless examination of my actions. *Could I have done anything differently? Would it have changed anything?* The doctors had said no, that nothing could have been done, Elliot had been dead within seconds. Even if I had been standing over him with a defibrillator and oxygen tank, I couldn't have saved him. It was a message that, even now, I wasn't sure had sunk in.

I stood with the wind hugging me and the rain crying alongside me. The nearest I got to physical contact these days, the nearest I could stand.

I suddenly felt very, very lonely.

'I see what you mean.' The words were shouted at me across the moor. 'Nothing left of the manor.'

'I did warn you.' I brought myself back from the brink of self-pity. 'The whole site was stripped bare more than seventy years ago.'

'I did have a bit of a poke.' Connor advanced on me, rain running down his waterproofs. 'And I found this.'

He came closer still and formed enough of a windbreak for me to be able to raise my hood to look at what he was holding out. Balanced on his palm, as though he were offering a lump of sugar to a nervous horse, was a tiny square object, with a glazed top.

'I give in.' I stepped again to keep my balance.

'Tessera.' The small square blew off his hand and bounced down into the heather and mud at his feet. 'Bugger and feck.'

We both crouched and began patting our way through the undergrowth, the wiry heather stems flicking more water up into our faces as the rain ran into new angles of our clothing. Connor was as black and shiny as a seal, rustling his way through the whin bushes in a desperate attempt to retrieve his tile, and it was all so incongruous and ridiculous that I let out a short laugh that I hadn't intended.

'You finding this funny?' He didn't sound as irritated as his words suggested.

'Ludicrous, really,' I said, tugging my hood further down over my face. 'So you've found a Roman mosaic? In the manor?'

'No, just a – ah, here it is.' He grabbed at the mud for a moment and then straightened up so suddenly that a raft of spray caught me in the eye. Caught by surprise, I flicked my head back and more rain got under my hood, blinding me, so I stayed down, shaking my head. 'Are you all right there?'

'Water in my eyes,' I muttered.

'Come on up, now.' Connor took my arm, oilskins crumpling into a greasy second skin under his touch, and pulled me to my feet. I rose from the depths of the twiggy heather, shedding water like Venus arising, and had to take several tiny steps to balance myself so that I didn't hurtle into him. I did tread on his foot but we were both wearing boots so stout that you could have shod a horse with them, so he probably didn't feel it.

I did. I felt the unexpected contact all the way from that clutched arm to the stompy toes. *Touch. A presence.*

'So...' I tried to keep my voice light, but it bent under the weight of worry and also a little from the water that ran into my mouth, channelled from my hood, '...there's definite sign of Roman occupation?'

Connor took half a step back so our waterproofs were no longer crackling against one another. 'A tessera does not a villa make,' he said. 'It could have come in on soil from somewhere else. But it does mean I'm going back to the documents. If there *was* a villa out here, then there's every chance there might have been a town close by. A farming settlement associated with the villa, anyway.'

I couldn't help it, I turned my head towards the site of my stone, still stretched out somewhere in the undergrowth further along the hillside. 'And... more research?'

'Oh, yes. Goes without saying. This could be a really important discovery, a Roman settlement out here. Not quite the "fringes of Empire", but close.'

Then he set off back towards the car, a stomping black object trudging over the shrubby undergrowth as the rain streamed down around him, leaving me biting my lip and worrying for the future of my folkloric stone.

13

I sat at my desk with the lamp illuminating the room, in a quiet puddle of simulated cosiness while the rain blanked out the sky. I'd laid out the format of the book, stories about the high moor with the stone at the centre of it all; stories about fairies and hobs, ghosts and spook lights, and if the teller hadn't mentioned the stone then I'd found a way to weave it in somehow, with cross references to fairyland. We had the man who'd encountered a fairy procession on a journey home from market, mysterious lights that led travellers astray and were said to be fairies trying to drown humans in bogs, the fairies apparently held regular markets on the stone and would occasionally pop up in farms, doing helpful chores. Things were going well. With some lavish illustrations of the moor in summer, lots of stretches of heather and trickling moorland streams, a scattering of 'it is said' and some spooky shots under a full moon – the book was all under control.

I pushed my chair back and turned tired eyes to focus out of the streaming window, practically seeing fairies myself now as the raindrops blurred into multicoloured stripes. It wasn't hard to envisage families out here, isolated and with a long five-mile trudge to the nearest town, using the otherworld as an explanation and descriptor for things in the natural world that they didn't yet have explanations for. Didn't we, even in the twenty-first century, ascribe actions to ghosts and poltergeists when we couldn't otherwise account for them? It seems that humans are naturally imbued with a tendency to want to co-exist with the paranormal.

I rubbed my eyes again and rested my head in my hands. Five hours in front of a screen wasn't doing my sight or my neck muscles any favours, and I hadn't even got Chess to bring me regular cups of tea or to bring magazines to my desk and point dramatically at outfits. Connor had gone out again, I wasn't sure where, but it was probably to impress some students on site, and I smiled at the impossibility of impressing anyone in a gale with rain that fell in every direction including upwards.

He had seemed genuinely excited by the prospect of Evercey Manor being built on a pre-existing Roman site. I glanced up at the window again, where the rain had smeared along the glass and occasionally splattered against it in a wind-driven frenzy, and wondered if his enthusiasm had been tempered somewhat by trying to garner student appreciation in a rainstorm. Then I spared a moment of pity for the Romans out here – even those from the north of the empire must have struggled with the short, damp, grey days. It was hard enough to find time to get anything done in winter even with artificial lighting. How much worse would it have been with nothing but firelight?

Poor buggers. It was horrible out there in oilskins. A wool cloak wouldn't give much relief from the wind, and how fairies were meant to get about, given their reported skimpiness of clothing, I had no idea. Then I stood up. I was beginning to ascribe human feelings to creatures that probably didn't even exist – and certainly not in the fluffy, late nineteenth-century depictions of wings, diaphanous clothing and cute baby-faces. Anything that flitted about on the moors would have to be sturdily constructed and wear big coats.

In the kitchen I put the kettle and the lights on, listening to the familiar creaks and rattles of the cottage with the wind caught in the eaves. A century ago, would I have been putting those noises down to ghosts? Would I have been imagining Elliot out there, tapping casements and knocking beams? I leaned back against the countertop that he'd fitted, sanded and oiled oak because the cottage demanded it, with lots of drawers and cubbies for storage because I had demanded it, and remembered again. All those months when I'd been so desperate for him that I would take almost anything as proof that he was watching over me. Random feathers, which found their way into the cottage unsurprisingly often given the number of duck-fights outside, were signs that Elliot was still out there. Butterflies and rainbows and every time the floors creaked – I'd tried to make them indications that my husband was a conscious, thinking presence and hadn't left me completely.

As I poured water into my mug I almost smiled at the way the steam rose, twisting into shapes that could have been a face, if I had been wanting it to be. Elliot was gone, I knew that. But there was a comfort in knowing that the cottage was his legacy; all his experience of sourcing materials for heritage properties had been brought to bear on it, all his knowledge and crafting ability and those of his friends had restored the little shell of a building back to life. He still lived among the salvaged beams and recovered brick, the lathe and plaster that had been carefully hand-mixed to insulate the internal walls. Elliot surrounded me in every plank and every surface. I didn't need his ghost to remind me he'd existed – I had memories and his house.

Behind me I heard a car splash into the yard, doors banging and voices, and then Connor appeared in a whirlpool of water at the back door, still in his rustling outfit and carrying a plastic bag.

'Hey!' He raised a hand of farewell to whoever had brought him back, and the car slithered a tight turn and headed back out up the hill to civilisation, whilst Connor came inside and dripped. 'How's the book?'

I flicked the kettle back on. 'Progressing nicely. How are the Romans?'

'Cold and wet, I should think. It's a grand day out there if you like drowning. Ah, you're making tea, that will be just the thing. I've been trying to engage enthusiasm in students all day, and I've got an idea that getting them to think about Roman town construction in a hurricane might have put them off the history for life.'

He peeled off the coat in the doorway and began stepping out of his trousers. I was very pleased to see that he was wearing something underneath the waterproofs. As I made him a mug of tea, he very carefully draped the soaked nylon over a chair back so that it would drip towards the door.

'You were well taught at an early age.' I handed him the mug and nodded towards the wet clothes.

'Ireland.' He grinned at me and took the mug. 'It's wet by tradition.'

Suddenly I found that I was enjoying myself. The domesticity I'd been missing as I'd rattled around the cottage by myself, tied in by memories of how things had been, swarmed in surrounded by tea steam and lighting. Having another presence here, even if it was the immensely annoying Connor, gave the cottage a 'filled' feeling and knocked away that dark emptiness.

I decided I really *would* get a cat when he went.

'I dunno,' he continued, pulling out a chair and slumping into it. 'I'm still undecided about what was going on up there. Town, settlement, farming community – I'm not sure which way to go.'

'Wouldn't a villa indicate a small community?' I sipped at my tea and restrained my urge to sit down alongside him, watching him waggle his socked feet against the tiles.

'It could. But villas were built with access to a road. They had to have a way of getting produce to the nearest sales point, and there's no road that we've found yet. If we can establish where the road went through your moor, we can start to narrow things down a bit. Rowan...'

I looked at his face. His usually friendly openness had taken a darker turn. He was squinting at me through the tea steam.

'What?'

'I'm afraid we're going to have to lift that stone.' He held up an appeasing hand. 'Just to check. If it's a funerary monument, then we've got a cemetery and they were built alongside the roads into and out of town. It would help us place the villa, if there is one.'

Had I really been settling into a companionable relationship with Professor O'Keefe? All the friendly feelings evaporated into the dank atmosphere. 'No. No way.'

He sighed. 'We've been here before. Look, we'd lift it, look at the underside, that's it. Maybe make some sketches, if it's worth looking at. I won't even tell you, if you need to keep plausible deniability. I'll let you keep thinking about fairyland being kept down there.'

'Don't you dare.' My voice was a low growl. 'Don't you *touch...*'

Outside there was a commotion as a subset of ducks flew, with alarmed quacking, across the river. We both heard it but ignored it in favour of eyeballing one another.

'We've got to know,' Connor said, obviously straining to keep his voice level. 'It could be really important to my research, Rowan.'

'That's Dr Thorpe, thank you,' I snapped. 'And the stone remaining untouched is important to *mine*, not that you seem to have considered that.'

There was something outside. A feeble light twirled as though someone was trying to read instructions by the light of a mobile phone. I registered it, but was too busy trying to communicate, through the medium of strained pupils and narrowed eyelids, that he was not going to lay so much as the tip of one finger on my stone. If he tried, I'd raise all the folklorists in the country against him, and that would *not* look good on his CV.

'But you *know* fairies aren't being kept imprisoned by the stone.' Connor sounded as though he was almost pleading. 'You're a rational woman. Well, mostly.'

'And what...' my eyes were so narrow now that even my lower lids were straining, '...do you mean by that, *exactly*?'

'Ah now, you've a wee tendency to hang on to the old memories, don't you think? You're using the stone as a symbol of the unchanging nature of things, when we all know things have to change. Otherwise, well, evolution would have been a dead loss, now, wouldn't it?'

I took a deep breath and tried to stay rational. 'The whole *point* of my research is looking to the past!'

'But it's not necessarily a healthy thing, now—' he began,

but, probably just as well for his own health, there was a knock at the door that stopped us both into rigid immobility.

'Was that...?' I asked, half holding my breath.

'Sounds like it. Out here, on a night like this?' Connor glanced towards the door. 'Should I open it?'

We stared at one another. And whilst I absolutely *knew* that it wasn't the sidhe come knocking to tell him that he disturbed their resting place on penalty of curses, I did have the tiniest hope that it might be.

'You'd better,' I whispered. Who the hell would be out here on a foul evening like this? I hadn't heard a car, the nearest bus stop was over a mile away, nobody would walk the five miles from town, not with the wind howling down the lanes and the rain turning every surface into a dark mirror.

'All right, now.' Connor sounded nervous too. 'If it's big and evil, I'll be the one under the table.'

He stood up, looking surprisingly vulnerable, I thought suddenly, in his socks, and shuffled over to the back door. A hesitation, and then he flung it open onto a flight of cold air and the increased sound of rain and agitated ducks.

There was a moment's silence. I found myself in a corner, reaching behind me for a weapon, but there was nothing on the worktop more alarming than a breadboard, so I wielded that, like a knight with no right to a heraldic design.

Connor was still standing blocking the door. Occasional draughts came past him. I could hear them rustling my paperwork in the other room and sending sheets to the floor. Finally he spoke and his voice was odd. Deep, but guarded, as though he didn't want to be talking.

'Saoirse?'

It was more of a grunt than a name.

I moved slowly around the edges of the kitchen, keeping the

worktop at my back until I could see around Connor's blocking of the door. Outside on the step, wearing a too-big parka that was clearly soaked right through, was a woman, nothing but pale skin and huge grey eyes in the illumination that made it past Connor's shape.

'Saoirse?' He said it again, and this time there was a response, but too low and mumbled for me to hear.

'For goodness' sake, let her inside,' I said. 'We'll be getting the ducks moving in if we don't close that door.'

I sounded sharp, and I hadn't missed the way that the possessive 'we' had slipped out, joining Connor and I in a domestic arrangement that we certainly didn't have. I didn't know who this was, but, from Connor's immobility and reluctance to step away from the door, I had my suspicions.

Without another word he turned and walked back into the kitchen, leaving the door open. No invitation, but then she'd clearly heard me and it would be stupid to stand on the doorstep any longer, given how the rain was still sluicing down and the unsuitability of her coat.

She shuffled over the step and into the kitchen, leaving the door flapping wide to the night. 'Hello, Connor,' she said, and her voice was soft with the same accent as his. 'I've left Michael and I came to find you.'

I closed the back door and went to hide in the bathroom.

14

It was surprising how much I could find to do upstairs. The shower needed a good clean and then I moved on to tidying my bedroom, putting away the heaped bedside reading onto the bookshelf, dusting the surfaces and rearranging the few ornaments across the beams. Then I plumped the pillows, shook out the duvet and refolded all the blankets, smoothed the sheet, picked up a few bits of fluff from the carpet, and sat on the end of the bed with my head in my hands.

Well, I should be happy, shouldn't I? Connor's lost love had come to find him. Done the decent thing, left her husband, and searched him out. Wasn't that lovely?

But a darkness rumbled underneath my attempts to feel satisfied that he'd leave me alone in my cosy house now. He'd disappear into the dark night with his lover, move on to a fabulous life and stop pestering me. It was what I wanted, wasn't it? Him gone?

A tiny, treacherous voice whispered into my ear, as though those fairies whose existence I fought to maintain despite everything were caught in my hair. *You expected him to stay. Until spring at least, when the nights are lighter and you can lose yourself in working until bedtime; you thought you could keep him here to alleviate the boredom and the loneliness. Besides, you quite like him, don't you? I mean, obviously, he's a Class A git with his threats to move the stone but he's easy on the eye and he cooks and he's chatty. And he seems to like you, even when you are an equal git about the stone. He's interested in it too, from the other side, and maybe you should try being less entrenched...*

There were voices coming up the stairs. Oh God, they weren't about to cement their relationship in my spare room, were they? I didn't think I liked the idea of Connor being all... all... *affectionate* on the guest duvet.

He tapped at my door. 'Rowan,' he half whispered. 'Is it all right if Saoirse has a shower? She's soaked to the skin here and I don't want her catching her death.'

I stifled a momentary urge to say that it would serve her right, walking all the way over here in a stupid coat, it would be a lesson to her, but I didn't. Of course I didn't, it would be cruel and my newly arisen possessiveness towards Connor was my own fault. 'Of course,' I said. 'Make sure she's got plenty of towels. And... here.' I fumbled at the back of my bedroom door for a moment and clutched down the spare dressing gown. It had been Elliot's, and I held it to me for a moment, but it no longer had the traces of him that I'd looked for so urgently before, 'Tell her to put this on afterwards.' I opened the door a crack and thrust it at him.

Connor caught at it and got my hand at the same time. We stood, him in the shadowed dimness of the landing, and me in the newly tidy bedroom with the bright lampshade swinging slightly in the draught. 'Thank you,' he said softly.

'No problem.' I disengaged myself and withdrew so fast that the draught caught the door and slammed it in his face.

I heard his bedroom door open and close then and, in a kind of silent horror that he might decide to get in the shower with her, I fled along the twilit landing and down the stairs, to stand in the living room. What did I do? Leave them alone to sort out their differences, possibly in my spare room, and loudly? Pretend not to be here listening to every word, gasp and sigh? No, the prospect was too dreadful to bear.

I'd go out, that was what I'd do. It was only – I glanced at the little clock, a wedding present from friends who'd bought it in an antiques shop and told us it would fit in right with our aesthetic, even though it was the wrong period and decorated all over with quite dreadful enamelled birds – half past seven. It might be as dark as midnight outside, but beyond this drenched valley with the hushed river, people would be going about normal life. Shopping and... well, yes, I could go shopping, couldn't I?

I scuffled my way into coat and boots and ignored the fact that I was wearing the fleecy tracksuit that I lounged around at home in. My bag, phone and cards were hunched on a corner of the worktop as though trying to hide from the conflict, so I grabbed the lot and flung open the kitchen door and then stopped on the step when a flurry of rain blew in and rebounded off my booted toes. This was *my house*! What was I doing, being driven out into the night by a soggy visitor? I should stay, call a taxi for the pair of them and send them off to a hotel with good wishes for the future and a sense of doom averted!

I rocked, hesitantly. Upstairs the boards creaked, and I heard Connor's door open again. There was a moment of pause, and then steps set off towards the bathroom, making each board groan under their weight as they went. The thought of having to listen to groaning of a more personal nature sent me flying out into the night to take myself and my car far, far away from here and to somewhere where bright lights and crowds would help me forget whatever might be going on in my poor, beleaguered cottage.

I drove to Malton, where it was late night shopping night, and a Christmas market was spread surprisingly around the streets, lashed by the rain and blown half sideways. Awnings thrashed and sent sudden dumps of collected water flying onto heads, everyone was huddled into the shelter offered by the bigger buildings, and an inflatable Santa dashed to freedom along the main road, pursued by a crowd of happily anarchic children.

It helped. There were things to do, there was shopping to get. I could convince myself that this was a necessary errand rather than an avoidance tactic. I parked the car among the others that had braved the night, gathered my coat close about my neck and, shoved along by a following wind, went for a browse.

I bought a bright knitted beret for Chess's Christmas present and realised that it finished off my Christmas shopping. My parents lived now in southern Spain, their card and presents had been despatched weeks ago to make the last posting day. The half-instinctive twitch towards 'things Elliot might like' had largely stopped now. This would be my fourth Christmas without him, and I'd managed to make myself a new routine, a day of TV and chocolate; building up the fire and sitting in front of the flames under a blanket with an M&S Christmas dinner on my lap, convincing myself that it wasn't so bad, really. Others had it worse. Opening the presents from my parents, making a Zoom call to watch them open theirs, stilted chat broken by my dreadful Internet connection, and then an early night to eat cake in bed and listen to the silence.

I really *was* going to get a cat. Sooner rather than later.

I bought a pack of freshly fried doughnuts and ate them defiantly in the middle of the square, dripping fat and sugar down my front as I watched some stallholders give up the fight with the elements and start to dismantle trestle tables and bunting. One man, standing under the banner 'Malton History Society', took a full-force gust to the goods and his entire collection was tossed into the air and bowled along the ground, so I stuffed the empty doughnut wrapper into my pocket and went to help.

'Thank you,' he panted, as we scooped *Roman Malton* into a basket, illustrations and booklets and pens all damp and crinkled. 'It's a rubbish night for the Christmas market. I did try to persuade them to hold it earlier in the month, but nobody listened.'

I nodded and fielded a collection of plastic figures that were all face down in a nearby puddle. 'I suppose that might have been worse.'

The man grinned. 'It's that time of year, isn't it? Can't expect twenty-degree sunshine in December.'

The figures were Roman centurions, about ten centimetres tall, all in full armour, with sandals and complete with cloaks flapping in a plastic breeze. On a sudden whim I bought one, a disgruntled-looking soldier with a plumed helmet and chilly bare legs, who had a most lifelike expression of utter disdain on his painted face. He could stand on my desk, I decided, and remind me that things endured. Roman remains under medieval buildings. Life went on, built on the ruins of what had gone before.

I roamed around the supermarket and bought a week's

worth of groceries, wondering whether Connor would be around to help cook them. Or, horrors, would he ask for Saoirse to stay too? I went to put another set of noodles into the trolley, then changed my mind and replaced them on the shelf. No. They could go to a hotel. I was only accommodating *him* under sufferance, any extra people would be masochistic, and besides… besides…

I couldn't stay out any longer without it looking sarcastic, and some of this food needed to be in the fridge, so I turned the car for home and the windscreen wipers to maximum. It was more like sailing a yacht than driving a car, coasting down the narrow lanes with the water spraying up either side and sudden blasts twitching the bonnet in an alarming way so that I had to concentrate hard all the way back.

I stopped at the top of the hill and looked down into the pool of black that was the cottage and the ford. I could hear the water rushing now, pouring down the leat and over the road, and there was, if I strained my eyes, one light on, at the back of the cottage. The living-room light.

Well, if Connor and Saoirse had packed up and gone, at least he'd thought to leave a light on for me to return to. I glided into my parking space and turned off the engine. No sound apart from the water. Good. At least there wasn't noisy sex going on.

Leaving my Christmas market purchases on the back seat, I grabbed the bags of food shopping and went to the kitchen door, which surprised me by being unlocked, and I burst my way in, in a flourish of carrier bags, water and boot prints. The door through to the rest of the house was closed, which was unusual. I normally left the whole ground floor open, so as not to worry myself with what might be *behind* any closed doors, and somehow it was nicer to come in to find the house open and welcoming me. I dumped all the shopping on the table and began to unpack, whilst crumbs of left-over sugar fell from my coat like fake snow.

The kitchen door opened slowly, making me jump, and Connor stood there, wearing pyjamas and thick socks, with his hair on end. 'Rowan?'

'Well, yes, I live here.' I carried on shoving food into the freezer, ignoring the slight lift that my heart gave on seeing him. It was the adrenaline of the door opening, that was all it was. 'Remember?'

He scuffled further into the room and closed the door behind him. I straightened, wondering what he didn't want me to see. Saoirse, spread naked in front of my fireplace? I was *definitely* going to have words if that were the case.

'Sorry, yes, I just woke up. I'm a bit...' He scrubbed both hands over his head as though he could scour himself awake. 'What time is it?'

'About ten. I think.' I went back to unpacking and, after a second, Connor came over and started to help, pushing tins into the store cupboard.

I wasn't going to ask. In fact, I wasn't even going to mention Saoirse. Mostly because I couldn't think of a single way to frame the question that didn't sound snarky. I kept quiet, and so did he, and in near silence we unpacked all the food, crumpled up the bags and put them away, and I put the kettle on. Connor sat at the table, hunched over his elbows.

'So,' he said, and then stopped.

'Yes.' It was all I could come up with. I turned my back to make tea, as elaborately as I could, to avoid looking at him. It was odd. He didn't *look* like a man who'd been passionately reunited with his lost love. If Elliot had come through that door right now, I would have stapled myself to him and never let him out of my sight again. Wouldn't I? The awkward thought that, if

Elliot *had* come through that door, I would have had a lot of explaining to do struck me. But then, so would he, so that would be all right.

'Saoirse is up in my room. I hope that's all right. I couldn't turn her back out on a night like this.' Connor had a note of justification in his voice and, when I turned to hand him a mug of tea, a look of total confusion on his face.

'I suppose so.'

'I'm on the floor in the living room.' He nodded towards the door. 'In there.'

'I'm aware of where the living room is in my own house, Connor.'

'You don't want her here.'

I sighed. 'I'm not keen on strangers pitching up out of nowhere and then staying, no.'

'Was that aimed at me?' Connor looked at me over his mug. 'Because I can go, y'know, if it's inconveniencing you.'

We both sounded odd, as though our words were covering something up, something that neither of us dared say.

'Look, she can stay for tonight.' I poured too much milk into my mug, debated remaking the tea and then decided that I didn't want to be here for one minute longer than I had to. 'But then the pair of you have got to find somewhere else to go. This place isn't big enough for three.'

Connor took a deep breath. 'You think I should go with her?'

He sounded so baffled and overwhelmed that I softened. 'Isn't that what you want? She came all this way to find you, she's left her husband, presumably for you. You told me that you'd never felt for anyone what you felt for her. It's got to be worth a shot, surely?'

He stood up and started pacing, sliding his socked feet up and down the tiles, with the toes elongating as he went. 'I don't know. I just don't know. I thought she was the one, y'know? We had such a good time and she was a laugh and all, but now – now I just don't know.'

I stood and watched him. He didn't seem to need my input. 'She lied, and I don't know if I can look past that. She wasn't who she said she was.' He spun a tight circle and tea slopped from his mug. 'What do I do? Rowan?'

'Do you love her?' I asked softly, and his head came up.

'Love her? I thought I did. Losing her was the most painful experience of my life.'

I remembered Elliot. Then me, standing in the hospital with a concerned nurse at my elbow, knowing that he would never come home again, and the way that felt. I would have given anything for him to have leaped up, shouted, 'Fooled you!' and to have been back with me. 'It's not just losing the person, it's losing the life you thought you were going to have,' I said softly. 'Isn't it?'

Connor looked me in the face now. His eyes were very dark, brows pulled together by uncertainty. 'We were going to get married. Buy a place in Clontarf, have a couple of kids, take them down to Granda's old farm and teach them to surf off Lahinch.' His voice was heavy with regret.

'She's got children already,' I reminded him. 'She'll want to keep them with her, I should think.'

He shook his head. 'I dunno,' he said, still heavily. 'I don't really know what she thinks is going to happen. She... Saoirse, she's not quite... I think she may have had some kind of breakdown.'

I thought of that wet shape in the doorway. The pale skin and those wide grey eyes. Nobody would turn up at a strange doorway like that unless they really, really wanted a reconciliation, would they? 'Maybe she missed you,' I said quietly.

It was disturbing seeing Connor so obviously upset and not knowing what to do. Up until now he'd been an irritating presence, occasionally good company; a dark streak of well-dressed professor-hood with an overhanging threat of spoiling my research and upsetting my folk tales. Suddenly he'd become an actual man, standing there in front of me with his mouth twisted and his eyes beginning to redden in the corners. He had emotions, he could be unsettled and confused and afraid; he wasn't simply the person-shaped thing that ate my toast and sang, he'd become *real*, somehow.

'I don't know,' he said again. 'I thought I was over her. I thought it was all coming together here.' Another shake of the head. 'But now she's arrived.'

'Look.' I put a hand on his arm. He was still staring into my face as though I had all the answers, as though I could tell him what to do. I remembered Elliot, walking out that morning, off to his wainscotting and a day of drawing plans, or so we'd thought. How much would I have given for him to come back? 'Ask yourself this. If she died tomorrow, how sad would you be? How much would you miss her?'

There was a long moment, in which rain hissed against the window. Then Connor leaned forward and kissed me on the cheek. Brief and soft, a contact of stubble passing my lips and the touch of his mouth on my skin.

'Thank you,' he breathed. 'Thank you, Rowan.'

Then he picked up his mug and went back into the living room to sit on the sofa with my spare duvet around his shoulders, while I scuttled up to my room to hide in the peace and quiet.

Next morning Saoirse was in my kitchen when I got up. There was no sign of Connor.

'Thank you for letting me stay.' She was sitting at the table, huddled over a cup of tea, wearing what was obviously Connor's jumper. Her bare legs, very white and long, jutted at awkward angles, and she looked about seventeen.

'That's all right,' I said, brazenly ignoring the fact that I hadn't really let her stay, that had been Connor, and I'd busily avoided the whole thing. 'It was a filthy night.'

We both looked out of the window at the newly calm day. The sun was breasting the rise and filling the little valley with pale light. 'You've got a lovely cottage. I'd love to live somewhere like this.'

I didn't know what to say to her. Saoirse had the wide eyes of a child, a small mouth and incredibly high cheekbones, and with her blonde hair loose around her shoulders she looked like a model after an all-night bender. I felt every strand of my uneven haircut; my indefinite-coloured eyes and just-about-there cheekbones sat sullenly in my face, retiring in the face of the competition.

'How did you find him? Connor, I mean,' I added, although who else I could have been talking about I didn't know.

'I went to the university and asked.' Her accent was softer than Connor's, with another influence. 'One of his students told me he was here and gave me directions. I got a bus and then walked.'

Another silence.

'You've left your marriage?' I tried to make it sound soft, just a query, but it was clearly more questioning than she could take, and she burst into tears.

'I don't know what to do,' she sobbed. 'Connor is so... he's great and my husband, well, he goes to work and comes home, and I've got the wee ones all day on my own!'

I absolutely was not going to give her any advice or tell her that it sounded as though she'd had an affair with Connor because she was bored and lonely. It would have been cruel, anyway. And it wasn't my business. *None* of this was anything to do with me. I was just the landlady.

But the memory of the graze of stubble, the sensation of lips against my skin made me shiver.

'Where is Connor?' I asked, and there must have been a trace of that remembrance in my voice, because Saoirse looked up sharply through her tears.

'Outside, on his phone. He's arranging us a lift back to York,' she said. 'One of his students, I think.'

'Oh. Right. Well, I'd better get dressed and go to work. It's been nice to meet you, Saoirse,' I added politely, and she waved a hand as though this were her house and I were an interviewee, failing to get a job.

I went back upstairs. The door to the spare room was open and I peeped around it, to see that Connor's belongings were all packed up in bags inside the door. The bed was stripped and the spare duvet he'd slept under last night was neatly folded and placed on the mattress.

Elliot's dressing gown was hung up behind the door. I stared at it for a second. Had I really given it to Connor to put on his girlfriend? I must have been in a state of panic – that dressing gown had been my Elliot substitute for months. I'd slept with it wrapped around his pillow so I would wake to the smell of him beside me, and the warm touch of towelling when I leaned over. Anything was less painful than the bland cold of an empty bedside. And I'd handed it over, as though it meant nothing to me, simply so that Saoirse wouldn't have to roam around the house wrapped in a skimpy towel. Had it *really* been for her comfort? Or because I'd feared what Connor might do?

I looked back at the bags, untidily packed and stacked around the bed. So, he was going, then. Fine. Good.

I dressed and went out, past Saoirse, who was still sitting at the table wearing his clothes. I didn't bother to lock the back door; I didn't even turn to look as I started the car and drove up the long hill away from the cottage. I didn't even stop to ask myself why I was crying. I turned the radio on to drown everything out and put my foot down all the way to the office.

15

'I'm back.' Chess snuffled her way into the office, divesting herself of layers of coat, scarves and hats as she came. 'Wow. You look crappy. Have you caught the cold?'

I sat with my head hanging over a handwritten book of charms. I wasn't reading it. I wasn't even attempting to turn the pages. I was letting myself settle back into my solitude.

'I do feel a bit off colour,' was as far as I would go. 'But I don't want to stay at home too often. They might do away with our office if I do that, and it's good to have somewhere to store everything.'

Maybe Chess was right, I thought. Maybe this feeling was what was it? A lowering of the spirits, as they would have called it back in the day; that sensation of the shine being taken off things, almost a disappointment in life itself. A ridiculous feeling. I shrugged my shoulders to try to lose the tightness in them, and turned back to the manuscript, a donated artefact from someone's grandmother, full of potions and spells from a farm near Durham at the turn of the twentieth century. That had been the pivotal era. People had gone past walling up cats as a house protection and putting shoes up chimneys but hadn't yet moved into the world of the telephone and artificial fertiliser. They had straddled the world of the past and the world of the now and lived in a time that was fascinating in its near modernity with a twist of superstition.

Chess brought me a cup of tea and I managed to avoid her putting it down on the crabbed pages only by a narrow margin. 'So—' she hitched herself against the corner of my desk '—what are you doing for Christmas this year? You know you're always welcome to come to mine – open house and cocktails?'

Christmas. Just under a week away and yesterday I'd been contemplating the solitary day with a measure of contentment. I'd been looking on it as a break from having Connor around – that he'd go back to Ireland for the holiday and then come back. Why did it now feel more like a life sentence?

'I'm not sure, Chess. But thanks for the invitation.'

'Or is Connor staying over? You're welcome to bring him too, of course. I have the feeling he'd liven up a party a treat!'

'Connor's moved out,' I said dully. Those packed bags still stood stacked in my memory, that empty room like a testament to the rest of my life. 'His ex came back and they were off to look for a hotel in York.'

'Oh.' She shifted. 'That's a shame.' Another shift of her weight. 'Are you sure you're okay?' This was said softly and with a measure of sympathy that I didn't want, and, besides, it was unwarranted. Connor leaving had always been the desired end result, and Saoirse's arrival had only precipitated it by a few months. It wasn't as though it were a huge shock, after all.

'I'm fine, honestly, Chess. It was a late night, and you might be right, I think I've caught something, making me feel a bit run down, that's all. Look, I'll head up to the records office. I want to look up some of the old maps and the fresh air will do me good.'

I stood up and my undrunk tea wobbled.

'If you're sure.' Chess's concern made my eyes water again. *Definitely rundown. Probably a virus.* 'Get some mince pies while you're out!' she called over her shoulder as she went back into her cubbyhole in the library.

I didn't go to the records office. Instead, I took a walk along the city walls, hoping that the chilly air and cold stone would clear my head. I'd got myself stuck in a revolving series of thoughts of how glad I was that Connor was gone and my house was mine again, and how quiet and empty it was going to seem now.

The potential cat crept a little closer.

Folklore suddenly felt pointless. A jumble of stories, a recited list of inventions and delusions with no more relevance to today than the narrow gateways that filtered ill-tempered traffic in and out of York, all traffic lights and hold ups. Once folklore had been useful. It had helped people make sense of their lives and given them an illusion of control over the natural world. Charms to help the cheese along and fairies to populate the high moors and watch over the cattle, to keep the water flowing and the bogs from sucking sheep under. They'd all meant something, once.

Now I found myself thinking of my years of study and my PhD as cute stories, fit only for pinning to the page to keep the tourists happy. Really, seriously, would it *matter* if Connor and his students lifted the Fairy Stane? There was no fairyland. There were no happy endings.

Roman, Viking, Norman, Tudor. I ran the rosary of the ages again. Connor was right, history was real, recorded facts. Folklore was myth and magic, so why was I trying so hard to preserve it?

I rounded the top of the wall, close to where there was a

large gap, where fishponds and wetlands had once prevented entry to York, and stared out over the city. Down the alleyway lay the headquarters of Elliot's workplace, the big salvage yard where materials were brought from all over the country when ancient buildings were demolished. I could almost see the roof of his office from here; that higgledy-piggledy mix of corridor and corner that had been my second home for such a long time, that had smelled of soup and microwave meals, where laughter had echoed at odd angles and Elliot had held chair races with his workmates on quiet days.

A place I no longer had a tie to. Elliot was gone. If I'd turned up there now, they would have been polite, pleased to see me in a baffled kind of way – they'd have fed me coffee and made enquiries into how the cottage was getting on, and how I was doing. All very concerned, but not *involved*. Then they would have turned away and got on with their work and I would have wandered back out into the chilly day, and Elliot still wouldn't be here.

It was just me. And that meant only me to remember the importance of things. Those witch marks that people had carved into wooden beams to keep the house protected from evil, they'd mean nothing more than random graffiti if people like me didn't list them, date them, keep the story alive. Shoes up chimneys, cats in walls, they'd all meant safety to the people that had put them there, and what right had we, as twenty-first-century people, to call them stupid superstitions? They'd made their own security back then, in a time of uncertainty, as Elliot and I had made ours. Those people were gone just as he was, and I was holding the memories of all of them, the fairy believers and my husband, to stop them from being lost.

I stared out over the city, where the brittle sunlight lay smoothly over ancient buildings, and shadows piled in corners.

Memory. All this came down to memory. Those things that were gone still existed, as long as someone remembered them. The folk tales, the myths, the fairies, they all lived on somewhere for as long as their stories were told. Elliot still lived on in my memory, in all those things in the cottage that he'd rebuilt. None of it was completely over, because I remembered. The quiet acknowledgement of the importance of never allowing anything to vanish completely ticked away in my head.

It was my job to remember.

I took a deep breath and carefully descended the steep and slippery steps that took me down to street level, then went in search of mince pies to keep Chess happy.

16

1910

Memmie climbed up out of the ditch cussing under her breath. 'Mazed Memmie', they called her, 'Mindless Memmie', but she knew. She knew a thing or two, more than those daft little girls who'd gone to school with her and now helped their mams in the kitchens and bakehouses; she knew about the fairy folk for a start. Her own mam had told her – you don't go out when the travelling folk comes through, you stays away, you turns your face to the wall and you doesn't listen to them calling you over.

She wasn't *quite* sure that they were fairies, but they came and went in the summer, with their vans and their fires and their songs, and all the children were told to keep away and not take anything they offered, so Memmie reasoned that they *must* be fairies, else what was they doing?

That hot summer night she'd leaned out of the window and heard the music and it had sounded so sweet. She'd heard the voices raised in song, and she'd climbed out and gone to them. Spent the night dancing and singing with them, drinking the harsh apple juice they gave her, but not eating, no, never eating, you don't eat fairy food else they'd take you away. That was what Mam said.

There had been the men, and she wasn't *entirely* sure what they'd done, mostly cos of the apple juice, which had made her head all fuddled. And now it was winter, and here she was in this ditch with her apron all ruined and this thing that they'd given her.

Memmie looked down at it. She didn't want it. She wasn't sure what to do with it now, and Mam would give her a belting if she took it home. Then Da would join in for good measure, and they'd know that she'd been out with the fairy folk.

There was only one thing to do. Memmie folded her apron around the thing and crept her way out of the village. Send it back. That was what she had to do, send the thing back to the folk it belonged to. Up, up onto the high moor, following the distant secret path that nobody was supposed to know, but that she'd seen the men walk only last week. Yes, the path was still here, still clearly marked by the tread of their boots. Out across the hill to the Fairy Stane.

Memmie felt her heart beat faster with the fear as much as the walking. Suppose the fairies was there? How did she tell them that she didn't want what they'd given her? How could she return the gift if they was there? But the stone lay, stretched and silent, alone in the dark, and Memmie relaxed. Nobody was here.

She crouched next to the stone and scooped great handfuls of wet, loose soil away from underneath it, digging until her nails were all dirt and her hands were sore, until she found the little bundle that the men had brought up here last week. They hadn't dug all the way down to fairyland, then. Just far enough to make sure everything was covered. Memmie nodded to herself. They wouldn't want to disturb the fairies down there, have 'em coming up around the village again. Once a year was all anyone could stand.

She rocked back on her heels and pushed the apron-wrapped gift into the new hole, on top of last week's offering, then used her forearms to push the excavated earth back in on top. There. Now it was back where it belonged and Memmie could forget about it and not get belted by Mam and Da.

It was the fairies' problem now.

* * *

Now

The lights were all on in the cottage. I could see them blazing out into the misty evening as I crested the rise of hills and began the swoop down towards the river, and I cursed Saoirse and Connor under my breath as I went. They could have made sure all the lights were off before they went! But I supposed they'd been hurrying, dashing out towards their wonderful new life, not worrying about my electricity bill.

The back door wasn't locked either and I cursed more loudly as I barged my way through, hoping that the place wasn't full of burglars or murderers, crouching behind my tiny loveseat or hiding under the beds. It would be vanishingly unlikely, of course, but it had been that kind of day.

'Bloody hell,' I announced to the kitchen, loudly, to give all the burglars time to get out of the upstairs windows, 'they really didn't care, did they? He could have locked the door and posted the key through the letter box.'

I dropped my work bag noisily on the floor. There was a reassuring lack of windows opening and black-clad figures jumping to the riverbanks, so the house probably wasn't being ransacked. I went over to fill the kettle to make tea while I got out of my coat and boots, and jumped. The kettle was half full and hot.

And then Connor walked in from the living room.

'Ah, you're back,' he said, as though last night hadn't happened and we were still existing in our landlady and tenant situation. 'I'll get some food on.'

'Connor?' I didn't know why I asked. It was obviously him, wearing an Aran knit jumper and his usual black jeans, looking as though he'd come from an evening of lecturing rebellious students. '*Connor?*'

'Who were you expecting? I hear Idris Elba is married, y'know, you'll have a long wait.'

'But you...' I gathered up my disobedient jaw, which wanted to gape. 'Is Saoirse upstairs?' I finished lamely.

He turned his back, fiddling with mugs and teabags and opening and closing the fridge. 'She's in a little B&B in Pickering,' he said, and it sounded as though the words came sieved through the sweater. 'She's not here.'

'So why are you?' I slumped into a kitchen chair. I'd so thoroughly convinced myself that he'd gone, that the cottage was back to being my place of solitude, that finding him here in the kitchen was nearly as hard to get my head around as it would have been should Idris Elba have turned up.

Connor turned around. He had a packet of feta cheese in one hand and an onion in the other, but, despite the fact that I was hungry, I found myself drawn to look at his face. His expression was – *clouded* was the best I could do. As though a thousand thoughts ranged at once through his mind and he couldn't sift out which ones should be given priority.

He took a very deep breath and then blew it out. 'Yes. Well,' he said, and then turned back to the worktop to finish making tea and begin chopping cheese. 'Is it always this hard?' he asked, his voice indistinct under the sound of the knife.

'It's probably been in the fridge too long.'

'I meant life.' There was a rise to his tone now, as though he was smiling. 'As I think you well know.'

I thought of my uncertainty this morning, as I'd stood on the city walls. My near dismissal of everything I'd studied and believed in the last ten years in a brief desire to have everything easily explainable, and then my sudden certainty that remembering the past was still important. 'It has its moments,' I said.

The kettle boiled, a pan clanged onto the stove, and Connor was a whirl of cracking eggs, pouring water, swirling and cutting, as though he was trying to think through movement.

'I'm sending her home,' he said at last.

'Saoirse?'

'No, my mother. Yes, of course Saoirse, who else would I be talking about, now?'

Good. Connor being irritated with me was better. I knew where I was when someone was cross, but he was vulnerable and uncertain and I didn't know how to deal with him. I didn't know how I *wanted* to deal with him.

'It's been a long day. There might have been fifty women since this morning.'

Now he laughed. 'Ah, you're right there. What with me being a playboy and wild, rampant seducer and all.'

He actually looked more like a mythical being than a playboy. There was something different about him, as though he were a selkie or dark sidhe wearing human form. As though he were moving through a mist of memories while he cooked, all the other times he'd cooked a meal overlaid on this present moment.

'So, what's happened?' I asked at last.

He didn't answer at once. Instead, he turned back from the stove, bearing two plates of cheese omelette and a small mixed salad. He laid one plate in front of me, sat down on the other side of the table, put his plate down, and stared at it.

'Connor?'

Another sigh. 'You know what you said?' He didn't look at me. He was prodding the omelette as though it were an unidentified creature that had come in through the window. 'About how I'd feel if she died?'

I did remember. I'd been thinking of Elliot never coming back. The feeling of loss and despair and how I would have given anything in those first months to have him with me again.

And then about Connor kissing my cheek. A brief, impersonal contact, and yet... and yet. How that touch had made me fire back into the kind of life that had been in abeyance for years.

'Yes,' was all I said.

'I thought about it. When I got upstairs, she'd packed my bags, she was so *sure*, so certain that it was the right thing. She'd left Michael, come all the way to England, found me...' He trailed off and poked the blameless, and delicious, omelette a bit more, keeping his eyes on the plate. 'I thought about what you'd said. And you know what?'

I stopped, a forkful of cheesy egg halfway to my mouth. 'What?'

He raised his eyes now. Focused first on the forkful, slowly making its way off the tines and back to the plate as it hung in suspended animation, then moving his gaze up to my face. 'I thought, if Saoirse died, right here, right now, what I'd mainly feel would be relief.'

I dropped my fork and pushed my chair back, suddenly

upright with alarm. 'Oh, God. You haven't... you didn't *murder* her?'

His dark eyes widened, his head jerked in panic and then he grinned. 'What? Ah, come on, woman, of course I didn't murder her. I took her in a taxi to Pickering, put her in a B&B and told her to fly back to Dublin. Not in so many words, of course, actually in a lot, *lot* more words, but I explained that I couldn't be with her. I only left her an hour ago. She wanted me to stay but it wasn't doing either of us any good.'

I felt a pull inside, an echo of loss. 'That poor woman,' I said softly.

'I know, I know.' Now Connor began to eat his omelette. 'I tried to be gentle. I told her that this was no basis to begin a relationship. That I'd loved her once but it hadn't been *her*, it had been who I thought she was. We'd been planning a life, but we'd been doing it from the basis of thinking we were two single people, free to do as we wanted, not taking into account an ex-husband and two young children.'

'How was she?' I thought again of that pale face, those huge eyes. 'I'm not sure Saoirse is entirely well, Connor.'

He shook his head. 'I know. I think it might be delayed post-natal depression. The wee one is only ten months, and Saoirse does get left alone an awful lot, two children under three and a husband who works away – I think she needs help, not me. I was a symptom, not the cure.'

I resettled myself at the table, feeling a bit daft for my overreaction. 'But you loved her,' I said. 'It doesn't just go away.'

'That I did. But she made me feel stupid, when I found out what she'd been playing at. There's nothing like knowing you've been fooled for making you see someone in a different light. She'd no need to have been spinning all those tales about travelling the world to take pictures and meeting all your celebrities, she could have told me she was a wee girl from Kerry who'd left her husband. It would still have been a lie, but not such a wild one.'

'I think,' I said gently, 'that she pretended to be what she wished she was. Free, travelling the world, meeting people. Not something that's easy to do with two small children. She used you to be her fantasy self.'

All the pity that I'd stopped myself from feeling this morning came flooding in. That confused, grey-eyed girl who'd sat at this table as though she'd owned the house wasn't quite the wilful liar I'd assumed, capturing herself a gorgeous professor in a net of untruths. She was a sick young woman who'd tried to escape a life that she was struggling with.

Then I had the awful thought that I had stopped myself from feeling sorry for her earlier *because I'd thought she was taking Connor away.* I pushed that thought away and squashed it hard under the knowledge that he was only here because he had nowhere else to go. He was a historian to my folklorist, and he wanted to move my stone. *Still the enemy. A good-looking, fun one, but. Still.*

'Which B&B did you leave her in?' I asked, putting my fork down on my plate with a clatter that rang through the room.

'The one next to the pub? On the road in, near the bridge.'

I knew which one he meant. A nice place, clean and boutique. 'I think I ought to go and make sure she's all right,' I said, grabbing my bag. 'I don't think she should be alone.'

Connor stared for a moment, then stood up too. 'I'll come with you,' he said.

I stared at him. '*Seriously?* You've dumped her, conclusively, and you think it will make things *better* if you turn up? I just want to make sure that she's all right. If she's ill I don't think she should be left alone just now.'

He nodded, slowly. 'I called her mother. When I left Saoirse, I got her to give me her mother's number and I told her everything. But she won't be able to get over until tomorrow. I stayed with Saoirse as long as I could and I did ask the people at the B&B to keep an eye out.'

I was glad he'd even thought about it. Connor wasn't the type to dump a girl and run, he'd wanted to make sure that someone would be there for her when he couldn't be.

'If it is depression then she's not thinking straight. Look, you call the B&B and ask them to check up on her with some excuse. I'm going over there.'

Connor's eyes were enormous with shock. 'D'you think she might...? Ah, no, come on, now, I'm not worth that.'

I thought back to those days after Elliot's death. The awful, aching hole that had suddenly opened in my life, that place that I had thought would be filled with parenthood, grandparenthood; that hole from which every lonely Christmas and special occasion, every Sunday morning walking alone, every evening in watching stupid TV programmes in silence, had stared back at me. I thought of those days spent lining up all the pills and tablets in the cottage and looking at them. Knowing that I could follow Elliot any time I chose, and it would stop this dreadful emptiness; the twitch every time a door banged, or a vehicle went past, when my heart would rise with the certainty that all this had been a mistake and he was coming home.

'She's very unhappy,' I said softly. 'And she might not be able to see any other way out.' I pulled on my coat and walked out of the door.

The B&B was a five-mile drive away. Connor phoned me whilst I was en route, to say that he'd called the B&B and they'd checked on Saoirse. She was in her room, and they could hear her crying.

I hesitated after he hung up. Should I be doing this? Maybe Saoirse was best left alone to come to terms with what had happened? A strange woman turning up out of the blue couldn't help her, could she?

But then I thought of how I'd felt. How anyone who had offered me understanding and company had been a lifeline back to the world that held coffee and cartoons, sunshine and *Strictly*. How talking about Elliot, about what had happened, had pulled me inch by inch out of that galactic black hole and back into real life. It had hurt, of course, but gradually the pain had eased, and I'd been able to crawl my way back into the world.

Maybe Saoirse needed that same lifeline.

I got to the B&B, under a crisp sky, where stars drilled their way through the night, and got the lady who was busy laying tables for breakfast to show me up to Saoirse's room, where I tapped on the door.

'Saoirse? It's Rowan. We met in my kitchen this morning.'

I could hear her breathing on the other side of the door. The gasping grunts of breath that told of recent sobbing, now abated but not far away.

'I came to talk,' I said, reasoning that this sounded better and gave her more agency than 'I came to make sure you were all right.'

'What about?' The voice was broken but distinct. She was sitting right by the door, from the sound of it. Probably on the floor.

'Whatever you like. I think you might need some company, that's all. It's not a good time to be alone, and the nights are the worst.'

A long pause, during which I could hear the ragged, uncertain breathing. Then, faintly, 'I don't know what to do.' Almost a wail, and I could feel the truth in the words. Hadn't I been there, only with a different cause?

'It gets better,' I said earnestly. Then, because anything was better than the silence, I sat on the floor on the landing outside her room and told her, through the carefully stripped pine panels of the door, how I'd lost my husband. Of the deeper griefs, of how we'd wanted a baby, how we'd tried, how it had seemed utterly hopeless. How we'd discussed IVF with the doctors and then, that morning, that miraculous positive test that I'd never had chance to tell him about.

'I still don't know whether I was actually pregnant,' I said to the doorknob. 'Whether I misread the lines, or whether the grief at losing Elliot made it not stick. I will never know, and it was just that one, extra uncertainty that felt so dreadful.'

'I've got two,' the voice confessed. 'Two girls. My two babies.' Her words split under sobbing. 'What have I *done*?'

I thought carefully. 'I think you've been very tired and very depressed, and Connor gave you a chance to escape for a while,' I said softly. 'And I think people will understand that you need help.'

Another moment of breathing. 'I wanted a bigger gap, you see,' Saoirse said. 'Maeve was only ten months when I fell for Fionnula, and she was such a difficult baby, and then I had the two of them and Michael off with the new job. We'd moved over to Dublin for him, with my mum back in Killarney and her not able to drive.'

Talking about her children seemed to help. Saoirse's voice had become a little stronger and she'd stopped gasping.

'Michael said it would be good to have them close, he's two sisters and a brother and all of them within the seven years. But I wanted to wait, let Maeve get a bit more independent before…

They're so hard and Michael not there most nights. I just wanted...'

'You wanted to escape,' I said gently. 'I wanted to. After Elliot. When the worst of the pain had gone, I wanted to move somewhere where nobody had known him. Where I could be someone else.'

'Yes! And I'd always wanted to do the photographs, you know. But then Michael came along, and we were buying a house and I needed to work for the mortgage. So I gave up the course I was doing and went to work for the airline so we could put a roof over our heads. Then I fell for Maeve so quickly when we started trying...' She stopped. 'I'm sorry.'

I felt my heart lift a little. She was feeling empathy, that was good. 'No, it's all right,' I said. 'I've often thought, if I *had* been pregnant, if I'd had to go through pregnancy and birth and then having our baby, all with Elliot gone, it would have been worse. I mean, yes, to have a reminder of him, but – all alone? I would never have been able to do it.'

'Ah, you would, now.' That almost sounded like a smile. 'You get on with it.'

'Well.' I couldn't follow that up, because the tears were in my throat now. I'd never know.

'When I met Connor he was so sweet and kind and funny, and – I don't know. I sort of slipped into being the Saoirse that I wanted to be. I'd leave the girls with Michael when he came back and I'd go to Connor, and...' A choke. 'I've ruined everything.'

'You can still fix some of it,' I said gently. 'Go back to Ireland. Get some help. Maybe you've lost your marriage, maybe it's saveable, I can't know that, but you've got your girls. Perhaps you can do photography when your little one is a bit older? But you need help first of all. You seem to have been so depressed you hardly knew what you were doing.'

'Oh, I knew.' The voice was bitter now. 'It was like I didn't care what happened to me. I didn't want to be *me* any more.'

I remembered that night in my bathroom. All those pills, lined up on the shelf. Knowing that I could work my way, end to end, and not wake up to this life on another morning of dark emptiness.

'Maybe you could see a doctor,' I went on, carefully not going back to the subject of children. 'See what they say. You might need a bit of help to get you back to yourself again.'

'I could move back to Kerry.' She sounded thoughtful. 'Back to Tralee, or to Killarney, near Mam.'

There was a scuffle and a click and the bedroom door opened. Saoirse stood in the gap, her face reddened with crying and her eyes bleary. 'I've got a kettle,' she said. 'Would you be liking some tea now?'

I spent the night sitting on the edge of Saoirse's bed, looking at photographs of her daughters on her phone, and making cups of tea while she spoke to her mother, who was clearly panicking wildly about *her* daughter. Saoirse seemed calmer, seemed to have taken on board what she'd done, but I knew that was only because I was here. If I'd left her to the dark and the long sleepless night, everything would have crowded back in again, pushing and shoving at her brain like a football crowd, letting all the doubts and the fear rise. She needed medication; she needed someone to listen. She needed to be validated as a woman, and that was what she'd used Connor for. He'd thought he was starting a relationship that was going to lead somewhere, falling for this fragile, pale woman and her fabricated life.

Somewhere around two or three in the morning, Saoirse fell asleep, curled up on the bed. I thought about tiptoeing away and driving back to my own bed, but then I thought of her waking alone again, to the memories and the horror, and tried to doze off myself in the little armchair by the window. But the dreams were here and wouldn't let me rest, as though they'd been given new life by my resurrecting the memories to help Saoirse.

I dreamed of Elliot, leaving that morning, complaining about a pain in his shoulder and feeling groggy. How I'd had little sympathy, hurrying him out of the door to work so that I could do the test in the bathroom and deal with the almost inevitable disappointment alone. I dreamed of that faint line on the pregnancy test, the astonishment and the sudden rise of excitement; the way I'd hugged that knowledge to myself like a longed-for present, and the way all the anticipation and joy had been forgotten when that phone call had come into my office, and I'd run for the hospital.

Then two days later, the bleeding, the dashing of hope, but I'd hardly been able to care, because my hope and joy had already gone, along with Elliot.

I woke to the surreal purple light of the Christmas illuminations under the window and the sound of Pickering starting its day. Saoirse was sitting up on the bed, back to being pale and troubled.

'What am I going to do, Rowan?' She rubbed her eyes with her knuckles. 'I was dreaming of Connor and Michael.'

I shook my head. The dream-memories were still with me too. 'I can't tell you what to do, Saoirse,' I said sadly. 'I really can't.'

'Michael is a good man,' she went on. 'He just doesn't know what it's like with two wee ones at home all the time. And Connor...' she went off into a reverie, staring at a corner of the room so hard that I wondered if there was anything about that illustration of the lighthouse at Flamborough Head that reminded her of Connor, '...he's lovely too. He makes me feel like I used to, before the girls.' A shake of the head. 'But it's not real. None of it was real.' She brought her gaze around to my face now. 'I think you're right. I need help,' she said. 'But I have to face reality too, and I don't know if I can.'

'It's not going to be easy,' I said gently. 'It will take time. But the girls will get older and easier, and you'll find yourself again.'

She smiled. 'When did you get so wise about all this?'

I shrugged. 'I've had three years to find out. I thought my life was over when Elliot died, but I've made another life since then. It's different and it's got holes in it, but it's there and it's up to me to do something with it.'

There was a noise outside on the landing, what sounded like a hushed conversation, and then a tap on the door.

Saoirse stared at me. 'What do I do?'

'Just open the door. Take it from there, I should.'

She opened the door. On the threshold stood a large man with flaming-red hair carrying a small child who had equally red hair and was asleep. Next to him stood a little woman in a mac she held the hand of a toddler who looked as though sleep was never going to be an option.

I assumed this was Michael, Maeve, Fionnula and Mam, but I didn't wait around to find out. I heard only a breathless 'We took the first flight we could get on...' and an enthusiastic cry of 'Mammy!' and I headed out, ducking under the arm of the tall red-headed man and off down the stairs.

What would happen, would happen. I'd done my bit. Saoirse had even seemed to be coming to terms with things a little and I hoped my company and empathy had helped.

I had another momentary flash of that line of pills on my bathroom shelf. If nothing else, I'd kept her from that desperation.

On the drive back home, the memories kept shouldering their way to the front of my mind. Memories I'd pushed down, kept away, held at bay using work and research as weapons to stop them snapping at my heels. Memories of the doctors telling us that Elliot had low-motility sperm and an unassisted pregnancy would be unlikely. His guilt at the results, telling me that I'd be better off without him and me telling him I'd rather have him and stay childless, than be without him...

One of our rare arguments, about, of all things, what we used as a worktop in the kitchen. His assertion that oak was best, would look right in the cottage, and mine that wood was a ridiculous substance to use for a surface that was going to be subject to heavy use and sharp knives. The raised voices as we held our positions – his for historical correctness, mine for practicality.

But I realised that I didn't ache as much as I had. Three years had worn away the sharp edges of the pain to blunt nudges rather than the incisions they had once been.

17

I got back to the cottage before the sun did. Connor must have heard the car because he was there in the doorway like a Victorian parent but wearing a tracksuit and with his hair on end.

'How is she?' He had one hand on the doorframe.

'I think she'll be all right. Her mum and Michael came over together to fetch her back, and she knows she needs help.'

Connor let out a huge breath and slumped. 'Grand,' he said, with his head practically on his knees. 'That's grand.' Then he looked up at me from under his hair. 'You look like you should be in bed.'

The dreams. 'No, I'm good,' I said. 'But I think I'll work from home today.'

He nodded slowly, breathing deeply as though he'd just come to the surface from a long dive. 'I've made such a fecking mess of things, haven't I?'

I hoped it was a rhetorical question, because the only applicable answer I could give was 'yes, actually you have'. 'If it hadn't been you, it would have been someone else,' I said. 'Saoirse was running away. She was pretty lucky that she ran to you and you're a decent human being, because it could have been much, much worse.'

'I dunno.'

'Well, yes, imagine if she'd run into someone who'd got really angry about being lied to? Or someone who used her vulnerability in some way?'

'I meant about me being a decent human being, but I see what you mean.' Connor clawed his way back up the woodwork and stood aside to let me into the cottage. 'I hope she'll get back on track now. But I won't contact her again.'

'No, I wouldn't.' I half fell onto the loveseat, desperate for a shower and a nap. 'Stick the kettle on, Connor, will you? It's been a hell of a night.' Then I stared at him. 'Why aren't you working?'

'Christmas vacs.' He went into the kitchen, and I heard tea-making noises. 'Another of the advantages of working in further education.'

'Oh, right.'

He came in carrying a steaming mug and pushed it into my hand. 'So, what are you doing for Christmas?'

I shrugged and hid my Billy No-Mates face in my mug. 'Haven't decided yet. What about you – are you flying back to Dublin?'

A tiny part of me hoped that he'd say no, that he was staying over here, flying home was too much trouble, he didn't know if he'd be welcome, the house would be full of his siblings and their offspring, no room at the inn.

'Yep, I leave in two days. Mam will be waiting to treat me like I'm sixteen again and I can't wait. I might even take all my dirty washing home, so she's got something else to berate me about.'

'Don't you dare.' But I laughed despite myself. 'I might go round to Chess's place. She has an open house over Christmas, cocktails and games, and it's always good fun.' I managed to say it like I knew. Chess made it *sound* good fun, but I'd never made it over in the two Christmases we'd known each other. I'd been too busy wallowing in my solitude.

I thought of Saoirse and her despair. Mine seemed old and tired in comparison, as though it had worn thin now. It was time to stop thinking about what should have been and start thinking of what could be. It wasn't as though Elliot was going to come back and complain about all the times I'd gone out or had fun without him. In fact, and the thought made the tea surface slide alarmingly close to the mug rim as my hand shook, Elliot would have been the first person to tell me to get out there and enjoy myself. Sitting at home under a blanket watching blooper reels on YouTube wasn't honouring his memory, it was allowing self-pity to rule my life. I'd lost my husband, but his life insurances had meant that I didn't have a mortgage and there'd been enough money to allow me to finish my folklore doctorate. I should stop giving Miss Havisham a run for her money and start living life.

'Yes,' I said again and more firmly. 'I could go to Chess's. Or I might volunteer somewhere.'

'Or you could come with me,' Connor said. 'To Dublin. Ma won't mind, one more in the house won't make any difference, and you can help even up the male-female split.'

I hesitated. *To Dublin. With Connor.* But then I conjured the idea of a house full of brothers, their partners, small children, all people I didn't know, and the noise. I shook my head. 'I don't think I'm quite ready for that yet,' I said. 'At Chess's I can come home when it gets too much.'

'Ah, you're probably right.' He picked up his mug. 'It can be a fair old ding-dong when they all get going. And I think we're even getting the sainted Eamonn with us this year.' But he said it with evident affection. 'I'm looking forward to a proper fight about the Second Vatican Council,' he said, with relish.

'Yes, I think I need to ease myself back into Christmas slowly,' I said. 'More on the crackers and pudding and less on the rows about Catholic dogma.'

'Ah, well. Don't say I didn't ask you.'

'I won't. Thank you.'

He raised an eyebrow at me through his tea steam. 'For?'

'Inviting me.'

'No trouble.'

From outside there came a splashy imperative sort of quacking. 'I'd better make some toast,' I said, tiredly. 'They'll only bang on the windows if I don't, and I could do with something to eat.'

'Here, I'll do it. You stay put, you look done in.'

But I didn't want to sit alone in the living room with memories of dreams in my head and the reality of Connor in another room. I followed him through to the kitchen again and sat on the edge of the kitchen table, looking out of the window at the sun, sloshing its light down into our little valley from a china-blue sky. Overnight a frost had iced the recent puddles into lace-edged solidity and crayoned around the edges of the windows in flaky white. The mud was solid ridges and even the river had a slow, jelly-like appearance as it curved across the ford, wide and dappled.

'Why did you go?' Connor asked suddenly, pushing bread into the toaster with some force, by the sound of it.

'Go?' I was tired, my brain wasn't processing words properly. I couldn't think of anywhere that I might have been that would have caused him to ask.

'To Saoirse. Last night. You seemed so worried about her. I mean, yes, I had my concerns but – she's a grown woman.'

I hesitated before turning back from the window. 'I know what it's like to suddenly find everything has turned upside down and the person you most want to talk to about it is the one who caused it,' I said. 'When Elliot died, what I *really* wanted – *all* I really wanted – was to be able to talk to him about what I should do. But he wasn't here, so I had to handle everything on my own. And that was... hard.'

The image of that line of pills sprang again, unwanted, into my head. Connor seemed to see it too, somehow. Maybe my expression gave it away, because he was watching my face very closely. When I let my eyes flicker from where tiredness had dragged them down to examine the tiled floor, he was frowning at my forehead.

'It was good of you,' he said at last, the words sounding slightly awkward. 'I knew she was unhappy, but it was me making her so. I couldn't stay.'

'No.'

'What else could I do?' There was an anxiety now in his tone.

I reached out and touched his shoulder. 'Nothing. Really, Connor, there was nothing else you could have done. But it wasn't just you making Saoirse unhappy. I think, deep down, she knew that it wasn't you, it was the whole situation. It can't be much of a joke, moving hundreds of miles for your husband's job, with two tiny children. Her mum helped her with the babies, but her mum can't drive, and two hundred miles is too far to pop round and babysit. Listening to her last night, it was like she separated herself off into two people: at home she was Saoirse, wife and mother, and she wanted the chance to be seen as the Saoirse she used to be, which was where you came in.'

The toast popped up but Connor didn't react. He stood, his

shoulder rigid under my hand. 'I feel so guilty,' he said quietly. 'I should have *known*.'

I let my hand fall. 'Brought up a Catholic? Of *course* you feel guilty. It's your default state.'

That made him laugh, and he was back to being the bright and breezy Connor again. 'Ah, you're right there. And it's probably the upbringing that's making me so interested in your manor there.' He pointed with an elbow, both hands being involved in toast, in the direction of the moor.

'I thought you were interested in the Roman remains underneath it?' I decided not to go back to the subject of Saoirse. He was beating himself up, I didn't need to add to the percussion, and, really, it hadn't been his fault. He'd come to realise that, of course, but for now the whole thing hurt and blaming Saoirse wouldn't help him.

The ducks were fighting a wet war under the window for prime crust-snatching place, and Connor glanced out at them as he buttered the toast. 'Well, yes, I am,' he said, opening the window and hurling the end of the loaf in the direction of the birds. 'But I'm also intrigued about how it all went out here. It's not my period, of course, but I'm looking at some documents. I've got a load of tangential stuff that applies to the area, trying to trace old buildings and references to old roads and suchlike.'

A brief prickle of ownership went down my spine. 'More my area of interest than yours, I'd have thought?'

'That's why I've been reading your books.' Connor licked his fingers, which were covered in badly aimed butter.

'Oh. Right.' A tiny dropping sensation in my midriff told me that I was disappointed. I'd hoped he'd been reading my books to find out what an erudite and amusing writer I was and how I could turn folk tales into a commentary on social history. To find that he'd only been doing it so that he could research his area more thoroughly was – yes, disappointing.

I ate the toast he handed me, in silence. Well, comparative silence. There was a flap of wings and the big white duck, the swaggering leader of the bunch, arrived on the outside window ledge. An orange eye angled in through the glass.

Connor watched the avian activity with a look of amusement, and then stood uncertainly, holding his crusts.

'Well, go on, then,' I said. 'That's what they're waiting for.'

'I know.' He stood, one hand on the window catch. 'But if I open the window, that one will fall off. He's in the way.'

I picked up my own crusts and opened the window, knocking the big white duck into flappy, panicked flight down to its usual spot on the water outside. 'Bird, Connor,' I said, very aware that my hand was on top of his on the window fastener. 'They fly.'

'So they do, now.' He didn't move his hand either. We watched the squabbling for a moment. 'I was forgetting there.'

I could feel his shoulder against mine, the gentle rise and fall as he breathed, and smell the fresh-laundry scent of the tracksuit that he was wearing, unflattering though it was.

The sun scythed its way in through the window, bouncing off the surface of the river in a thousand moving reflections, and still we stood there, hands on the mechanism of the window catch, unmoving.

'D'you think they actually *like* each other?' Connor asked. 'The ducks, I mean.'

'They seem to. They're quite free to go somewhere else if they don't. There's plenty of river.'

He nodded slowly. 'Perhaps they *pretend* not to,' he said, keeping his eyes focused on the water. 'Maybe they think they'll lose face if they just admit that they're really good friends.'

'Do ducks have faces?'

'You know what I mean. The pointy bit at the front of their heads that they look out of. Maybe they're worried that it's admitting defeat if they stop being antagonistic.' He looked at me sideways from around the dishevelled hair.

Reluctantly I dropped my hand and moved away. 'Fascinating as ducks are, Connor, I ought to do some work. I must give Chess a ring and tell her I'll not be in, and then get stuck into some more writing.'

He picked up the toast plates and moved to the sink. 'I'll clear up and then I'm off up on the moor for a bit.'

I stared at him. 'I thought you were on holiday.'

He shrugged. 'There's not a lot else for me to do, to be honest. Thought I'd go and pace around a bit in a moody, Irish fashion among the heather. Try and pick up a contract modelling for Burberry.'

'Shut up.' But he'd made me smile, and, as I went to grab a shower and change my overnight-worn clothes, ring Chess and settle into writing, I thought that Connor could actually be quite good fun at times.

The thought that he hadn't really been talking about ducks only grabbed me by the neck about two hours later.

I'd made myself a coffee to try to stay awake, and was rummaging through the cupboard in search of biscuits, when Connor's words came back to me. 'Maybe they think they'll lose face if they just admit that they're really good friends.' I turned, seized with a sudden horror that made my face heat up, and stared out of the window.

Had it really been about ducks? Or was he talking about us? Had I, in my sleep-deprived state, missed an allusion? My cheeks were now so hot that my face felt as though it were on fire. I didn't know which was worse – that Connor might have been talking about us, about *me*, not wanting to take a step away from my 'All Historians Are Myth-Busting Bastards' stance and admitting that he was actually quite a decent human being, or that I had been carrying on talking about ducks whilst he'd been meaning something else, *and I hadn't even realised.*

At least, I thought, banging my forehead gently against the reclaimed wood of the cupboard door, he wasn't here to see my mortification. And maybe, *maybe*, it really *had* been about ducks, and I was tired and overthinking the whole conversation.

Yes. That was what it was. It had all been about ducks all along.

18

'Snow's forecast,' Chess said cheerfully as she breezed into the office an hour late the following day.

'Is it? Oh, bugger.' I folded up the ancient map I'd been scanning.

'I'd have thought you'd watch the forecast like a hawk, being stuck out where you live.' She folded up the copy of *Cosmo* that she'd been reading on the bus and tucked it away into her bag. 'Coffee?'

'Better not, I've had three already.' I was still suffering from the lack of a night's sleep, and the avoidance of Connor that had followed my Duck Doubts. Luckily, he'd been out for most of the working day, and I'd used getting an early night to excuse myself from his company in the evening. I'd got up to come into work extra early today and had left him making packing noises in his room.

'Yes, supposed to be a white Christmas this year, apparently,' Chess went on, making an extraordinarily long business of hanging up her coat. 'I've got your present here, by the way. We *are* closing the office for Christmas today, aren't we?'

'Yes, yes,' I replied testily, having forgotten completely when I'd said we'd have our Christmas holiday. Four days to go. Four days at home, Connor in Dublin and me trying my best to break out of my widow's weeds and celebrate. 'And I might well come and drop in at yours over Christmas, Chess, if that's still all right.'

Chess stopped uncoiling the gigantic scarf she'd got wound around her neck, and stared at me. 'Oh, good,' she said. 'No, that's really good, Rowan. If you don't get snowed in, of course.'

'Is it supposed to be that much snow? It's a bit early.'

She shrugged. 'Take it up with the Met Office and don't shoot the messenger.'

'Yes, sorry. Bugger. I'd better do a quick food shop, then, just in case.' I stood up and reached for my jacket. 'I can pop round Sainsbury's quickly and leave the stuff in the car.'

'I'm glad you said that.' Chess began rewinding the scarf again. 'Only if you're going out you can't mind if I head into town and finish the last bits of present buying, can you?'

'I suppose not. But back here by twelve. I've got a Zoom call with the grants people who want to know how the book is getting on, and I want you to be bustling around in the background looking busy.'

'Oh, the usual.' She sighed. 'You want me to interrupt with a phone call from...'

'Wales. Wales is good. No, outside the brief for the book. Um, how about Northallerton? That's in my area, they might fall for that one.'

'Okay, phone call from Northallerton, what, half an hour in?'

'Please. We should have gone over everything by then, and I can offer to send them the manuscript so far, if they're really desperate. But I should think they'll all be wanting to go home for Christmas too, and it might all be over in ten minutes.'

I pulled my coat back on and grabbed my car keys, then Chess and I shared a smile of complicity and went off into York.

I was back within an hour, having elbowed my way around the hell that was a supermarket in the run-up to Christmas, leaving the food in the freezing confines of the car, where I reasoned nothing could possibly go off, as it was basically a metal box in sub-zero temperatures.

Chess hadn't returned yet, and I still had time to kill before I had to appear frantically busy in front of the grants people, so I sat at my desk with another coffee, and flipped pages. Someone had written to me wanting some information on an old story that I'd covered. It was about a ghost at a well possibly being a hangover from tales of water spirits, and I had to reacquaint myself with the story before I replied. So, when I heard the outer door bang, I assumed Chess was back and called out to her to bring some coffee through.

A few minutes later, Connor put his head around the door, carrying two cups of hot chocolate from the market just down the road. 'Thought these might be more appropriate.'

'Thank you.' I glanced at my screen, set up for the Zoom call and waiting for the other parties to join. 'Are you off, then?'

'Sorry? Off where?'

'I thought you were flying tomorrow. I thought you'd be heading to the airport tonight, what with snow forecast and everything.'

He sipped his chocolate. 'Ah, no. I'll head over tomorrow, plenty of time. I've got a late afternoon flight – I'm not really up to spending more time than I have to surrounded by the budding sisters-in-law all asking when I'm going to get myself partnered up and start reproducing, and the brothers slapping my back and telling me that I don't know how lucky I am not to be.'

'And Eamonn, who presumably won't be doing either.'

'No, no, true. He'll be asking me when I last went to confession.'

'Tough crowd, then.'

'Yep.'

'Look, I have to do this Zoom thing, then I'll wait for Chess to get back and tell her we're closing the office early. Is that all right?'

'Grand.' Connor went and sat in the corner of the room, flipping casually through some notes, while I spoke to the grants people, who all seemed to be very happy and smiley today. I put it down to the proximity of Christmas, and, since they all seemed happy with the progress of the potential book, I finished the call without needing any intervention of the 'emergency phone call' kind.

When I'd disconnected, Connor stood up. 'Well, they all seemed very jolly,' I said.

'Probably because you've got chocolate all over your mouth,' he replied.

'Shit, no, I haven't, have I?' My camera wasn't particularly good and the lighting in the office was dreadful, and I hadn't been looking at my own face, assessing the mood of the grant board. But when I checked, Connor was absolutely right and I had a noticeable ring of hot chocolate across my top lip. 'Oh, bugger. Now they're going to think I've got the mental acuity of a five-year-old.'

'No, no, you sounded very professional.' He grinned at me, and then Chess came banging in.

'Sorry, sorry! Meant to be back earlier but there was a hell of a queue in Seasalt and – did you know you've got chocolate all over your face?'

She began unwinding the scarf again, raising her eyebrows

at me under cover of the enormous woolly beanie hat she was wearing and jerking her head towards Connor in a 'I see you've brought a friend' kind of way.

'Yes, thank you, Chess, twenty minutes ago that would have been great advice.'

'Oh. Did I miss the Zoom?'

'Yes, you did, but it was all right, I had Connor there squatting in the corner to make the office look occupied. Don't take your scarf off, I've decided it's home time.'

Chess made a moue of surprise, and the eyebrows went up again. 'Really? Wow, Rowan, that's decent. You're really...' Then she stopped and began making a huge performance out of rewinding the scarf and adjusting her hat.

'What am I "really", Chess?' I asked, trying to keep my voice level. Connor was still grinning.

'You're really beginning to loosen up a bit,' she said eventually, talking into the several layers of wool around her mouth. 'Like, nicely, I mean. You've always been a bit keen on keeping the hours and all that.' She glanced sideways at Connor. 'Something is doing you good. You're not nearly so much of a slave-driver these days.'

I felt a cringe of guilt begin. I'd had nothing else in my life, apart from work, so I'd made a habit of being here early and leaving late.

'I mean, in a good way, obviously,' she added quickly, although how one could be a slave-driver in a good way I quite failed to see. Maybe by using tea and cake as an incentive, rather than whips? 'We've got an awful lot done in these past two years.'

I pretended not to be appalled, and handed over her Christmas present, before I dragged Connor out into the afternoon's chill. He was still grinning.

'So, you're a fair slave-driver, then,' he said. 'But you're loosening up. That's a decent thing.'

'Chess is overstating her case. She regards not being allowed to watch *Loose Women* at work as being oppressive.'

The puddles cracked ominously under our feet as we crossed the car park. I glanced up at the sky, which was grey, darkening to a yellow tinge around the edges. 'Oh, bugger, it looks as though it really is going to snow. I was hoping we'd miss it.'

Connor settled into the passenger seat. 'Nice though. Very seasonal. Festive.'

'You won't be saying that when you've been stuck in the cottage for three days and the cheese is running out.'

'Come on, now, you're exaggerating. Nobody gets snowed in these days. There's the big snow ploughs and... and... well, they come and dig you out, don't they?'

I gave a dark and sarcastic laugh. 'Well, it might not be too bad. It's too early for much snow – we usually get it all in January if it's going to come. We'll get a covering, that's all. You had better book your taxi to pick you up for the airport though. There'll be loads of Christmas parties going on and they might all end up too busy to fetch you. And I'm not driving all the way to Leeds Bradford to drop you off, not when I'm on holiday.'

'I'll do that.' He settled into the seat in a way that irritated me slightly.

'You need to learn to drive, Connor.'

He turned to watch me easing us out of the little car park and onto the road. 'Why would that be, now?'

'Well, it's... I mean, I don't always want to drive and... there's no public transport around here.'

Connor crooked up an eyebrow and turned to look out of the window, but I thought I saw a smile beginning before he did so. 'I'll be back in Dublin by April, and we've all the buses. There's no need. Anyway—' now he turned back to me with a straight face again '—by the time I passed my test I'd be gone. I've *seen* me drive, Rowan, and it's not something a couple of lessons and a bit of practice is going to sort.'

'Of course,' I said, feeling hot and stupid. Why would he need to drive? He was going back to Dublin. Out here in the wilds of Yorkshire, where buses were infrequent, the nearest railway station was fifteen miles away, the taxis had to come from the towns, people learned to drive early. Many a twelve-year-old could be found bombing around his dad's fields in a clapped-out Fiat. They were on the road in tractors as soon as they were sixteen, test passed on their seventeenth birthday, and parents breathed a sigh of relief and opened a bottle of wine in the evenings.

'What's Dublin like?' I asked, negotiating my way off the ring road and out into countryside.

'It's grand. Wonderful city. All-night bars, music and architecture and poetry and all that.' I got another proper smile. 'Buses too. Are you regretting saying you won't come? You can change your mind, y'know. We'll get you a ticket and we could be there for Christmas.'

Out of the corner of my eye I could see him sitting there, long legs bunched up and his ubiquitous big black coat wrapped around him, and I thought of Christmas in a house full of people. Company and shouting and children and coming and going at all hours; Eamonn, who had taken on a kind of Father Brown persona in my head, wandering about being kindly and a bit vague and possibly detecting crime in his spare time. Connor's parents, who seemed to be a dichotomy between faith and high-flying, not quite knowing what to do with this odd, quiet friend of their son's. And then there was Connor's status as still being in disgrace for involving them all with a married woman who was being unfaithful.

'I think I'll stay at home this year,' I said. 'I've only just started to pick up my life where I left off when Elliot... well, I think I need to ease myself into things. I've spent three years basically being a hermit, so I think I ought to take it one person at a time.'

'You're finding life a bit better now, though? It's getting easier?' He was watching my face but I couldn't return the look. This was a tricky bit where cars parked either side of a narrow road, there were no streetlights, and the road was slippery with the detritus of the long-gone autumn.

'A bit,' I admitted. 'I think it's having you around. It's made me realise that I don't like the quiet as much as I thought I did.'

'Well, I'm glad I—'

'I'm thinking of getting a cat in the spring.'

He closed his mouth and raised his eyebrows. 'Good that I can be replaced so easily.'

'A big tom, all swagger and yowl, I thought.'

'Is that me, or the cat?'

We lapsed into silence as we headed out across the dark countryside. A few flakes of snow dropped lazily into the headlights, and I concentrated ferociously on getting home before more arrived to join them. These narrow, twisty roads with a covering of snow over the ice that still crusted the puddles could be treacherous.

'I'm not promiscuous,' Connor said suddenly, making me jump, as we rose to the top of the hill before the cottage.

'Er. That's nice to know, although I'm not quite sure why it would come up,' I replied, trying to remember whether I'd left the porch light on before I left.

'Tomcat. Me. I'm drawing a parallel here, as I suspect you intended.'

'Did I?'

'Rowan.' He shifted in his seat, and I nearly drove into the hedge. There was a patch of ice that had frozen right across the whole road – water that had poured from overflowing drains had formed a slick surface where the car had no grip. 'Saoirse fooled me. If I'd known she was married, if I'd known that she was making it all up, do you think I would have gone near her?'

I muttered something and drew the car up into its usual parking spot. I went to open my door, but Connor put a hand out to stop me. 'I know you think I'm a bit of a dick, and I hold my hands up to having been an idiot. But she was telling me what I wanted to hear and future-faking it all down the line. Now, tell me that if I were a woman and I came to you having been fooled by a married man who told me all the stories of how we'd get married and have a few children, live by the sea and all that – you wouldn't be sympathetic? You wouldn't call him a bastard and berate him for having lied?' He moved a little more, so that he could see my face properly. 'So why is it different because I'm a man?'

It wasn't different. Of course it wasn't. But I was so used to seeing Connor as breezily careless that it was hard to get my head around the idea that he had been fooled. He always seemed to know exactly what he was doing – like with his historical research. He was sure that there was something Roman up there on that moor so he was working hard to get to the bottom of what it was. He researched, he investigated. And yet, one pretty woman came along and told him what he wanted to hear and he'd fallen into believing her without any question.

'You always seem to know what you're doing,' I said. 'You're always so sure of yourself. Like... like with the Fairy Stane. You research and you check all angles and you're desperate to get to the bottom of it. I have the feeling that if I turn my back you'll be up there with a crowbar, to give yourself the advantage over other historians. You're single-minded. So that's why it's hard for me to see how Saoirse managed to fool you, because you could have blown her story open with a bit of research and a few questions – like "where are your photographs published?" – but you didn't ask.'

His hand dropped away from me and I got out of the car. I was shaking slightly from the flare of adrenaline that was currently sending emergency signals to my entire body. *Why did I care?* Connor was just a man who was taking up my spare room and cooking great meals. He would, as he repeatedly reminded me, be gone in four months. Why should I care why he fell for Saoirse?

I went round to the boot of the car and began hauling out plastic bags of groceries. Connor had begun to stalk off towards the cottage, but, seeing me lifting out bag after bag, he came back and took a bag in each hand before he did the Indignant Stomp again.

I caught up with him as he used his key to open the door, and we stormed inside together, on a gust of wind-blown snowflakes and irritation.

'Look.' He put one bag on the worktop and began unpacking it, almost as though he wasn't thinking about the actual shopping but needed something to do with his hands. 'I can tell you think I'm a fool for going along with Saoirse.'

I was unpacking on the other side of the kitchen, with my back to him. 'I don't think you're a fool, Connor. People can get caught up in situations. But I do think that you went into that relationship with your eyes closed. A photographer should have a portfolio of published work, a website. You're a historian. You check everything. But with her, you never *checked*.'

I slammed the freezer door, having shoved in more bread than the drawer could really take, and there was a sharp crack of plastic breaking. The sound annoyed me.

'Are you telling me that you check out every man you're dating? You look them up? On the Internet?' He sounded aghast.

'Well, no, but only because I've been with Elliot since forever, and I didn't date much before him.' I'd used the present tense again, I noted. *Elliot's gone*. 'But it's a sensible thing for a woman to do. We don't know if a man has a criminal record, or pictures of himself with his wife all over Facebook, so we check.'

'That's... that's *weird*.'

'No.' Beans into the cupboard. I'd bought an awful lot of beans. 'It's common sense. No one wants to go on a date with a bloke only to find out he was headline news in the *Mirror* for murdering his landlady or something.'

'Right.' Connor put the last packet of biscuits – I'd also bought a lot of biscuits, for some reason – into the cupboard and closed the door definitively. 'Come on.'

'What?'

I followed him through into the living room, where my computer blinked at us. Connor didn't even turn on the light. He wiggled the mouse to wake the computer, and then typed 'Connor William Patrick O'Keefe' into the search bar.

'Connor, what are you doing?'

He didn't answer again. He stood back, waving a hand at the brightness of the screen, where his name was listed in blue above a whole host of sites.

'There,' he said at last. 'That's me. No secrets. No murders, no newspaper headlines. A load of research, some publications, a couple of awards and a mention when Mam got to be head of her department.'

'Well, that's...' I started weakly.

'I was lonely, Rowan. I was lonely and she was pretty and funny and bright – a touch brittle, but I thought she worked too hard. I told her what I was looking for and she echoed it all back to me, and when you're living for your work and your family are all doing the good Catholic thing of marrying and producing children...'

'Except Eamonn,' I felt bound to add.

'Ah, but Eamonn is exempt, he's got his own trajectory, being a priest. So there was I feeling a failure and left behind, and all I can see is a future of being an academic, burying myself in the journals and reviews... Do you see how I fell for her?'

He was talking fast, pointing at the screen showing his name every now and then as though to punctuate his words. It felt a little as though the easy-going Connor I had got to know had been subsumed under this wild-eyed, gesticulating man, trying to make me see something when I didn't know what I was meant to be looking at.

'Connor, you don't need to prove anything to me,' I said softly. 'It's fine. I *know* you weren't stupid. You took a woman at face value. You believed her because you had no reason not to. That's not stupidity, that's just good-natured optimism.'

He turned away from the screen, slumping his shoulders and with his head falling forwards, as though he'd received the biggest rejection in history. 'But I,' he said, and, in contrast to his previous tone, his voice was very quiet now, '*I* feel stupid, Rowan. All the brothers now, they've managed to find someone to take them on, with their bloody daft *Star Wars* slippers and their addiction to Lego, two married and Finn engaged to that wee girl from Dungannon. While I find myself someone, the family all approve, it's all going great – and then she turns out to be married with kids! I might be a professor and have an encyclopaedic knowledge of Roman building techniques, but I'm still a fecking idiot where women are concerned.'

'You're not.' I tried to keep my voice quiet too. 'But are you telling me that this is all about sibling rivalry? That you want to find yourself a partner just to keep up with your brothers?' There was something so intense about him right now that I felt a stab of pity. He *really* wanted me to understand why he'd fallen for Saoirse.

'Of course,' he said, but it sounded as though he might be smiling, only a little, but still.

'So you were lonely and feeling left out, and Saoirse – well, she's very pretty. Then she told you that she wanted exactly what you wanted… why wouldn't you fall for that? You're a man, you're not in danger from being alone with someone, so you'd no need to do any searches, you *believed* her. That's not stupidity, Connor, honestly. It's wanting something so hard that you can't help but go after it when it's put in front of you.'

He took in a breath so deep that I worried in case he burst out of his coat, but then he blew it back in a sigh that told me how bad he felt more than any number of words.

'Thank you,' he said. 'It's not sibling rivalry, not really. I mean, I'm a professor, and that's ranked pretty highly in the family. It must be hard for you to understand as you're an only child.'

He'd remembered, then. 'Well, yes, but Chess has got two sisters, and I know far, *far* more about the Great Boyfriend War of 2022 than I could ever want to.' I watched him now as he slumped onto the loveseat, his coat flopping as though it too were exhausted. 'But how come you're lonely? I mean, looking like you do, you can't be short of female company, surely?'

He looked up at me for a moment too long. *If this were a romantic movie,* I thought, *he'd stand up and kiss me now.* Then, horrified at the thought, I took two steps back until my legs were against the desk.

He didn't stand up. He leaned forward, elbows on his knees, and rubbed his face. 'I don't know,' he said. '*I* think I'm okay, women seem to differ on that point. Maybe I work too hard.'

'You can be a bit single-minded about Romans,' I said, not sure whether I felt relieved or not about his non-standing state.

'I can that.' He nodded gravely, staring at the floor. 'And I'm getting a bit old for the partying and the running round town at two in the morning. It's all very well for a while, but I'm more for the sitting in front of the fire with a well-crafted dinner, a good bottle of red and a conversation.'

'About Romans,' I put in helpfully.

'I've got other pet topics.' He glanced up and saw me, backed into the corner. 'I'm not bad at medieval religion and I've a working knowledge of Viking incursions.'

'Anything to say about *Strictly, Cosmopolitan,* or Tom Hardy?'

Another small smile. 'Not notably.'

'You're no good for Chess, then. She likes her men to have popular culture at their fingertips. Being able to talk about popular culture two millennia ago probably won't cut it.'

The air felt thick all of a sudden, as though it were setting, like jelly, or icing up. We'd already looked at one another for too long, freeze-framed into a moment, and the adrenaline fired another warning flare into my nervous system.

'Rowan...' Connor said, standing up now, and taking a small step towards me.

'We've left the dairy out,' I said suddenly. 'On the side. We need to get it in the fridge.' My voice sounded a bit breathless, as though I'd run round the room before speaking. 'The... the butter and... things.'

With a swerve that any rugby fly half would have been proud of, I dashed around Connor and into the kitchen, where the fluorescent light buzzed like an extra layer of reality. I started to unpack the final couple of bags, trying not to think about what might have happened. Did I want it to happen? Did I want *anything* to happen with Connor?

No. No. He wasn't Elliot. He wasn't my lovely, sandy-haired, bristly cheeked husband, with his bad jokes, his calm accepting nature and his practicality. Connor was too lanky, too dark. Too sharp and bright and, besides, he was going back to Dublin. I didn't know what he'd intended when he'd said my name and looked at me as though I were someone he'd never seen before, but whatever it was, I didn't want it.

Tomorrow couldn't come quickly enough.

19

1915

They'd all seen the telegram arrive, the boy on his bicycle coming all the way from Pickering to deliver it. This was one of the worst things – nobody knew what to do. Should they go round, offer some comfort? Or pretend not to know yet, let Lilian break the news as she saw fit?

'Let the poor girl be,' Mrs Dobson said, settling her arms comfortably on the top of the pigsty. 'We all know what it'll be, her young man, that one from York as she was courting, he's been shot down over France or somewhere. She'll need a bit of time.'

But when Nell saw Lilian setting out to walk up onto the moor, she knew where she would be going.

'Lil!' Nell ran to catch her up but Lilian didn't slow down. 'Lil!'

'I'm going up to the stone.' Lilian didn't sound herself at all. Her voice was broken and strange, as though she were an old woman now. 'I have to go and tell them.'

Nell ran faster. 'Lil!'

'I have to tell them he's gone.'

'What, them as is under the stone?'

Lilian stopped and turned. Nell took a step back. She'd never seen her friend look like that before, red-rimmed eyes and a face so white that her freckles stood out like pebbles. 'I have to tell them.'

'That's bees, Lil. You tells the bees when someone is... when something happens.'

'He was going to marry me, Nell. He really was. He said so before he went away, he said, when he got leave first thing he'd do was find me and marry me.'

'I know.'

'And I have to go to the Stone and tell them he won't be coming.' Lilian stumbled and then crumpled to the ground. 'He won't be coming, Nell. Not ever.'

Nell sat down on the damp tussocky grass and put her arms around her friend, while she sobbed and sobbed herself into blank-faced acceptance.

* * *

Now

We unpacked, cooked and ate whilst chatting about weather and childhood pets, nothing meaningful, and went to bed. I lay in my chilly room, listening to the water run past over the ford in the quiet air, and tried not to think about Connor, lying similarly quietly in his room, a wall's thickness away.

He's not Elliot.

But Elliot's gone.

I like him. He's rather sweet, in a peculiar way. Great cook. And his conversations aren't that bad.

But he's not Elliot.

Am I so lonely that I'd fall for any man that was nice to me? Any man that made the nights feel a little less dark and long?

Elliot wouldn't mind. He wouldn't want me moping and weeping forever. After all, if I had died, would he be still living alone? Or would he have kept my memory but moved on in the real world? He was pragmatic, he worked with wood. He saw how life didn't have to come to a dead stop just because of death – it might take a different shape from that moment, but it went on.

Am I so lonely that I'm seeing something that isn't there? He's kind, he didn't want me spending Christmas alone, that's why he invited me to Dublin. He's never so much as put a toe over the landlady/tenant line. He's been nothing but friendly, and I'm mooning over him.

And he's not Elliot.

But Elliot's gone...

I fell asleep and woke late to a chill grey light and a sense of relief that Connor was flying to Dublin, and I'd got at least a week to get my sensible head back on. By the time he got back I'd be deep into the book, I'd be busy and casual and dismissive. I'd have fixed that damp patch over the door, and he could be as friendly and cook as many meals as he liked, but I'd be looking forward to his eventual removal back to Ireland.

Besides, he still wanted to lift my stone.

I stretched and yawned into the quiet. Maybe Connor had already gone? A late flight didn't mean he might not have wanted an early start. I pulled on my dressing gown and padded down the stairs to the kitchen for tea, with a sense of relief.

Connor hadn't gone. He was sitting glumly at the table, staring alternately out of the window and at his phone. He hadn't even put the kettle on yet.

'What's up?' I asked cautiously.

In answer, he waved at the window. A duck perched on the ledge, waiting for crusts.

'Yes? They can't get in, you know.'

'No, beyond the duck.'

I crouched to see past the feathery bulk and saw the snow. It lined the river edges, so that the water cut through its deep whiteness like a black thread. Further back the hills wore a uniform white. The track was invisible and the trees that overhung it had branches so heaped with snow that they bent beneath its weight as though the wind had become visible.

'Oh, bugger,' I said.

'Bugger is right. I've rung every taxi company for twenty miles, and nobody is moving today anywhere off the main road.' He stared at his phone screen again as though a miracle might be about to burst forth. 'The amount of snow seems to have caught everyone by surprise,' he said, glumly.

'What are you going to do?'

'Well, I've had a shout at the Met Office so that was therapeutic.'

I stared at him, kettle suspended halfway to the tap. 'You rang the Met Office to tell them off because it snowed more than you thought it would?'

A half-laugh. 'No, no, of course not. It's not their fault. I shouted at the app. Then I checked the news and the forecast, and it's set to freeze. Looks like we've got another Beast from the East.' Another mirthless laugh. 'All the planes are grounded anyway, so I might get my money back for the missed flight.'

'Urgh.' I filled the kettle, glad that I'd closed the office now and didn't have to even pretend to try to struggle up the hill out of the little valley. 'Chess did say they were forecasting a white Christmas.'

'So, anyway, I rang home and cancelled myself.'

The kettle wobbled as I had a momentary panic. He *had* to go! I needed to get my thoughts in order and my equilibrium back. 'Can't you go tomorrow? Or the day after?'

Connor gave his phone another resentful look, as though it were responsible for the sudden change of plan, and then put it firmly down on the table. 'Tomorrow doesn't look much better, and the day after is Christmas Eve,' he said.

'Yes, but things still move.' My voice had a slight note of terror, it was high and a bit strained. 'People travel on Christmas Eve. They're noted for it, in fact. I think there's even a film about it.'

He looked at me curiously. 'I know. But it's hardly fair to Mam and the family, to have them all on edge about whether or not I'm going to come walking in like the return of the prodigal, is it, now? Better for their planning to say I'm not going to be there, than to have them panicking about the number of sprouts and puddings they need.'

'Oh.' This sensible and considerate thought hadn't occurred to me.

'But I won't be a nuisance. I won't interfere with your Christmas plans; I can make myself a cheese sandwich and get some work done.'

'I don't *have* any Christmas plans.'

'You were going to Chess's open house, I thought. Cocktails, wasn't it, now?' He put his head on one side and looked at me from under a flap of hair.

'I only said I might,' I said defensively, aware that I knew as well as he did that the chances were high that inertia would have kept me in the cottage. I might have *intended* to drive the twenty miles to Chess's place, and throw myself into partying and playing daft games, but, ultimately, would I have really done it? Or would I have walked the silent lanes and come back to wrap myself in a blanket and remember past Christmases, as I'd done for the last three years, because it was easier? Easier to live with memories than make new ones.

'Ah, well. If all this melts tomorrow I can take myself off to York or somewhere. I've a few of the lecturers who have offered me Christmas dinner and a sofa if I want, if I couldn't make it back to Dublin.'

'That's... nice of them.' I didn't know what I wanted in that moment. The snow to instantly vanish, and Connor miraculously to be able to go back to Dublin? Or a forecast thaw, with him heading to a Christmas lunch in York, where they would discuss current historical theories over a turkey and drink thick red wine with pudding and talk about Romans?

Or him, here? Captive, in the cottage over Christmas, which sounded disturbingly like the title of a Hallmark Christmas movie – that, or a Stephen King book.

I became aware that I was staring at him, blankly. 'You can stay here,' I said. 'There's food.'

'I know. I put most of it in the cupboard last night.'

My confused thoughts were interrupted by a peremptory rapping on the window. An orange eye was angling in, and feet paddled on the ledge.

'The ducks are waiting for their toast,' Connor observed neutrally. He didn't seem upset by my seeming lack of enthusiasm at probably being stuck with him, snowed up for Christmas.

'Yes, yes, we ought to have breakfast. Of course.'

He stood up. I thought he was going straight for the toaster, but he came across to me and touched my shoulder gently. 'It's okay,' he said. 'It really is.' Then he scuffled over to the bread bin and began making toast and tea, without elaborating on what it was that was okay.

Did he mean that it was all right that we hadn't exactly got a complement of Christmas foods? Or was he reassuring me that his family wouldn't mind this sudden change of plan? Or that his presence wouldn't disrupt my own Christmas festivities?

Or was he telling me that this Christmas was going to be different? Which, of course, it was, obviously. I was trapped in my own house with a man who... well, he was still my adversary in the matter of folklore versus history, but apart from that... I didn't quite know how I was meant to be reacting to him.

'I'll probably be up in my room for most of the day today,' Connor said eventually, bringing the toast over to the table. 'I've got a little bit of work to do – I was going to sort it out over in Ireland, but I can do it here as well as anywhere. So you don't need to worry about amusing me.'

'I wasn't in the least worried about amusing you,' I said briskly. 'You're stuck here, you can amuse yourself.'

He laughed. 'Ah, go on, a little bit of amusement between us wouldn't be a bad thing!'

I wondered what form he thought this amusement would take, and concentrated very hard on my toast.

'I might need you too. I'm looking into the Evercey Manor thing,' he went on, not even the slightest bit abashed by the fact that my cheeks were beginning to heat up. He might not even have noticed, hopefully. 'Big Catholic house, all the workers in the faith too. You know that a lot came over from Ireland in the 1840s?'

'Makes sense.' I swallowed a painful crust. 'Fleeing the famine, freedom of worship, all that.'

'It's made me think.' Carelessly he opened the window and

flung out a crust. 'Your Fairy Stane stories, would they have begun around then?'

I thought. 'Early to mid-nineteenth century, so, yes, I suppose so. That's about as far back as I can trace a lot of the stories, because that's when people started to write them down rather than pass them purely through word of mouth. It's when folklore began to gain some traction – people could see the rural ways of life being lost to industrialisation so they started recording some of the tales.'

Connor nodded. 'Well, I'm thinking there may be a crossover with some Irish stories and legends, y'see.'

I boggled. 'I thought you thought folklore was a waste of time?'

He gave me a level look. 'I never said that.'

'No, but you... you're a *historian*!'

Connor stood up. 'I'm a Roman historian by training but I'm an Irish boy by birth, and my granda was one with the songs and the stories. I've got Irish legends in my blood, the fairies and the *bean sidhe* and all.'

'But you want to lift my stone!'

He stood for a moment, staring out of the window at the white acres that stretched off into the distance. 'I've got an idea about the Fairy Stane,' he said. 'Not so sure about my Roman settlement but it could link Evercey Manor to your folk tales. I need to do some reading, and possibly talk to Eamonn first. And *then*, well, then I think we might need a wee look at what's underneath.'

'The land of the Little People,' I said grimly. 'Fairyland. The otherworld.'

'But don't you want to *know*?'

'No!' I snapped, slamming my plate down onto the table. 'No, I don't. There has to be mystery and the unknown – that's why the supernatural is so popular! People *need* their fairies and their ghosts, because if we discover everything – then what have we got to be curious about?'

Then I turned and stormed out of the kitchen and stomped up the stairs to shut myself in my bedroom.

20

My hopes for a swift end to our joint imprisonment were dashed by the frequent snow showers that came and went throughout the day. The air would darken and the windows became claustrophobic with the dashing of snowflakes against them. Then the snow would whirl away and leave the day a brilliant gold and white for a few minutes before the next shower drew in.

I could hear Connor rattling on his keyboard in his room, while I dragged a huge velvet eiderdown out of the cupboard and wrapped it around me on the loveseat, so I could sit and stare moodily out at the snow. It was nice not to have to work, but Connor's extreme productivity made me feel both guilty and resentful and his occasional forays out for tea or biscuits sent me scurrying to my computer to try to look busy, even though I hadn't much to do, apart from look up the weather forecast every ten minutes just in case an unexpected thaw was due.

But at least the winter's day was short. By three, Connor was back downstairs again, now wearing his all-purpose hoodie and jogging bottoms.

'It's the day before Christmas Eve tomorrow,' he announced,

as though I'd been living on the moon for the last six months and had become unaware of the calendar. 'We should go out for a walk.'

I stared at him from under my voluminous wrapping. 'Have you seen "out", Connor? There's three feet of snow and counting. Why would we want to go for a walk in that?'

His face creased in a moment of apparent confusion. 'Well, it's... What are you going to do, sit in here until the snow all melts? We always go for a walk on the twenty-third. It's traditional.'

'Your traditional, maybe. Not mine.'

'What are your traditions? Should I expect you out cutting greenery to deck the halls?' Connor looked around at the obvious lack of any decoration in the house. The only sign that Christmas might be happening at all was two Christmas cards, one from my parents and one from an aged aunt, on the shelf above the log burner.

'I haven't really done Christmas for the last few years,' I said, slightly defensively. He was right, it could have been any season in the cottage, apart from the two squares of card showing robustly secular winter scenes on the shelf. 'Elliot... well, he died in early November, so I wasn't up to anything that first year. And after that – there didn't seem to be any need. I've just holed up here with the TV and a big bar of chocolate and got through it.'

'And before?' Connor put his hands in his hoodie pockets, tilted his head to one side. 'What did you do before?'

I unhuddled a little. The velvet of the eiderdown stroked my cheek like a caress. *Elliot is gone. But life goes on.* 'We'd get up late.' I smiled at the memory of *why* we'd got up late. 'Have a big breakfast, open our presents, walk up on the moor and then come home to cook a massive dinner.' *Walking until it got dark, and then the lights of the cottage beckoning us home to the cosy warmth. Fairy lights swinging above the doors, the smell of meat roasting as we walked in, the fug and steam of dinner. Music and laughing and Elliot never knowing how to cook potatoes properly and the annual half-serious half-amused arguing over Monopoly late into the evening while we ate an entire box of chocolate mints as the papers crackled in the fire...* 'It was nice,' I finished.

'Well, then.' Connor didn't seem to know what to say next. 'Well.'

'But you might be right,' I admitted. 'I can't sit here on my own every Christmas for the next sixty years. Elliot was always one for the next thing, moving on to the next stage, looking forward. He wouldn't have liked the idea that I sat here remembering him forever.'

Connor smiled. 'No.' He nodded slowly. 'I can see that. I mean,' he added quickly, 'I wouldn't want anyone pining away after me if I were gone. It would be nice to know that I was remembered with a smile, but not with the memories held up like paragons to aspire to. So, walk tomorrow, then?' Then quickly, because I'd opened my mouth to object and my expression must have given me away, 'We could away up to your stone, and have an argument about it, if that would make you feel better?'

I laughed. I couldn't help it. Connor was very good at taking the irritated wind out of my sails. 'I suppose so. It's quite a hike through snow though.'

'The exercise will be good for us.'

'And we can't go if it's blizzarding. People get lost in the snow on the moors all the time.'

'Seriously? *All* the time?'

'Well, no, but sometimes. I'd rather not be a frozen corpse for Christmas, thank you.'

The light was almost gone from the room, what little illumination remained was mostly evening sky bounced off the snow; an unearthly whiteness reflecting off the walls and ceiling. It meant Connor was a shadowy shape, his face hidden in the depths of his hood. 'Saoirse messaged me,' he said.

I jerked my head up. 'Saying what?'

He shrugged. 'Mostly goodbye. She put in a message for you too. I have to say thank you to you. She's getting help and she and Michael are trying to make a go of things. She said it's because you talked sense to her.'

There was a moment of snow-kissed silence. 'And you're all right with that?' I asked eventually, keeping my voice quiet and level.

'It's the best thing,' he said, although there was a thickness to his voice that told me he was struggling a little with the emotional fallout. 'No, really, it is. She and I were never real, so what I felt for her wasn't real either. It couldn't be.'

'Doesn't mean you didn't love her, though, does it?'

I couldn't see his reaction. It was too dim, despite the snowlight. 'I didn't love *her*,' he said slowly. 'I loved who I thought she was. Sending her away was the only thing to do.' Then, with his voice a little stronger, 'And it sounds as though she's getting herself sorted, which is grand. She was running away, and I'm not the person to run to, now, am I?'

'Aren't you?' I said and could have kicked myself. 'No,' I added hastily. 'You're right. It might have felt real, but it wasn't, and how would you have felt if you *had* gone off with her and only found out about the husband and children later? It could have been far worse. I sat with her in that room, and she was tearing herself apart over the children and what she was doing to them. It wouldn't have worked. You did the right thing, Connor, honestly.'

He stood for a second longer, unmoving. 'Thank you again, Rowan,' he breathed. 'For understanding.' Another moment of silence, and then, 'Shall I do us something to eat now? We've not got long before the ducks start looking in and wondering why we're not throwing out the leftovers now.'

He was back to being the Connor I knew, with a smile in his voice and movement surrounding him as though someone had drawn cartoon lines to show his energy. But there was a dip to his shoulders and a ferociously over-the-top nature to his bustling into the kitchen.

'You'll get over it,' I said, following him into the brightly lit room. 'It hurts, I know, but the pain starts to fade after a while, like an injury. You never lose the scar, but that awful grinding agony really does mitigate.'

I watched him rummage in the fridge. 'You're not one for meal planning, now, Rowan, are you?' He moved cheese and bottles around.

'And it's no good disengaging. You have to face it square on. It's the best way.'

Quite what I was doing, giving advice on getting over a lost relationship, I had no idea. I still held the idea of Elliot to me like a cosy comfort blanket.

'They'll all be talking about me.' Connor withdrew from the depths of the fridge carrying some pork chops. 'At home. Ah, I was never sure about the going back. It'll be all hushed conversations in corners and Mam a bit tight-lipped while Da gives me a beer and pats my shoulder and whispers not to worry. I *know* it'll blow over and they love me really and that it was a bit of stupidity, now, but... there will be the *looks*, y'know?'

'You really care what they think of you, don't you?'

'Doesn't everyone? Deep down? Even those yokes that

pretend to be all careless and casual and free spirits and everything? It's hard to hear the disapproval when it comes *en masse*.'

The chops went into a pan and I cut up some veg without really thinking about it. Connor moved back and forth across the kitchen behind me, restlessly searching the cupboards, but, I thought, to really keeping moving because it was easier than standing and letting the memories hit.

'The disapproval is their problem though,' I said, slicing carefully. 'You can't legislate for what everyone else thinks of you, you only have to be able to live with yourself. That Catholic upbringing is giving you some grief, isn't it, for all you say that you've left it behind?'

I turned around and saw him frozen at the far side of the kitchen, a spatula in hand, arrested in the movement of turning the chops, which were sizzling in a way that spoke of slight burning. 'You might be at the heart of it now,' he said slowly. 'Me feeling an idiot, losing the woman I thought I loved and the whole future, it's all tied up with the guilt and letting the family down.' He poked the spitting chops. 'You sound as though you know what you're talking about here? From experience?'

I paused, knife blade suspended over the pak choi. 'A little, perhaps. My parents didn't altogether approve of Elliot. I mean, they were nice enough to him, very accepting when they met him, but I always got the feeling that they thought I could have done better than what my mother called "a builder". He wasn't "just" a builder, of course he wasn't, he was a skilled tradesman. He was trained in historical methods of reconstruction – he could build a wattle and daub wall the old way.' I smiled at the memory. 'Treading the dung and straw into the clay with bare feet to get it to mix properly.'

'Sounds like you're well in recovery,' Connor observed.

'Like I said, you never really get over it. Every single

reminder picks away at the scab. But—' I turned and he stepped back – I was flourishing a really big knife '—you learn to live with it. Like... like giving yourself a bad knee from ice skating. It aches away in the background and every now and then you do something strenuous and it kicks up big time, but it always dies back to that general background ache that you put up with, because it reminds you of what you once had.'

'"Ice skating"?'

'You know what I mean. Sometimes it's nice to have that little bit of pain. It links you to what went before. Elliot's never truly gone, because I remember him with that little ache. And you can remember the good times with Saoirse. It will hurt, but it reminds you that you *had* them.'

'Lies that they were.'

We went quiet. The chops spat and sizzled a bit more, and I cooked the vegetables in water that roiled and boiled and added more atmosphere to the silence.

'What about making new memories?' Connor said eventually.

'I'm starting to try. I know that I can't live in stasis any more; I need to move on with my life, not despite Elliot, but because of him.' I drained the vegetables while Connor ladled out the chops. 'He loved me and I loved him and that's gone now. But he left me with the memory of what love can be, and how much fun life is, so I should honour that memory and enjoy myself again.'

Even I noticed the hesitancy in my voice. I'd done the thinking and I was speaking the words, but I wasn't quite sure how I was supposed to carry out the actions. Here I was, talking like some kind of women's magazine heroine with all the 'I must learn to love again' stuff, but deep down I knew that it wasn't that simple. It was *never* that simple.

'But you're going to worry, every time any man walks out of that door, that he might not come back,' Connor said, succinctly. 'And that sort of worry isn't going to be good for your health or your relationship.'

It stung somewhat to hear it laid out like that, but he was right, damn him.

'While you're going to worry that every woman you meet is keeping massive secrets about a whole other life,' I responded in kind. See how he liked it.

'Ah, well.' Connor slid the plates onto the table and we sat down and eyeballed each other over the slightly singed chops. 'We're a right pair of romantic disasters, aren't we?'

I nodded. 'We're practically a rom-com.' I began to eat my dinner.

'That we are.'

There was cutting and chewing now taking the place of conversation, but it actually felt rather pleasant. The lamp on the dresser shone a cheerful pool of light and even the overhead fluorescent bulb didn't feel quite as stark as usual.

The window threw a patch of brightness into the darkness of outside, illuminating a square of white snow, dark and slow river, and a few spare ducks pecking idly at protruding growth around the edges. Everywhere else was almost silent. There wasn't even the usual distant sound of cars travelling the road along the top of the ridge, only the far-off whirr of a generator on one of the farms as evening milking continued.

'What do you think, then,' Connor said eventually, when the plates were nearly clear.

'About what?' I leaned back. He really was a good cook – those chops weren't as burned as I'd feared.

'About making new traditions? Doing things differently so it's not a matter of stirring up old memories but making new ones? Because I was thinking, there's no point now in raking over the old stuff and trying to make it *feel* different. How about breaking new ground instead?'

He opened the window to scrape the plates out and the ducks fell upon our scraps with much quacking into the snow-shaded dark.

'Why have you been thinking about new traditions? I mean, you're fine, aren't you? The snow won't last forever, you aren't going to be stuck in the cottage for the next fifteen years.'

Connor paused, elbows on the open windowsill. 'No, no, you're right.' He said it lightly and cheerily, but with an undertone that I couldn't place. 'I'm not, am I?' He came back inside and closed the window. 'But my reluctance to go back this year is opening my eyes to a few things.'

'Such as?'

He sighed. For a moment he looked tired and a little disillusioned. 'I'm trying too hard to fit in,' he said and then turned away, bustling with the dishes. 'To be the son that they want rather than who I am. Why don't you get a dishwasher?'

'I've already told you, because there's only me and I don't make that much washing up.'

He clanked a few more plates and ran hot water without answering me. I stood with my back to those carefully argued-over oak worktops and looked at my lovely kitchen, built by my wonderful husband. When my parents had come on a visit after Elliot and I had bought the place, when it was still a building site filled with planks and holes in the wall, I'd proudly showed them around. My mother had pursed her lips and frowned and said, 'It's a bit small, isn't it? For the money you paid?' Unable to see beyond what it was, and into what it could be, and coloured by her disapproval of Elliot's profession, she'd put a damper on my excitement and enthusiasm that day.

I'd been so determined to prove her wrong. I'd sent pictures of the cottage in every stage of construction; photos of the huge oak dresser being put together – Elliot had found it in a salvage yard and trimmed bits off to make it fit our room – anything I could think of to show her that I'd been right. So maybe I wasn't quite as innocent of the crime of 'wanting family approval' as I thought. I'd wanted my mother to see Elliot as I saw him, a hard-working, kind, practical man who loved me and had a vision for our future. I knew she saw him as stolid and unimaginative, not a high-flier. Unsuitable for her educated daughter, even though that daughter was pushing forward with such an esoteric field of study, not something she could boast about to her friends, such as jewellery or royal palaces. 'Fairy tales, darling?' she'd said, when I'd told her about my doctorate. 'Aren't you a bit old for that sort of thing?'

But she, and my long-suffering father, who had enjoyed Elliot's company, and who had cornered him to talk about football at every chance, were in Spain now. Too far for me to need to make any accommodations for them.

'What you said, about going for a walk tomorrow.' Connor spoke again, his back to me now as he sluiced water into the sink. 'And traditions. Yes, going for a pre-Christmas Eve walk was one of ours but, y'know, maybe you could make it yours too. Different from what you did before, with Elliot. Something for *you*, a new Christmassy way to be.'

I let myself imagine all those lost Christmases that could have been. The cottage alive with lights and a tree and small plastic toys scattered over the rug. Stockings hung, turnips put out for the reindeer, and Elliot making boot marks in soot by the chimney to let the children know that Father Christmas had been. Hopeless laughter over badly cooked sprouts, a handmade rocking horse, and nights cuddled under a blanket while we watched the stars.

'Are you all right?' Connor had turned suddenly and caught me with the memories sparkling in the corners of my eyes and the imagination of what ought to have been running down my cheeks.

'Yes,' I said, choked. 'I'm just – oh, it's so *unfair*! We had plans, we had a life! I wanted... more, so much more. All those years we'll never have...' The words stopped, caught up behind the regret and the grief, which I always thought I was getting over, but which would ambush me at inopportune moments.

'Hey,' he said. And the next thing I knew I was being embraced, gathered into a tight hug. 'It's fine, now.'

'I keep thinking I'm over it.' I sobbed out the words. 'But then it finds another way to get me.'

Connor adjusted his hold so that he could poke the corner of a tea towel into the hug for me to wipe my face on. 'That's a big life change to get used to, widowhood, and you so young. You're allowed to feel that life can be a proper feck when something like that happens.'

I cried on for a bit longer. Oddly enough I didn't feel embarrassed at breaking down in front of Connor, and the way he seemed to take my tears in his stride was reassuring. I blew my nose on the damp tea towel, noisily.

'My mother thinks it was my fault for marrying him.' I sniffed loudly. 'If I'd married some history graduate with a professional pathway and a life plan, we'd have four children by now and a Georgian rectory in a village somewhere. I wouldn't be a widow with a precarious grant writing books about things nobody believes in any more.'

'Hey,' Connor said again, taking half a step back and putting a hand under my chin so I had to raise my face to look at him.

'*You* believe in it. Ah, you might not believe in the fairy folk or the black dogs walking the night, but you believe the stories are important, and that should be enough.'

His eyes were smiling, but his mouth was serious, as though he was teasing me lightly.

'That's not what my mother thinks,' I said.

'Ah, well, y'see, *my* mother thinks I'm a wild lad for heading off to England. I'm the black sheep already for what happened with Saoirse, so I believe she thinks I've gone right off the rails. I suspect Eamonn has only been invited for Christmas to try to talk sense into me.' He was still holding me close, tipping my face so he could see my expression. 'So maybe it's not just you that needs the new traditions and the new memories. Maybe we *both* have to start new lives.'

My heart started to beat very hard, as though it had enlarged and was forcing twice as much blood through my body.

'Connor, I...' I began, and then all the lights went out.

We stood in the dark for a moment, and then disengaged slowly. 'Power cut,' I said, not sure how I was meant to feel about this. 'It happens. Snow brought down the power lines, probably.'

Connor stepped towards me, crashed into me in the pitch black of the kitchen and rebounded to hit the table. 'Ow! Have you any candles?'

'Of course. And a big torch. I'll dig them out if you can put your phone torch on so I can see.'

There was a moment of fumbling and the bright light of Connor's phone torch illuminated the side of the kitchen. I bent down and pulled the candles, matches, torch and holders out of the drawer where they lived, ready to hand for the not-infrequent moments like this.

'There. That's better.' I lit several tealights and dotted them around the kitchen. 'But we'd better get to bed – the cottage gets quite cold when the heating goes off.'

'We could light the logs?' Connor sounded hopeful.

'We could, but we should save them really, in case the power stays off.'

'It *stays off*?' He sounded indignant.

I was busy being practical, moving candles, fussing around with saucers to stop tealights dripping wax. I didn't even want to think about what I might have said to Connor if the lights hadn't gone out. I didn't want to think about what I might have suggested, or how it might have gone down. Even I didn't know what I'd been about to say. 'You're squashing me.' 'Have I got snot all down my face?' 'Will you take me to bed and help me stop thinking?'

No. I'd only been going to ask how new memories got made. How, given that we were stuck here without proper Christmas food or preparations, we were supposed to make any memories at all, other than those occasioned by malnutrition and hypothermia.

'Well. All right, then.' He sounded reluctant, although quite what he thought the alternative might be I had no idea. We were hardly going to be sitting here by inadequate candlelight reading peer-reviewed journals to further our studies, were we? 'Goodnight, then, Rowan.'

'Goodnight, Connor.' I blew out the candles. I'd leave them there for tomorrow, in place ready to be lit once darkness crept back.

There was a brief moment of kerfuffle as we both tried to leave the kitchen at once, carrying our phones, torches beaming in front of us like a couple of techno Wee Willy Winkies, and we squeezed our way through into the living room with the lights whirling and causing shadows that loomed in a terrifying way.

'So, walk tomorrow?' Connor asked.

'Oh, all right.' I sounded less than excited about the prospect.

'It could be a new tradition.'

'I suppose it could.'

We were both standing at the bottom of the stairs, but neither of us moving to go anywhere. After a few seconds of this, Connor lowered his torch, so it lit up his feet.

'To hell with it, Rowan.' His arms came around me, unbalancing me so that I had to put one foot on the bottom stair so as not to fall over. 'Would you mind very much if I kissed you, now?'

I froze. 'I... I'm not sure,' I said, suddenly wanting him to kiss me very much, but not sure if my face would allow it. It had been a long time – a *long* time – since anyone but Elliot, as though I'd forgotten how my lips worked with anyone but him.

'Ah, you're right.' The arms around me loosened. 'Bad idea all round.'

But then I thought 'new traditions'. I remembered how alone I was, that Elliot, loved though he'd been, wasn't here. I thought of the silence and the cold of the long night and that I still hadn't got a cat. I reached up, put my arms around Connor's neck and stretched myself against him.

We kissed in the narrow confines of my staircase, me with my back against the wall and Connor with one hand in my hair and the other on the newel post to prevent him from falling upwards. His mouth felt strange and yet very comfortable, as though we'd kissed our way through many previous lives and this was just the first time for us in this life. Outside, through the living-room window, the moon peered in like a peeping Tom, bouncing off the snow and illuminating enough of the hallway to let highlights shine in Connor's hair.

He was warm and tall and there was a lanky firmness to him that contrasted with my memories of Elliot's gentler softness. The whole experience, this whole new body and smell and taste, was at once alien and familiar. But while my body was losing itself in the closeness and the comfort of kissing Connor, my mind would not shut up, and kept whispering to me that it was only a kiss, it didn't have to mean anything. This didn't have to go any further than a mutual admission of frailty and attraction. Elliot was still safe, hidden away in that corner of my memory, with our relationship still unique and protected.

Eventually gravity got the better of both of us and I toppled gently over onto the staircase, while Connor rotated around his hand on the post until he hung over the banister. It drew our lips apart and wrenched a gap between our bodies, which was just as well because my lungs needed some space to properly expand.

'Well,' I said. There wasn't much else I could say.

Connor cleared his throat but didn't speak.

Moonbeams crept around the lower stairs as though afraid to go any higher for fear of what they might see, and then we both spoke at once.

'I can't...'

'It's too soon for us to...'

We both stopped. We were looking at each other in the vaguely lit space as though neither of us had seen the other before, and we tried again.

'I think we should...'

'Let's not rush...'

We stopped again, in a spirit of muted annoyance. Finally, and cautiously, in case he was going to do it again, I spoke.

'Perhaps we need to think about this. I'm going to go to bed.'

When he was sure I'd finished speaking, Connor started.

'You're right. We need a bit of time here. This doesn't have to be... a thing, Rowan. Let's sleep on it. Er. Separately.'

I heeled my way up another stair and then turned so that I could clear the entire staircase in two bounds, then shut myself in the bathroom with my phone clutched so tightly in my fist that the light gleamed out from between my fingers in little ripples. I was breathing fast, and my cheeks, when I held the torch up to the mirror, were flushed with a mixture of excitement and stubble burn.

No, no, no, no, no. This can't have happened. He's not Elliot. And I can't... It would be disloyal.

But Elliot has gone.

Connor is nice. And he kisses well. And he doesn't try to make you go further faster than you want.

But he's not Elliot.

ELLIOT ISN'T COMING BACK.

For the first time in all these years it hit me properly. As though I'd been sitting here enduring the passing time, knowing that Elliot was dead and gone but secretly waiting for him to come back to me. As though a tiny corner of my mind had been tapping its foot and keeping the faith with a secret knowledge: that Elliot couldn't – *wouldn't* – have left me, not *really*. If I kept my life the way it had been and kept the cottage as he had known it, somehow I could call him back to me from the land of the dead.

Maybe *that* was what was really behind my obsession with the Fairy Stane. Not that I wanted to keep those folk tales alive with the hint of mystery, and that whispered undertone of *nobody really knows what's down there*. Maybe I wanted to convince myself that Elliot hadn't died in that hospital, that miserable Wednesday afternoon. In reality, he'd heard the fairy pipes playing and been summoned by the music to descend beneath the stone to the land of the fey, the world of the Little People. But if I held firm and truly loved him, I could bring him back into the land above, the human world.

Now, in this torchlit bathroom with my face glowing and my eyes bright, I felt the pull of the attraction to Connor and knew that I'd been lying to myself. Only very deep down, only in my imagination and those thoughts that allowed 'what ifs' to dwell in dark pools and secret groves, but I'd kept myself apart just in case Elliot came back.

But Elliot was never coming back.

21

I spent a very disturbed night, falling in and out of dreams that hinted at guilt and recovery, letting go and holding fast. The brightness of the moon didn't help either, squinting between the curtains with its light enhanced by the glistening snow beneath it, so that the bedroom felt as though daylight were haunting the night.

I woke up late, disorientated, embarrassed and bleary, with my head still full of Connor and last night's kiss.

I liked him. A few of the dreams had proved that, allusions of moist heat and another weight in the bed. There was still the matter of his being a historian and diametrically opposed to some of my beliefs, but I'd lived with him here long enough to know that he was reasonably house-trained and, unless that kiss had unleashed a foul-mouthed, slobbish boor that he'd been keeping well hidden, he was pleasant to have around. It didn't have to be a 'thing', anyway, did it? Just a brief encounter. Something to take away the ghost of Elliot in a nice way. A gentle exorcism.

I lay stretched across the bed, listening to ducks arguing and feeling the hole where Elliot had existed as one pokes a newly absent tooth with a tongue. The wound was less painful than it had been. Elliot wasn't coming back. I could have a new, different life with his memory as a comfortable place in the back of my mind, like childhood or a lovely holiday.

From outside I could hear a crunch of footsteps in the snow. Connor must be outside, and I wondered what he was doing. The thought that he might be going for that walk alone, uncertain of my commitment to tramping three miles in knee-deep snowfall, struck me and I leaped out of bed to look out of the window.

The door to the woodshed was ajar and a stamped path showed that Connor had been up and down a few times with the wonky wheelbarrow that existed solely for the purpose of transporting logs to the back door. I frowned, wrapped my sturdy dressing gown around me and went onto the landing.

There was an instant smell of 'green', and warmth, as though the house had been filled with tree spirits, scenting the air with their perfumes. Cautiously I went down the stairs and stepped into the living room, where the log burner was pushing out a constant heat and a huge pile of logs had been stacked neatly in the holder ready for stoking the blaze.

And the walls were hung with branches. Greenery from conifers and yew, jewel studded hawthorn twigs with the berries gleaming in the firelight, were on every surface and hanging from the overhead light fitting. The bare black of twisted hazel and birch adorned the dresser and the table bore the bright fluttering chestnut of beech, still holding the last leaves of summer now dried to a leathery tan.

As I stood staring, Connor came in with another armful of logs. 'Good, you're up,' he said cheerily. 'I hope you don't mind but it was looking a wee bit unseasonal, so I thought some midwinter décor might be just the thing.'

'Connor?'

He looked uncertain for a moment, standing in the doorway with his clothes dusted with a mixture of snow and log detritus. 'Er. Sorry, was I wrong? I didn't mean to upset you, now, I only wanted...'

'It's beautiful.'

I watched his face collapse with relief into a smile that seemed more relaxed, more open than it had before. 'Now, I'm relieved to hear that. I was a bit worried there for a moment that you might start throwing things.'

I turned, taking in the artful draping of the fir branches that hung around the window and let the sun's rays filter through in a green net that caught the light and released it gradually across the floor. It smelled like Christmas. 'It really is gorgeous.'

'Thank you.' He sounded humble, which wasn't like Connor at all. 'When we spent Christmas with Granda, when I was very young and before the rest of the boys were born, he used to bring the green in at midwinter. I remember the smell of the peat fire and the branches and the whisky and he'd play the pipe and sing. Mam was always a bit tight-lipped about the whole thing. I thought it was just that she didn't get on so well with Granda, but later I realised that it was the pagan thing she couldn't deal with. Not really "Church", all this.' He indicated with his elbows, his arms being full of wood. 'But I thought it would be more "you".'

'You are amazing,' I breathed, my breath puffing out in steam because the back door was still wide open, propped by the barrow full of logs.

Connor tried, without notable success, to look modest. 'New memories. Old ones resurfacing, in my case.'

I shook my head, dizzy with disbelief at the beauty and artistry of it all. 'You are wasted as a historian, Connor. You need to come to the dark side of pagan mythology.'

'There's a fair bit of that in Irish history, to be fair.' As though becoming aware of the cold creeping in behind him, Connor stepped back and closed the door then came through brandishing his armful of logs. He tipped them down onto the pile in the fire grate and bent to stack them neatly. 'I thought I'd light the fire too, it's fair freezing in here now. And the electricity isn't back.' He reached up and flicked the switch for the desk lamp, which clicked and did nothing. 'How long is it usually off for?'

I shivered and came closer to the blaze. 'Could be hours. Not usually days though, unless it's this small area and they forget about us. Shall I make some tea and toast?'

He frowned. 'Electricity is off.'

'But the log burner is on. I've got a stove-top kettle and a toasting fork for just such eventualities.'

Now Connor nodded, slowly. 'Of course you have. Here's you all practical and sorted and the folklorist, with the historian imagining eating cold soup and hunks of cheese.'

I laughed and hunted out the big iron kettle, and we sat in front of the flames and ate slightly crunchier than usual toast and drank our tea. Beyond the kitchen window the ducks grumbled.

Then we went for a walk. Through thigh deep snow, alternately stepping carefully and toppling into gulleys, we made our way up onto the high moor where the snow had scoured and drifted, and some places wore only a couple of centimetres of covering and in others the snow was piled higher than a housetop. Because we kept slipping and tripping and falling and having to pull one another out of drifts, it seemed natural and time-saving for us to go hand in hand along the icy path out across the moor to the Fairy Stane, which lay docile under its white blanket, visible only because of its edges and the way the heather and rushes fringed around its corners.

I let go of Connor's hand and walked out to stand by the side of the old stone. There were no fairy footprints in the snow, only the runic lettering of pheasants' feet across its surface, and the stammering prints of a hare that had run across on its way elsewhere.

'The Little People,' Connor said quietly. 'Lovely spot for them.'

I looked around at the smooth humps of the moors stretched out around us, like carefully made beds covered in the purest linen. The sun was shining visible ice from a Wedgwood-blue sky. 'It is, isn't it?' I replied. 'Who needs fairyland when you've got this up here?'

'Bit chilly for the fairies now.' Connor jiggled on the spot and rubbed his arms. His big black coat didn't allow enough room for the layers beneath it that I was wearing under my sturdy waxed jacket.

'Maybe they knit themselves clothes out of moonbeams and mist,' I said whimsically. 'Or rabbit fur and blackbirds' feathers.'

'They'd more likely wear the whole rabbit, the murderous little bastards.' Connor continued to jiggle. 'You're a folklorist. You know what the Victorians did to the fairy myth now, dressing it up as babies with wings and all that gossamer nonsense. You know what the fairies were before that lot got at the stories, all wilderness and blood and stealing the newborn from the cradle.'

I looked down again at the Fairy Stane, smooth and unblemished, decorated by nature. 'These fairies were prime Victorian fodder,' I said. 'All the stories I can trace go back to that mid-

Victorian era, so strictly rose-petal skirts and cobweb wings down there.'

We stood in silence a little bit longer. From a very long way off came the mew of a buzzard rising on a thermal, but there was nothing else moving anywhere. 'Doesn't sound as though they're partying down there today though, does it?' Connor said. 'Not big fans of Christmas though, your average elemental.'

'No,' I said, slightly sadly. 'I used to come up here after Elliot died and will them to take me down to fairyland.'

Connor looked at me, then took a couple of steps in to close the gap between us. 'And how do you feel now?'

I kept my eyes on the stone. 'I'll always miss him.'

'Of course. That's natural.'

'But I'm beginning to let myself believe that life goes on. Just a little bit.' I didn't dare look up at him. 'And I don't have to wait any more.'

Connor let out an enormous breath that clouded the air for a moment, then tattered at the edges and dissipated into the white-cold of the air. 'I'm a wee bit glad to hear you say that,' he said quietly. 'Because I'd really like us to... I dunno what the modern language for it is, to "have something" here.' I did glance up at his face now, but he was focusing somewhere out in the distance, watching the rising black V shapes of the buzzards climbing the thermal ladder into the vast blue of the sky. 'Still as the grave,' he said under his breath.

'No graves here.' I pointed, my arm wobbling slightly under the weight of clothing I had on. 'Over there is the church – you can see the top of the spire. That's where all the graves are.' The sudden memory crashed in: a dark, wet day in early November, where the rain had hidden my tears. 'Elliot's ashes are there, in the churchyard.'

I felt Connor flick me a look. 'Do you visit him?'

'He's not there.' I was surprised at how strong my voice sounded. 'He's out here.' I waved the pointing hand, at the moors which lay all ridges and dips beneath the smooth lightness of the snow. 'He's everywhere he ever was.' And I didn't cry this time.

We stood for a while longer. I didn't look at the stone again. Connor was right, it was just a stone, but maybe I could look at getting some kind of plaque put on it? So visitors would know why it was here? One of those information boards that dotted the Roman roads or the wells, giving a potted history and a children's activity, would look nice and mean that everyone knew that this was the Fairy Stane.

Eventually Connor caught at my hand again. 'Shall we go back?' he asked. 'I'm fecking freezing, and we don't want the fire to go out, now, do we?'

My legs were tired with the strain of stepping through the snow, I was soaked to the gusset and my feet felt as though all my toes had been welded together in liquid nitrogen. 'Yes.'

I felt his fingers wind through mine. 'Then I can give you your present,' he said. 'I was going to leave it on the table for you to find, when I flew off to Ireland, but, well...' He nodded out at the snow, which was unavoidably filling my boots again.

'Oh!' I was suddenly struck with horror. 'I didn't get...'

'It's fine. Honestly, Rowan, that's not what it's about. This is us, making new memories, remember?'

Ireland. His home. His job, his family. All a few hundred miles away. 'How long for, though?' I sounded despondent and I didn't want to. I wanted to sound upbeat; fine with the prospect of this 'something' we had being temporary, a small step I had to get over before I could properly start living my life again. So I added, 'Not that it matters,' in as insouciant a tone as I could manage.

My hand got a little shake and his fingers squeezed for a second. 'For as long as we want,' he said softly. 'It's not just you that's lost something, you know, Rowan.'

I stopped walking. He pulled up alongside me and turned me into an embrace that was ninety per cent coat. 'Saoirse has made me afraid to trust my own judgement now. I used to be so sure... so *certain* of myself, probably a little bit cocky, if I say so myself, a wee bit...' He tailed off.

'Arrogant?' I supplied. 'Because I'd not put that so much in the past if I were you.' I hoped the half-laugh in my voice, muffled as it was by acres of wet wool, told him that I was only a bit serious. He *had* been arrogant, when we'd first met. Had he changed, or had I?

'That whole business, falling for her and realising that it was all fake, it's given me a touch of a complex. I'm not quite so keen to throw my heart out there for a tumble and a weekend, do you understand me?'

I couldn't see his face now it was hidden beyond the embrace.

'I'm not sure,' I said slowly.

There was another, puffed-breath pause. I could feel his body swaying slightly; the rough fabric moved against my hands, which had been gathered in and lay in loose fists on his chest. 'I need this to be something real,' he said at last.

I had a sudden moment of knowing. As though the thin rays of the sun brought me an insight I hadn't had before and beamed it directly through the top of my head into my mind. *I'm not the only one who's lost something here. Connor has lost his innocence, his naivety about people, and for him that's nearly as painful as losing a person.*

'I need it to be real too,' I said.

The embrace tightened until my nose was squashed against

his collarbone and I had to squeak until he let me move back.

'Well, now.' His voice was back to its jaunty confidence-filled self. 'That's a good thing. Shall we go back and thaw ourselves out now? Only I've got the horrible feeling that your cottage is going to be largely made of wet socks for the next day or so.'

He doesn't want to dwell on it. My mind continued to tick over the thoughts as we walked on, heading down the hill towards the cottage in its snow-lined bowl with the river a dark crack through the perfection. *He knows what Saoirse did to him, and he knows I understand.*

I can't keep bringing Elliot into everything. Connor knows. It's turning-the-page time.

22

'But it's not Christmas yet,' I tried, as Connor pressed a package into my hands. 'Shouldn't we at least wait until tomorrow?'

He'd propped a branch in the old log bucket and hung it with duck feathers. We were sitting underneath it, illuminated by the flick and twist of candlelight and the steady roar of the log burner, heating soup in a saucepan on its hot metal top.

'New memories,' he said cheerily. 'Remember?'

I stretched my feet, now in dry socks, towards the blaze. 'Well, all right. But next year we get a proper tree.'

He didn't look up, he carried on prodding the wrapped package along the floor in my direction. 'New memories,' he said softly. 'I'll bet you've got all your old decorations tucked away in the loft, now, haven't you?'

I had another of those jolts of memory. The last Christmas Elliot and I had had, and packing away the carefully chosen ornaments and baubles, tissue-wrapped, into their box in the corner of the attic. I hadn't even looked at them since. 'Yes.'

'But it would be a touch of bad taste for me to get them out and hang them, wouldn't it?' he went on. 'They were yours and his. It would be like me editing myself into your wedding pictures.'

I laughed. 'It wouldn't be *that* bad. But I see your point.'

'New memories, Rowan.' He picked up the parcel. 'Sometimes it means other things need to be new. Ah, well, next year, as you say.'

Neither of us mentioned Dublin, his job or the distance.

'I didn't get you a present, but there's this.' I handed over the badly bundled heap, which was more tape than paper. 'You might like it.'

Solemnly we opened our presents. Despite the amount of tape, Connor got into his first and laughed. 'Ah, now! He's got the expression that I always assume when I'm faced with a big pile of research to read through!'

I'd dug the disillusioned Roman soldier out from his position guarding the crease in the back seat of my car and given him to Connor. He did, indeed, look like someone being faced with a distasteful task – his painted plastic face was realistically pissed off.

'He's very accurate too.' Connor turned the figure over. 'Yep, they've got the clothes right, maybe not quite enough hobnails in the boots, but, otherwise, pretty good effort there.' Unexpectedly he leaned over and kissed my cheek. 'Thank you.'

My face had gone hotter than the fire could account for. 'Sorry I didn't think to—'

'Hush. It's fine. Now open yours.'

It was a beautifully printed book of illustrated folk tales. Nothing new, no stories I hadn't already heard, but the pictures were gorgeous, deep and dark and layered. 'It's fabulous.' I ran my finger over the embossing on the cover. 'Really beautiful. Thank you.'

He did one of those shrugs that mean the shrugger is quietly pleased with the result but wants to look as though it was nothing, whilst wanting the shruggee to know that it took them weeks to find that exact thing. 'You're welcome. Now, for the love of God, can we have something to eat that isn't toast?'

We drank our soup and we played cards until the darkness got too much for us and the fire started to burn down low into a bed of ash. The shadows of the hanging branches made us look as though we were lost in a forest.

There was a silence. I became very aware of the feel of Connor's arm alongside mine, the flex of his fingers on the deck of cards and the way his skin looked pale and unearthly in the firelight against the darkness of his hair when he pushed it back.

'Rowan.' His hand left the cards and found my forearm, tracing a complicated pattern on my skin as though he were putting an invisible tattoo on my wrist.

I blinked at him. My breath had gone thick in my throat, as though I were breathing water, and my heart had risen to somewhere just under my collarbone, from where it was trying to tunnel out.

'Rowan...'

'Yes.'

He leaned across, bracing his weight on his arms, and his mouth found mine. My hands were in his hair, and then we were stumbling our way upstairs together, limbs wound around one another, kissing and tugging at clothes until we reached my bed. When we fell together under the duvet, we laughed as if a little shocked at what we were doing. The darkness helped – I didn't have to think that nobody had seen me naked since Elliot, because we couldn't see anything anyway. Even the moon had got the evening off, replaced by a sheet of cloud that kept even starlight from reaching us, and the dark was so thick that we occasionally elbowed one another in the eye or put a knee into an unfortunate place.

But then...

'Are you all right?' Connor had stopped. We were pressed together. Everything had been fine, everything *was* fine. There'd been kissing and hands everywhere and we were naked, and I was...

I was crying.

Just tears leaking out of my eyes, no drama. No huge, body-heaving sobs, but definitely crying, almost without being aware of it.

'I... yes. Yes, I'm fine.' I wiped the back of my hand over my eyes, surprised at the volume of tears.

Connor sat back, scrunching the duvet around himself. 'No, you're not fine, are you? It's all right.'

In silhouette his hair was on end, his face a pale smudge in the darkness.

'I don't know why I'm crying.' I pulled myself away so I could sit with my back against the pillows, gathering spare bits of cover to my chest. 'I don't know!' Tears overspilled and fell onto my neck and I mopped at my face with a corner of the duvet. 'This is ridiculous!'

'No, it's not.' Connor bent forward and groped around on the floor, then got out of the bed. He was, the writhing shadows told me, pulling his underpants back on. 'Really, it's not.'

'But I want to... I mean, I'm here, I'm naked, it's all going well, and I have absolutely no idea what's wrong with me!'

Connor clambered back up the bed, sat beside me and put a comforting arm around my shoulders. 'That's better. I was not going to talk any sense with my willy flapping about, now, was I?'

I snorted a laugh that was half muffled by duvet. 'Now that's an image designed to put anyone off sex.'

'Well, good. Because sex is – well. It's only a part of things, isn't it? A good relationship doesn't depend on how hot the sex is, or how often you have it or in what positions. A proper relationship can break down in tears and say, "I haven't done this since my husband died and everything feels different. And I actually feel a wee bit guilty even though I know I'm a widow and therefore technically not cheating even a little bit," can't it?'

'Is that me?'

'It is, now.' The arm tightened. 'It's too fast for you. You don't think it is, but your body has got other ideas.'

He smelled nice. Clean and with a little hint of woodsmoke; a friendly, domestic sort of smell. I snuggled against his shoulder. 'I don't *want* my body to have other ideas. I'm going to sleep with men that aren't Elliot, I know that. I'm not hastening to a nunnery at thirty-five.'

'Ah, but knowing and *knowing* are two different things. Tell me that there's not this little corner of your brain telling you that you're being unfaithful.'

I slumped and his arm caught me, holding me in against his bare chest. 'Why is it all so weird and complicated, Connor? Why can't we just have a lovely time? And how do you know so much about all this?'

He laughed, but it was almost ironic in tone. 'Catholic guilt. It does a number on you, Rowan.' He sighed. 'So I know all about deep, ingrained shame, even when there's nothing to be ashamed of.'

'Does that mean you're ashamed about Saoirse and what happened?' I asked, trying furtively to wipe my face so that I didn't have trails of snotty tears all over it.

Another sigh. 'Shame is probably the wrong word. I couldn't

know, how could I? But, like you said before, I took her word for everything without asking the questions – I was so bowled over that this attractive, successful woman wanted to be with me that I was very uncritical. I should have been at least a wee bit sceptical; I'm not *that* great.'

I turned to look at him. He was a big blob beside me, one smooth shoulder under my cheek and hair everywhere. 'You are pretty great,' I said quietly. 'You might want to hoick up my Fairy Stane, but apart from that you're pretty damn great, Connor O'Keefe.'

'*Professor* O'Keefe, if you please,' he said but his voice was laughing. 'Maybe there's a way around this whole "lifting the stone" thing. Like I said, I need to do a bit more research and have a chat to Eamonn, but I think, maybe, there might be a way.' He gave me a quick, one-armed hug. 'We need to find out what's going on, but without letting your fairies out into the world, now. The last thing we want is those flying bastards all around the place.' The arm dropped away from my shoulders and Connor clambered out of the bed.

'Are you going?' I noticed how my voice trembled slightly. Urgh. I cleared my throat. 'Where are you off to?'

Connor straightened from where he'd been raking the floor, with half his clothes over his arm. 'I think that we'll put tonight down to a trial run,' he said carefully. 'I'm going back next door so that we can both get a proper night's sleep. Next time I'll stay over. Er...' He stopped talking and seemed to go back mentally over what he'd said. 'If you want there to be a next time, of course. And if you can bear to have me around overnight.'

I thought about the way his hands had felt on my body, and the firmness of his lips on mine. 'I think so,' I said.

'Right, then. I'll bid you a somewhat Shakespearian goodnight.'

Not at all like a man who'd been sexually disappointed and who was wearing only his underpants, Connor strode from the room, carefully closing the door behind him, which caused a pair of trousers to flop to the floor, and I could hear him swearing quietly on the landing.

'Goodnight,' I called softly.

'Sleep well, Rowan,' came the reply from beyond the door, and I heard him head into his own room and close that door carefully. Then I punched the pillow very, very hard a few times and finished the cry that I'd started earlier, only this time with a good deal of annoyance mixed in.

23

When I got up the next morning, Connor had gone out. Where he had gone out *to*, bearing in mind the grey, overcast snowfield outside the door, I didn't know, but I was quite glad of his absence.

It meant I didn't have to look at him and remember last night, hungry mouths and hands and the kind of longing I had thought was in the past. I did some housework, called my parents, phoned the electricity company ('power should be back by lunchtime!'), banked up the fire and watched some TV when the power finally reappeared.

The greenery still festooned the living room, giving it the look and smell of a forest glade. The branch in the bucket, which Connor had decorated with the fallen duck feathers, had a wild, random appearance, as though a festively inclined hurricane had blown through and deposited it where it could be appreciated. It kept snagging my attention, although I tried to lose myself in Christmas episodes of programmes I usually liked. Out of the corner of my eye I kept seeing the scarecrow version of the Christmas tree, its tufted twigs skulking. In the end it irritated me so much that I gave in.

'All right,' I told its stick-waving form. 'You're a Christmas tree. I get it.' And I went upstairs, pulled down the ladder and squeezed myself up into the attic space. The cold and dust lay thick up there so I didn't hang around. I raided the box for a random collection of baubles and brought them downstairs, carrying them cupped in the palm of my hands like precious eggs.

When Connor came in, red-faced and stamping the snow off his boots, I was sitting, firelit, the tinted glass balls rotating and reflecting in the draught from the warm air.

'Oh,' he said, draping his coat over the table. 'Oh!'

I didn't say anything. I thought the Christmas tree was suitably illustrative of my desire to move away from my past relationship and really hoped that he wasn't going to ask any questions – I was a touch wobbly on the subject and still not entirely sure I'd done the right thing.

'This is grand.' He toed off his boots in the doorway and kicked them across the kitchen, then, obviously with the voice of his mother in the back of his mind, he went over and put them neatly together by the back door.

'Remind me to thank your parents at some point,' I said. 'The training stuck.'

'Five boys.' Connor bounced across to stand in front of the fire, warming his hands. 'If it hadn't, we'd have been living in squalor after the first five years. You've reminded me, I need to speak to Eamonn. You all right here?' As though his socks had springs in, he moved across, touched me briefly on the top of my head, and went out. I heard him rattle up the stairs and then, after a moment, the muffled sound of his voice talking in his bedroom.

He hadn't acknowledged the tree with its old decorations causing multicoloured lights to spiral around the room like a seventies disco. He'd seen it and knew what it meant. There would have to be new baubles, some of these had too many memories attached for them to be truly assimilated into any new household I might make, but they would do for now. Spun glass in seasonal colours, jewel-coloured birds, two pinecone hedgehogs and a plus-sized acorn made of balsa hung innocently from their pine supports, ushering in Christmas but showing out my old relationship in a carefully understated way. They'd been there that last Christmas when Elliot and I had been reading up about IVF and the possibilities it invoked. When we'd dared to dream that the impossible might actually become possible or, at least, more probable that it had been. When he'd given me the eternity ring that now languished in its tiny box upstairs, guarding the wedding ring that I'd torn off in a fury the night he'd died, so angry that he could have left me. That tiny box that I'd put under my pillow and slept with, with the memories wrapped around my mind as I'd wrapped Elliot's dressing gown around my body.

Gone. Elliot was gone.

But that didn't mean I had to stop living. His ending was not my ending.

I leaned back against the sofa, listening to the sound of Connor pacing up and down, his voice a rise and fall of Irish cadences in the background. Elliot hadn't been able to talk on the phone without walking either, I thought with a smile. It must be a guy thing.

Outside the cottage the wind was getting up. I could hear it slapping the river surface against the old mill supports and humming its way through the trees down the lane. The weather must be changing. I looked out of the window and the snow that had ironed the scenery flat beneath its weight was tattering at the edges into icy lace as a thaw moved in, borne on the wind and hastened by the splatter of rain that came with it.

Good. We'd be able to get out. Maybe even tomorrow the hill would have enough clear patches for me to be able to drive up, and Christmas Day could be diluted by Chess and cocktails.

I wondered what Connor would do. Whether we had moved into the kind of relationship where he would come to Chess's with me, hold my hand on her sofa and drape himself casually around me to the music playing in her living room. Or whether we were still at the cautious distance stage, and he would go to his lecturer friends for food, make Lego models with their clever ten-year-old children on the floor in front of the fire and sleep over in the careful décor of their spare room.

Which version of Connor did I want?

Feet rattled on the stairs, and he erupted into the living room, making the branch-tree sway dangerously in its bucket.

'Eamonn is coming over,' he said, as though this were the result of a conversation we'd already had. 'After Boxing Day though. Mam will have a stupendous amount of leftovers and she'll probably kill him if he doesn't eat his own weight in turkey before he leaves.'

'Oh,' I said weakly.

'Ah, now, it's fine. He won't stay here. After all, we're an unmarried couple, cohabiting under the same roof. He might spontaneously combust.'

My expression must have been one of startled horror, because Connor started to laugh. 'Your face! No, Eamonn likes his creature comforts, he's not one for the spare bed or the sofa. He'll take himself to a hotel around abouts. And you've no worry, he's a twenty-first-century man, he's not going to castigate us for living in sin. He's got a great line in censorious frowning, though, I'll warn you now.'

'But why,' I asked faintly, 'is he coming at all? Not just to bring you your share of the leftovers?'

Connor wandered over and sat down beside me, close enough that our bodies touched all down one side. He didn't look at me but stared ahead with his eyes focused on the flicker of flame in the log burner. Reflected red light caught his hair from the glass baubles and his eyes were very dark.

'I think we might need him,' he said.

'I'm not bloody marrying you,' I said snippily. 'And there's no other conceivable reason to bring a priest into this.'

Connor turned his head and gave me a little wink. 'Ah, sure, you're not meaning that,' he said jauntily. 'I'm irresistible. But—' and my shoulder got a little nudge '—that's away in the future. For now – well, I was up at your Stane today, for a wee bit of the research, and I think I want my brother here.'

'It's...' All I could think of was fairies, breaking through into the world and being fought off with the power of the Church, but the whole idea was too Gothic even for me. 'What on earth for? Bell, book and candle?'

He opened his mouth as though he wanted to say something, but then closed it again and shifted his weight to put some space between us. 'I'm not quite certain yet. I'll tell you when I am.'

'Get you, man of mystery.' Then, after a moment's consideration, 'You didn't lift the stone, did you?'

Connor reared back and stared at me, then lifted one arm to demonstrate his unbulging biceps. 'Er, I said I was irresistible, not Thor. Have you *seen* the weight of that thing?'

'So what were you doing up there? You were gone ages.'

'Oh, you know. Looking. Bit of scrabbling in the old bog there. Checking sightlines, nothing important.'

'No Romans, then?'

'There's three feet of snow, Rowan, what could I be doing for them?' Connor stretched himself out towards the fire, a faint blush of warmth showing on his cheekbones above the dark lines of stubble.

'Isn't that what you're here for? Discovering the settlement?' I tried to keep the emotion out of my words. What would he do after that? He was here for six months, to map out and uncover the putative Roman settlement, and then he'd be gone back to Dublin. Did I really want to start anything with a man who would leave? Despite last night, or maybe *because* of last night, I had a choice to make and for all my talk of moving on and making new memories, none of those memories or new life had to include Connor. I could make my own life.

The cat was still a possibility.

He gave me another small sideways look. 'You know the Romans were a bit of a ruse, now, don't you?' he said. 'I'm not going to be the one digging – I do the research and the paperwork, the archaeology department takes over from there. I came for a look at the site and to get a better idea of the topography. From here on in I can work from anywhere.'

'But you're still here,' I said. 'Eating my food, sleeping in my spare bed and annoying the ducks.'

'And paying for the privilege,' he replied, his voice still calm. 'I think you know why I've stayed now, don't you, Rowan?'

He turned to look properly at me and I returned the look with eyes fresh from new knowledge and realisations. The light reflected from the baubles glowed across our faces. 'You stayed because of me?'

He smiled, a softening grin that made his face crinkle in an attractive way. 'I did. And I don't want you to think it's just physical, although I do have to say that I find your whole person quite pleasing. You've a way with you, Rowan, and I like who you are.'

The flames crackled and almost as sudden as the thaw outside came the realisation that I really, *really* liked Connor.

Our mouths met, and this time it was frenzied, hungry. We tore at one another's clothes without finesse and the sex was almost desperate, as though the end of the world had been announced and we had to celebrate what life we had left; desperate, but very, very satisfying, and we collapsed back on the living-room floor gasping for breath and both slightly surprised.

'An unexpected conclusion to a conversation about my brother.' Connor held me against his chest as we scrambled for space in front of the fire. 'And probably as close to sex as Eamonn will ever get.'

I pulled a rug down from where its drape across the sofa had been meant to indicate that I lived a carefully curated existence in my impeccable home. Scattered cushions on the floor and the way the sheepskin in front of the wood burner had been rucked against the grate now blew that illusion, so moving the rug wasn't going to cause Instagram panic.

'I think it helped, not being in my bedroom,' I said, wrapping the rug around us both. 'Not so many memories.'

'You're not telling me you never had a good shag in here.' Connor pushed my hair off my face. 'Go on, I'll not believe that.'

'Oh, no, we did. But it was different. *You* are different. This whole thing is different. And you've still got your socks on.'

'Sorry about that.' Connor wiggled a foot that stuck out from the end of the rug attached to a hairy ankle. 'I've yet to master a sexy way of taking my socks off.'

I started to laugh. It *was* different. The ghost of Elliot had left me, not in a hauntingly sad leave-taking, but quietly evaporating to condense softly in a corner of my memory. He would always be with me, of course he would. But he had no need to sit in the front seat any more. He could merge into memory and only appear on anniversaries and holidays to be gently taken out and dusted down with a smile.

I had a glimmer of a future again, with this lanky dark Irishman who was laughing alongside me, or, rather, underneath me, wobbling the covering rug so hard that it slithered off us and I had to grab it back with my spare hand.

Different. As though happiness had more than one shape, and I hadn't realised.

24

We slept in my bed that night and woke to the distant sound of Christmas bells chiming through the valley from the little church so far away. The snow was leaving, waving a reluctant farewell in tatty little piles and ice fragments, and dripping its way out with the coming of a warmer wind and gusty showers. Connor and I stayed in bed.

'We could go to Chess's,' I said thoughtfully, from my position; I'd got out of bed to lean on the windowsill to watch the melting snow receding from the river edge. 'If we wanted. I think I could probably get the car up the hill.'

'Do you want to?' Connor asked from the bed behind me. 'We can. Or I can rummage in the freezer and create a culinary delight from whatever miscellany is in there.'

'Or we can stay in here, with a sandwich.' I turned around.

'Ah, now, you're insatiable, woman!' Connor laughed, flipping back a corner of the duvet to reveal that insatiability wasn't unique to me.

'Three years. More than three years,' I said. 'I've got some making-up to do.'

But it wasn't just the sex, although that was a not inconsiderable part of it. It was the lying close with someone, breathing in their scent and watching the way their hair caught in stubble, or their sleepy bundling of the duvet. It was laughing at awkwardness and talking – about stuff. Nothing important, no futures had come into our conversation, but we talked about our pasts. We talked about history, about folklore. I told Connor some of the stories about the area, and he talked about the Roman occupation of Britain. It was a lot more fun and a lot sexier than it sounds.

We got up and cooked, draped in dressing gowns. My lack of real Christmas preparation meant that we didn't have the full table-groaner of a Christmas dinner. Instead we had a weird scratch meal of assorted foods fried, and the ducks glared in at us with an antipathy built of a lack of toast crusts and leftovers.

'Was this Christmas different enough for you?' Connor asked as we got back into bed, replete in many different ways and satisfied in many others. He'd stood his little Roman centurion on the shelf, from where he watched our activities with his vaguely censorious painted expression conveying the same emotion as my mother did about my life.

'Oh, yes. *Very* different.' I settled back into the comfort of his embrace. 'I mean, there were some similarities, of course. Starting the day with sex isn't totally unknown to me, and at least one component of Christmas dinner has to be burned or it isn't really Christmas, is it?'

'Hmmm.' Connor had been a bit sensitive about burning the noodles, although it hadn't been entirely his fault as I'd been showing him a folklore book at the time.

'But what about you?' I turned to face him. 'You've talked a lot about me making new memories and everything, but what about *your* memories? They must be mostly good, surely?'

He sighed and his gaze went from my face to a space above my head, a distant, inward-looking stare. 'When we were kids, yes. Very. But then, when I decided that the Catholic faith wasn't for me any more, so Midnight Mass wasn't really a thing, well, then the magic sort of evaporated as it does when you get older – it got to be a bone of contention with Mam. Dad goes along with anything for a smooth ride, and the house full of the brothers and their wives and fiancées and then the kids...' His focus moved back to my eyes. 'You're not the only one to want new memories, Rowan,' he said. 'Saoirse and I, we'd planned out our Christmases. The little cottage, hopefully a couple of kids, just us as a family without having to include every passing congregation member and Father MacDermot, a man who I am convinced had at least fifteen Christmas dinners whilst "visiting his parishioners".' He squeezed me gently. 'All those lies. They've made me a bit wary of forward planning.'

'I think...' I began, and then paused to make sense of my thoughts before starting again. 'I think too much forward planning might be a bad thing. It kind of leaves you open to disappointment when everything doesn't fall into place like you wanted. Elliot and I had our lives planned out – house, children, careers, all that, but then the children weren't happening...' Another memory: that bathroom, that morning, that *hope*. 'Then he died. And, in some ways, it was twice as bad because I didn't just lose Elliot, I lost a whole future life. If we'd been a bit less rigid about things, had more of a "take it as it comes" attitude, maybe I wouldn't have felt so lost for so long.'

'That's the folklore talking.' Connor squeezed me again. 'History is all about the documentation and the proof, a bit like planning, only backwards. But I know what you mean. If Saoirse hadn't been one for the talking about what we'd do in the future, I'd have taken it more in my stride. Just a wee thing that happened, a mistake. But it wasn't just *her*, as you say, it was the whole of my future life went "pop" when I found out about her.' He sighed. 'Future faking. Only yours wasn't faking, it was a genuine expectation of how things would be.'

I pushed his hair back from his face, grinning at his expression, at the fact he hadn't shaved for two days, at the whole dark package that was so uniquely *Connor*. 'So, this time round I think we should take it as it comes, don't you? No plans, no expectations, no certainties. Just us.'

'Ah, and there's still the matter of your stone up there.' An elbow jutted to indicate the distant hump of moorland beyond. 'I'd like to know what's going on with that.'

'And your Roman settlement.'

'That can wait until summer. The archaeology boys can get up there and see if my theories are right.'

I ran my hand down his cheek, feeling the sheer realness of his cheekbones, his jawline, that stubble. 'Does that mean you're not going to lift my stone to prove your case?'

He sighed. 'If I'm right, we might not want to. But let's wait until Eamonn gets here for that.'

'Fairyland,' I muttered as I started to drop into sleep, feeling Connor's breath and his arms tight around me. 'We can't let fairyland out.'

I heard him say 'the Little People ought to be known' before I fell into dreams of joyful little winged fairies bouncing around and granting wishes.

25

Before we knew it the Christmas holiday had passed, and that charmed, secret time was over. But that was all right, I reminded myself. Life couldn't all be bed and giggling and making our own timetable. Reality had its place.

Reality was dropping Connor off near the university and heading into my office, where Chess was working, pink and enthusiastic after the break. I sent the Fairy Stane book off for editing and half planned some trips out for when winter gave up and let spring in.

Chess had, of course, taken one look at me and known *exactly* what sort of a Christmas I'd had.

'I knew it!' She punched the air triumphantly on my arrival into the office on our first day back. 'I *knew* it!'

'What did you know, Chess?' I asked, playing for time as I sorted through post and checked that my chair wasn't growing mushrooms.

'You're glowing! And if that isn't stubble burn, then you ought to go and see a dermatologist. Connor, right? I *knew* it! You're made for each other.'

There was absolutely nothing I could say, so I did the annoying little smile that neither confirms nor denies, to keep her on edge a little longer. She obviously took it as confirmation, because she spent the whole morning fluttering about singing 'I knew it!' and bought me an extra-large coffee and a bun from the little café down the road.

When we'd been back about a week, Connor turned up in my office at the end of the day with someone in tow.

'This is my brother, Eamonn,' he said, poking a young man through the doorway. 'Go on, Eamonn, she won't bite you, now.'

Eamonn, whom I'd consistently pictured as a rotund, placid little man with a beatific smile and a natty line in those cape things that priests always seem to wear on TV, turned out to be the most stunningly attractive man I'd ever seen. Connor was, of course, subjectively more attractive, but Eamonn's sheer beauty took my breath away.

'Er. Hello there,' he said.

Chess, who hadn't left yet although she'd got her hat and coat on, was glued to the wall of my office, boggling. When Eamonn and Connor leaned over my desk to look at a map, she looked over at me, her mouth and eyes wide in a silent scream of astonishment.

Wow! she mouthed and fanned herself with her hand.

Priest, I mouthed back and mimed a dog-collar.

No!

I gave her a rueful smile and nodded, but she still couldn't take her eyes off Eamonn, who wasn't only astoundingly gorgeous, but also had Connor's height and long-limbed frame. Then I grinned to myself at the thought of the whole of Eire coming to a halt every time he walked down the street. He'd never be short of an offer of a Christmas dinner, anyway.

'Is it all right if Eamonn comes over tomorrow and we take

him up to the stone?' Connor asked, propping himself against my desk. 'He's staying in York tonight.'

'Of course.' I frowned. 'But how will you get over there?'

Eamonn grinned, and it was the white-toothed grin of a Hollywood star. I gave myself a talking-to. 'I've hired a car,' he said. 'Connor is the only one of the family who can't drive.' Then he gave his brother a very unpriestly smack around the head. 'You need to learn, my friend,' he said. 'You're not five.'

'I've tried! You know what happened when Mrs O'Donahue took me for a spin around Dundrum. Newspapers everywhere, and a poodle that will never be the same again.'

'He'll certainly look over his shoulder next time he hears a Fiat Panda coming towards him.' Eamonn nodded. Then he looked at me, and I was surprised by the depth of expression in his dark eyes. He loved his brother and was assessing me for suitability – it was a mother-in-law look, not a look I would have expected to see from a man of the cloth. 'Perhaps Rowan can teach you.'

I wondered whether the family had sent him to check me out. Then I remembered that Connor had summoned him, and again I wondered why. As far as I knew there was nothing ungodly about the Fairy Stane, although the position of fairies within the paranormal canon might contravene something biblical. Not my field of study, thankfully.

'Tomorrow morning?' I gave Chess *A Look*. 'I'll work from home tomorrow, Chess.'

She was still boggling. 'Oh, do you have to?'

'Yes.'

Then she brightened. 'Maybe tonight I could take Eamonn out? Show him the sights of York?'

Eamonn and Connor exchanged a similar *Look*. Women falling over themselves for Eamonn's attention was clearly not an unknown occurrence. 'That would be nice, thank you,' Eamonn said brightly. 'There's a couple of churches I'd like a look over before I go back.'

Chess's smile faded a little, but she gamely breezed on. 'Here's my number. I'll pick you up from your... hotel?'

'That would be grand.'

Connor and I left the two of them arranging a meet-up, and I clutched at Connor's arm as we walked through the car park. 'She's going to try to seduce a priest! Oh, that girl is going to hell.'

'Which you don't believe in,' Connor said, smoothly.

'No, but... should we leave them alone? Chess can be – persistent.'

Connor gave me a hug in the darkness. 'Eamonn has been there before, trust me,' he said. 'He's a great one for letting them down gently. Now, I've got some fish here – would you like a Goan fish curry tonight?'

I drove home to the cottage and marvelled at the way we'd fallen into this routine and how comfortable it was. We still hadn't spoken about any kind of future. I was aware that he'd got a six-month secondment and that the Romans and their possible settlement couldn't keep him here forever. Did I even *want* him here forever? Even if he was great company, cooked like a dream, was completely house-trained and had even struck up an uneasy alliance with the ducks?

Did I? Could I see a future, a new, different future, with Connor? I looked down into the valley as we breasted the rise that took us down to the river and the mill cottage. Everything was dark, apart from the little glimmer of light that was the kitchen lamp, a tiny, summoning beacon across the acres of night. 'Allegorical,' I said to its shining hint of hope in the gloom.

'Sorry?' Connor twitched upright.

'Nothing,' I said, and steered the car down the hill to home.

The next morning was bright and sharp with frost, the ground diamond-hard and our breaths clouded the view as we stepped out over the moor towards the stone. Connor and I were wearing thick jumpers and boots, but Eamonn was evidently unprepared for the conditions in his borrowed wellingtons and a waxed jacket that didn't have nearly enough layers underneath.

Connor pointed out sights of interest as we went. Well, of interest to him, anyway.

'That's where the medieval manor was, up there past the hill.'

Eamonn nodded as though this had already been discussed. Maybe it had, although I had no idea why it would have been.

'And there would have been pretty much a whole village up here somewhere,' Connor went on. 'The cottage was part of the mill for the entire settlement. Probably got Domesday origins.'

Eamonn nodded again as we tramped out over the cold-crisped grass and heather.

'This is the stone in question. Gateway to fairyland, apparently.' Connor looked meaningfully at Eamonn.

'Ah, no, it's just a marker now,' Eamonn replied. 'The stone isn't symbolic.'

'If it is what we think…'

'Still only a place to come. To remember.' Eamonn's tone was very even, his voice level, but I suddenly had a tremor of intuition. They were having a conversation about something that had been discussed, and I didn't know what that was.

'If you lie here at midnight…' I began.

'You can hear the fairies under the stone,' Connor finished.

'The Little People, partying away. And what do you think that might be about, Rowan?'

I put my hands on my hips. 'Well, the theory that the fairies might be a folk memory of the earlier peoples of the British Isles has been more or less discredited now. So we're left with wondering whether they're a common myth to make sense of various meteorological phenomena or a completely contrived creation for some reasons that we don't yet understand.'

Eamonn was staring at the stone, his eyes very dark. Connor stood next to him, taller and wirier, but his eyes were also fixed on the slab of gritstone, as though it meant something to both of them.

'The little people,' Eamonn said, quietly.

I had a tingle of foreboding. 'Is this where you perform some ritual and call elemental beings into life?' I asked, only half joking.

'He's a fecking priest, not Aleister Crowley,' Connor observed mildly. 'And anybody less likely to perform any rituals you're never going to see.'

'Mass is ritual, Connor,' Eamonn said, not looking away from the stone.

'Oh, well, if we're going to bring religion into it...'

'Will you two stop bickering and tell me what's going on?' I used my best 'getting Chess to do some work' voice. 'We're clearly not up here for our health, and, as we've brought a priest with us, I'm guessing there's a bigger reason for all this than just a nice walk.'

Both of the men looked at me wearing identical expressions of sorrow and sympathy. Connor put an arm around my shoulders. 'What do priests do, Rowan?' he asked me, so gently that I began to really worry that the stone was about to split and reveal a Creature from the Pit.

'They pray,' I retorted.

'And?'

'And exorcise. If that's why we're here then I need to go home and get some better underwear on because I am *not* wearing my Banish All Evil knickers today.'

Connor snorted and Eamonn looked over his shoulder at both of us, rolling his eyes.

'Not even a suspicion about what might have gone on here?' Eamonn asked Connor, nodding in my direction.

'No, but she's folklore, not history. Folklore tends to deal a little more with the *conjectural* side of things. I'm on the bricks-and-mortar side of the old speculative razor wire.'

'Show me where you dug.' Eamonn moved around the edge of the stone and Connor followed him, pointing at the soft ground slightly off to one side, where the boggy, reedy soil did show signs of disturbance and there were still small piles of snow melting slowly in their heaps.

I marched up and caught Connor's arm. 'You dug? You didn't tell me you were digging.'

There was an almost unbearable expression of sympathy on his face now. As though there was some terrible, dreadful secret that the two of them knew – that the whole *world* knew – and I wasn't in on it.

'I did tell you I'd been up here, scrabbling about, when I walked up, in the snow. And, to be honest, a bit before that, when I still thought the stone could be a Roman marker. I just did a wee bit of poking around under the edge there.'

'But...' I was too confused to be truly annoyed. 'But this is *my* stone!'

'I think...' Connor led me gently away from where Eamonn was crouched now, pulling at the roots of some reeds carefully and staring down at the soaked earth, '...that you might be glad I did. What do priests do, Rowan?'

'I told you, they pray and they—'

'Exorcise, yes. But there are other things.' He was looking at me as though he was willing me to come to my own conclusions, so he didn't have to fill in the gaps.

'Well, they marry people.'

A sudden laugh. 'And, when and if the time comes, I was thinking a civil ceremony might be more the mark. But there's time, Rowan. There's time.' He hauled me into a sudden hug. I saw Eamonn look up, smile and shrug himself back down into the bog, his jacket scraping the stone. 'So, what else do priests do, Rowan?'

'Why don't you tell me?' His persistent questioning was raking claws up and down my spine. That feeling that there was a huge joke, an enormous answer that absolutely everyone else knew, was oddly familiar. It reminded me of just after Elliot died, when I lived in a dislocated world, a planet with the centre gone. I'd felt then as though everyone else had the comfortable, settled lives that had been ripped from me, as though they all knew what was going on while I didn't even know what day of the week it was.

Connor looked at my face. My doubts, my memories must have been showing, because he gave me a gentle kiss on the forehead. 'I'm sorry about the folklore, Rowan,' he whispered. 'But we need to close this story down.'

I shivered. His tone was soft, but there was a kind of dark import behind the words, as though there really were a route to hell under this stone. 'I...'

'What else do priests do?' Still quiet, still low, but spoken with such *weight*. 'They baptise.'

And suddenly everything came together, with an almost

audible click. Eamonn stood up, and he was holding brown and twisted stems that I could now see weren't stems at all, and my stomach dropped.

'Do you know what a *cillín* is, Rowan?' Eamonn asked and he sounded as gentle as Connor. 'You'll need your Irish folklore for this one.'

The name rang a vague bell, but as I'd concentrated on the folklore of northern England and my knowledge of Irish was sketchy, I had to admit defeat. I shook my head.

Connor sighed, but it didn't sound like a sigh of annoyance, more of sadness. 'Literally, it means "little church",' he said. 'We've a number of them all over across the water there. I've never seen one in England before, that's why I didn't know what I was looking at for a long time.'

He turned me by my shoulder until we were looking out across the moors. 'The house that was out there. The manor. The *Catholic* house.' Then he turned me around until we were facing more or less the direction of my cottage. 'The village associated with the manor. Full of Catholics, displaced from Ireland in the mid eighteen hundreds.' Then he turned me again, just a degree or two, until we could see the spire of the local church, only the tip and the weather-vane prodding the sky from the town three miles further down the valley. 'The church. Not Catholic, but it illustrates the point.'

Eamonn joined in now, sitting carefully on the edge of the stone, nursing those brown tangled things in his lap. 'Back in the day, if you died without the holy sacrament of baptism, you were deemed to remain eternally in limbo and the Church, in its wisdom, wouldn't allow a proper burial.'

They both went quiet, and I looked out across the broad landscape of the hills, patchy with melting snowdrifts and the re-emergence of the skeins of heather and grassy stretches. A sheep baa rose through the stone-cold air and there was a distant noise of something mechanical working, but otherwise silence. My mouth had gone dry, and I couldn't have said a single word if Connor had gone down on one knee and proposed right then.

He didn't, of course, it was far too soon for that. But he did enfold me in the drapery of his big coat, firm and warm against me. 'When a baby was stillborn, or died before they could get the holy water to their heads, the men of the settlement would carry them out to a well-marked local site and bury them with all the ceremony they could manage,' he said. His voice echoed inside my head. 'They tried to do the right thing, even though the Church denied them.'

Again, that silence. That blank hole in the world as I tried to comprehend the incomprehensible.

'They weren't allowed to bury their babies?' I whispered.

'Not in consecrated ground, no. They weren't members of the Church until baptism, you see.'

'That's horrible.'

I saw Eamonn drop his head. Then I realised what those bundled root-like things were, and I sprang away from Connor and stared at the Fairy Stane. 'They buried their *babies* under the stone?'

'With reverence, Rowan,' Connor said. 'With love. They will have said prayers and made a little ceremony of it. They didn't just dig a hole and hide them away. And the stone was here, when they wanted to come and pay their respects, it was here. The graves were marked in the only way they could. The Church...' and he glared at his brother as though the whole thing were his fault, '...might have denied them, but their parents did what they could.'

'The little people.' I half whispered the words over the blockage in my throat. 'It was a literal thing. I never thought…'

'No. Nobody did. I don't think we've seen a *cillín* outside Ireland, have we?' Connor stopped eyeballing Eamonn. 'I'd guess they brought the idea over with them when they escaped the Great Famine. Usually the babies were buried at night, in churchyards where those who oversee such things turned a blind eye. But with this being so isolated and the church so far to travel over bad ground back then…'

'It's not great ground to travel even now,' I put in, feeling a little more robust. 'See how we got snowed in last week.'

'Exactly. And, what, a hundred and fifty years ago, how much worse would it have been? So they did what they could. They made their own safe, sacred place.'

'And you knew? All this time, you *knew*?' I rounded on Connor.

'No. I began to suspect, what with you and your folk tales of the Stane, which started to sound more and more like a metaphor, and with me knowing about the *cillín* from Granda and his stories – well. I put two and two together. Then I found…' He trailed off. 'I knew I was right.'

We all looked at the tiny fragments in Eamonn's lap. He was nursing them as though the children were still here, still alive.

'So it's not a Roman grave marker, and it never was?'

Now Connor grinned, his usual, relaxed smile. The worst was clearly over. 'It still could be, y'know? But I'll not be for lifting it. It's a sacred place. We'll look for official protection for the site. I'm not *quite* sure how, but Eamonn is well up on these sorts of things.'

'Not in England, I'm not,' Eamonn replied. 'But I know a man.'

'God?' I asked.

'Well, he's a professor of Irish studies, so, you're close.' Now Eamonn grinned at me too, and the resemblance between the brothers was incredible. 'He'll know how to deal with all this. In the meantime...' He pulled a small bottle out of a jacket pocket.

I was baffled. 'We all have a drink?'

'It's holy water, Rowan,' Connor said, carefully. Eamonn had gone pale. 'Eamonn will perform a service of baptism for the babies. The baptism they never got.'

I *wanted* to say, 'Well, that's a fat lot of good to them now, isn't it?' but didn't. Just because I didn't believe, and thought that the religion that had caused grief-stricken parents to have to bury their babies secretly in a resting place marked with what they probably thought was a heathen symbol ought to keep very, very quiet right now – well. It wasn't my place. Through recording people talking I'd heard what previous generations had had to go through. Folklore wasn't a synonym for pretty. It wasn't all household charms and lights guiding you through a bog. There was blood at the heart of it. Folk tales were the smooth edge that made you not notice the razor underneath.

Fairyland beneath the stone. The stone that must not be lifted for fear of disturbing the Little People, who lived a life away from man, that could be heard at midnight if you put your ear to the stone. Stories told by the grieving, to help ease their consciences and their sorrow.

My throat squeezed. 'What do we do?'

His head came up, watching his brother, who was walking around the stone now, gently sprinkling water on the site and praying in Latin. 'First, we watch and remember,' he said quietly. Then, with a lift of his chin and a sideways look to me, 'Then we all head into town and have a bloody good meal, quite a lot to drink, and we talk about the future.'

I opened my mouth to protest, but a quick kiss came out of

nowhere to silence me. 'Eamonn can drive us. He doesn't drink.' A fond glance at his brother, who was standing praying now. 'He's a great lad, except for the Church thing.'

I thought of all those parents, all that guilt. All that sadness. It would have been there, even if their babies had been properly buried – they would still have felt a guilt and an awful aching unhappiness for that hole in their lives. The loss bound us together somehow – my loss of a husband and the desire to keep the Fairy Stane intact for the sake of my memories. Their loss of their babies, and the Stane standing for all the graves that would never be marked.

Grief and loss. Then I looked over at Connor, who was watching Eamonn continue to perform a baptism ritual and thought, *And a future. They might have gone on to have more children, children who lived. I can go on and have a life. An end doesn't have to mean the end of everything.*

These parents had done what they could and I thought, with a tingle of possibility, to honour them I could write the story of those parents; maybe even find out their names and where they'd lived. I could give them another life, linking the folklore of the stone to what had *really* gone on here. Maybe, wherever they were now, they'd know that their children were not forgotten.

26

1963

Mr and Mrs Turner followed the old sexton up along the overgrown path. Ironically, this was the 'new' part of the cemetery, although to them it looked less cared for than the old part, which bore jutting monuments of staggering Victorian hideousness.

Eventually he stopped and held out a hand. ''Ere is where we puts 'em,' he said, coughing around his Woodbine. 'Nice spot. Lovely view.'

Mrs Turner mopped at her eyes. 'They never told us…' she half whispered, her voice competing with the wind. 'They took her away and we never knew…'

Her husband put his arm around her. 'Now, lass,' he said, not unkindly, his own voice somewhat thick. 'Don't take on.'

'I'm sorry, Peter.' She made an obvious attempt to straighten her back and take in her surroundings. 'It's just that seeing the place…'

'I know, love.' He patted her arm. 'I know.'

'We buries 'em proper.' The gravedigger nodded, wiping his hands down his shiny trousers. 'Reverent, like. Not so long ago they wouldn't have been allowed in...' he took a run at the word, '...con-se-crated ground, but—' he coughed liberally '—now they've changed the rules. Babbies can go straight to heaven now, 'parently. Dunno what was stoppin' 'em before, like, but there you go.'

He looked at the bereaved parents, him in his good suit and overcoat, her in a two-piece and tidy little slingbacks that were all stuck up with the mud. They'd dressed up smart to come out to see where their little one lay – that was nice, he thought. Respectful.

'But no headstones.' Mr Turner addressed him directly.

'Nope.' The sexton thought about spitting but decided against it. 'Mass grave, y'see. All the babbies that doesn't...' Showing unusual sensitivity, he changed tack. 'All them little ones, they keeps each other company. All in there.' A grubby fingernail indicated the tiny plot. 'I keeps it nice.'

Mrs Turner bent and put her tiny posy of primroses on the shorn grass. 'She wasn't christened,' she said, through tears. 'She never got to be christened. But we were going to call her Primrose, weren't we?'

Mr Turner and the gravedigger, united in male embarrassment, watched as she gently touched the ground next to the flowers. 'Sleep well, our little Primrose,' she said softly.

Then she took her husband's arm, and they walked back to the waiting car, past all the properly marked graves of those who had lived and died.

* * *

Now – A Year Later

'Put your hand there... that's it. Move it gently... careful now.'

'Is that it?'

'Nearly. There. Can you feel that? Now, here, lift this, very, very slowly, until you feel...'

'I think I've got it... oh, feck!'

The car leaped forward, jerked and stalled again. Connor pulled a face. 'I told you, I'm not cut out for this driving yoke,' he said.

'Hill starts are always difficult.' I tried to sound sympathetic, but, in reality, teaching Connor to drive would have tested the patience of a saint, and I decided to buy him some more driving lessons for Christmas this year. Last year's Christmas present, the plastic centurion, had pride of place on the new shelving in the living room, but this year there would be *proper* presents. A proper dinner – I'd already bought and stuffed the turkey. We'd asked Eamonn over but he was doing the official 'family' thing, and I still hadn't met the rest of the O'Keefe clan, because we were 'taking things slowly', according to Connor, or 'avoiding them', as I put it. Connor was working on researching other *cillín* in England, being a visiting lecturer in Irish History at York and generally achieving a medal in 'not going home to be nagged'.

I felt the writhing inside me and put a quieting hand across my stomach. We weren't taking things *that* slowly, and our unborn son was clearly keen to meet the rest of the family too. 'Just stay put for another three months,' I whispered. 'You don't want to arrive at Christmas, the precedent isn't exactly stellar.'

'Sorry?' Connor ground the gears again and made another brave attempt to get the car ten centimetres further forward.

'Nothing.' I smiled at him, although the smile came filtered through a worry about my gearbox. 'Thinking aloud.'

'Ah, let's forget this, shall we?' The car lurched forward and stalled again. 'Let's go for a walk instead. We've not been up to the Stane for a week or so.'

With relief I accepted the end of the lesson and clambered inelegantly out of the car to take his hand. 'We need to take some more flowers up,' I said. 'The old ones will be withered by now.'

'Good idea. There's a bit of life left in those roses in the kitchen that I got you.'

'You don't have to buy me flowers every week, Connor, honestly.'

There was that sudden embrace again, that careful hug as though I might be china and prone to breakage. 'I do,' he said fervently. 'Trust me, I do.'

And hand in hand, watched by a coterie of suddenly interested ducks, we walked into our cottage. Behind us, the car, smelling of burning brake pads, ticked its engine cool into the oncoming evening.

Above us, the moor stretched itself into the dwindling light. Meanwhile, beneath their blanket of stone and flowers, now recognised and hopefully at peace, the little people slept on.

ABOUT THE AUTHOR

Jane Lovering is the bestselling and award-winning romantic comedy writer who won the RNA Contemporary Romantic Novel Award in 2023 with *A Cottage Full of Secrets*. She lives in Yorkshire and has a cat and a bonkers terrier, as well as five children who have now left home.

Sign up to Jane Lovering's mailing list here for news, competitions and updates on future books.

Visit Jane's website: www.janelovering.co.uk

Follow Jane on social media:

facebook.com/Jane-Lovering-Author-106404969412833
x.com/janelovering
bookbub.com/authors/jane-lovering

ALSO BY JANE LOVERING

The Country Escape
Home on a Yorkshire Farm
A Midwinter Match
A Cottage Full of Secrets
The Forgotten House on the Moor
There's No Place Like Home
The Recipe for Happiness
The Island Cottage
One of a Kind
The Start of the Story

LOVE NOTES
LOVE IN EVERY CHAPTER

WHERE ALL YOUR ROMANCE
DREAMS COME TRUE!

THE HOME OF BESTSELLING
ROMANCE AND WOMEN'S
FICTION

WARNING:
MAY CONTAIN SPICE

SIGN UP TO OUR
NEWSLETTER

https://bit.ly/Lovenotesnews

Boldwood

Boldwood Books is an award-winning fiction publishing company seeking out the best stories from around the world.

Find out more at www.boldwoodbooks.com

Join our reader community for brilliant books, competitions and offers!

Follow us
@BoldwoodBooks
@TheBoldBookClub

Sign up to our weekly deals newsletter

https://bit.ly/BoldwoodBNewsletter

Printed in Great Britain
by Amazon